Teresa Halikowska read Polish and English at Warsaw University and Comparative Literature at Oxford. She has taught Polish Literature and is at present engaged in freelance writing, reviewing and translation.

George Hyde read English at Cambridge and Translation Studies at Essex. He is Senior Lecturer in English and Comparative Literature at the University of East Anglia. He has spent four years lecturing at Polish universities, including a year as Visiting Professor at the Jagiellonian University, Kraków.

The Eagle and the Crow

Modern Polish Short Stories

Edited by Teresa Halikowska and
George Hyde

This book was published with assistance from the
Arts Council of England

Library of Congress Catalog Card Number: 96–69161

A catalogue record for this book is available
from the British Library on request

First published 1996 by Serpent's Tail,
4 Blackstock Mews, London N4, and
180 Varick Street, 10th floor, New York, NY 10014

Typeset in 10pt Times by Intype, London, Ltd
Printed in Great Britain by
Cox & Wyman Ltd., of Reading, Berkshire

Contents

Introduction

Why an eagle? That's easy: it is Poland's most revered icon. Not very original? Perhaps not: but rarely has a national symbol acquired more significance. After almost a century and a half of 'suspended animation', when the Polish state was wiped off the map of Europe (1795–1918) and the brief interlude of regained sovereignty (1918–1939), the eagle lost its crown to the communists. After communism, the crown was regained. What was the logic of this new coronation? Would the monarchy be restored? If not, why was this poor over-burdened symbol of nationhood given the extra weight of a crown? Was an uncrowned republican or democratic eagle unimaginable? Maybe the Polish eagle, unlike its American counterpart, has too much to lose by lowering himself to the level of *hoi polloi*. Poland is a country where the passion for liberty is matched only by the deep-seated respect for hierarchy and precedent. This dichotomy is reflected in Polish culture.

But why a crow? The editors' choice of this bird may appear idiosyncratic: yet it has its own rationale. A crow is rather like a raven. Edgar Allan Poe's raven inaugurated, critics tell us, the aesthetics of the short story. Poe's raven was a bird of few words: in fact, just one: Nevermore! Crows, in contrast, are noisy creatures. Poland is full of crows: they caw and croak an accompaniment to the eagle's flight of fancy; they presage doom and destruction; they mock the heroism and romance which the eagle embodies and proclaims; they mimic, in their grotesque way, the aspirations of the king of the birds. 'Crow' was a nickname given to General Jaruzelski's military council, during the period of Martial Law in the 1980s, from the acronym WRON (formed from the initial letters of the Polish words that made up its name); 'wrona' is Polish for crow. Some crows eat carrion; they are scavengers and gravediggers; they are also not averse to pecking one another to death. Polish crows are wintry birds; they were there when the doomed January Uprising of 1863 failed, as in the searing story by a 19th-century writer, Stefan Żeromski: *Rozdziobą nas kruki, wrony* (And They Will Peck Us to Death, Ravens, Crows). Poland has, for most of its modern history, been full of corpses: the victims of history, haunting the living.

Polish writing is (as all agree) steeped in Romanticism and nationalism. The Romantic trope of the *Doppelgänger*—the split self—meant, in the Polish context, that for every fine gesture or flight of fancy, there is an equal, and parallel, lapsing back, and a malicious overview of humanity's 'puerile utopias' and recipes for 'paradise now'.

This anthology sets out to present modern Polish literature in the light of the profound impact which history and politics have made on it during this century. The present collection of short stories, dating from the period just before the Second World War to the 1990s, offers the English reader a selection from literature which—although restricted in its impact by the minority status of its language—has a distinctive contribution to make. Most of the writers included here reflect, some anticipate, major developments in European culture, while at the same time articulating a specifically Polish experience. In particular, the sense of existential exposure, the grotesque and the absurd, which runs through postwar writing in Europe and America, is prefigured in Polish writing, embodying, as it does, a culture profoundly moulded by the traumatic events of this century and therefore constantly having to renegotiate its boundaries and its sense of identity.

Teresa Halikowska
George Hyde

The Eagle and the Crow

Bruno Schulz

Birds

Came the yellow days of winter, filled with boredom. The rust-coloured earth was covered with a threadbare, meagre tablecloth of snow full of holes. There was not enough of it for some of the roofs and so they stood there, black and brown, shingle and thatch, arks containing the sooty expanses of attics—coal-black cathedrals, bristling with ribs of rafters, beams and spars—the dark lungs of winter winds. Each dawn revealed new chimney stacks and chimney pots which had emerged during the hours of darkness, blown up by the night winds: the black pipes of a devil's organ. The chimney sweeps could not get rid of the crows which in the evening covered the branches of the trees around the church with living black leaves, then took off, fluttering, and came back, each clinging to its own place on its own branch, only to fly away at dawn in large flocks, like gusts of soot, flakes of dirt, undulating and fantastic, blackening with their insistent crowing the musty yellow streaks of light. The days hardened with cold and boredom like last year's loaves of bread. One began to cut them with blunt knives without appetite, with a lazy indifference.

Father had stopped going out. He banked up the stoves, studied the ever elusive essence of fire, experienced the salty, metallic taste and the smoky smell of wintry flames, the cool caresses of salamanders that licked the shiny soot in the throat of the chimney. He applied himself lovingly at that time to all manner of small repairs in the upper regions of the rooms. At all hours of the day one could see him crouched on top of a ladder, working at something under the ceiling, at the cornices over the tall windows, at the counterweights and chains of the hanging lamps. Following the custom of house painters, he used a pair of steps as enormous stilts and he felt perfectly happy in that bird's eye perspective close to the sky, leaves and birds painted on the ceiling. He grew more and more remote from practical affairs. When my mother, worried and unhappy about his condition, tried to draw him into a conversation about business, about the payments due at the end of the month, he listened to her absent mindedly, anxiety showing in his abstracted look. Sometimes he stopped her with a warning gesture of the hand in order to run to a corner of the room, put his ear to a crack in the floor and by lifting the index fingers of both hands, emphasize the gravity of the investigation, and begin to listen intently. At that time we did not yet understand the sad origin of these eccentricities, the deplorable complex which had been maturing in him.

Mother had no influence over him, but he gave a lot of respectful attention to Adela. The cleaning of his room was to him a great and important ceremony, of which he always arranged to be a witness, watching all Adela's movements with a mixture of apprehension and pleasurable excitement. He ascribed to all her functions a deeper, symbolic meaning. When, with young firm gestures, the girl pushed a long-handled broom along the floor, Father could hardly bear it. Tears would stream from his eyes, silent laughter transformed his face, and his body was shaken by spasms of delight. He was ticklish to the point of madness. It was enough for Adela to waggle her fingers at him to imitate tickling, for him to rush through all the rooms in a wild panic, banging the doors after him, to fall at last on the bed in the farthest room and wriggle in convulsions of laughter, imagining the tickling which he found irresistible. Because of this, Adela's power over Father was almost limitless.

At that time we noticed for the first time Father's passionate interest in animals. To begin with, it was the passion of the huntsman and the artist rolled into one. It was also perhaps a deeper, biological sympathy of one creature for kindred, yet different, forms of life, a kind of experimenting in the unexplored regions of existence. Only at a later stage did matters take that uncanny, complicated, essentially sinful and unnatural turn, which it is better not to bring into the light of day.

But it all began with the hatching out of birds' eggs.

With a great outlay of effort and money, Father imported from Hamburg, or Holland, or from zoological stations in Africa, birds' eggs on which he set enormous brood hens from Belgium. It was a process which fascinated me as well—this hatching out of the chicks, which were real anomalies of shape and colour. It was difficult to anticipate—in these monsters with enormous, fantastic beaks which they opened wide immediately after birth, hissing greedily to show the backs of their throats, in these lizards with frail, naked bodies of hunchbacks—the future peacocks, pheasants, grouse or condors. Placed in cotton wool, in baskets, this dragon brood lifted blind, wall-eyed heads on thin necks, croaking voicelessly from their dumb throats. My father would walk along the shelves, dressed in a green baize apron, like a gardener in a hothouse of cacti, and conjure up from nothingness these blind bubbles, pulsating with life, these impotent bellies receiving the outside world only in the form of food, these growths on the surface of life, climbing blindfold towards the light. A few weeks later, when these blind buds of matter burst open, the rooms were filled with the bright chatter and scintillating chirruping of their new inhabitants. The birds perched on the curtain pelmets, on the tops of wardrobes; they nestled in the tangle of tin branches and the metal scrolls of the hanging lamps.

While Father pored over his large ornithological textbooks and studied their coloured plates, these feathery phantasms seemed to rise from the pages and fill the rooms with colours, with splashes of crimson, strips of sapphire, verdigris, and silver. At feeding time they formed a motley, undulating bed on the floor, a living carpet which at the intrusion of a stranger would fall apart, scatter into fragments, flutter in

the air, and finally settle high under the ceilings. I remember
in particular a certain condor, an enormous bird with a feath-
erless neck, its face wrinkled and knobbly. It was an
emaciated ascetic, a Buddhist lama, full of imperturbable
dignity in its behaviour, guided by the rigid ceremonial of
its great species. When it sat facing my father, motionless in
the monumental position of ageless Egyptian idols, its eye
covered with a whitish cataract which it pulled down sideways over its pupil to shut itself up completely in the
contemplation of its dignified solitude—it seemed, with its
stony profile, like an older brother of my father's. Its body
and muscles seemed to be made of the same material, it had
the same hard, wrinkled skin, the same desiccated bony
face, the same horny, deep eye sockets. Even the hands,
strong in the joints, my father's long thick hands with their
rounded nails, had their counterpart in the condor's claws. I
could not resist the impression, when looking at the sleeping
condor, that I was in the presence of a mummy—a dried-
out, shrunken mummy of my father. I believe that even my
mother noticed this strange resemblance, although we never
discussed the subject. It is significant that the condor used
my father's chamber-pot.

Not content with the hatching out of more and more new
specimens, my father arranged the marriages of birds in the
attic, he sent out matchmakers, he tied up eager attractive
birds in the holes and crannies under the roof, and soon the
roof of our house, an enormous double-rigged shingle roof,
became a real birds' hostel, a Noah's ark to which all kinds
of feathery creatures flew from far afield. Long after the
liquidation of the birds' paradise, this tradition persisted in
the avian world and during the period of spring migration
our roof was besieged by whole flocks of cranes, pelicans,
peacocks, and sundry other birds. However, after a short
period of splendour, the whole undertaking took a sorry
turn.

It soon became necessary to move my father to two rooms
at the top of the house which had served as storage rooms.
We could hear from there, at dawn, the mixed clangour of

birds' voices. The wooden walls of the attic rooms, helped
by the resonance of the empty space under the gables,
sounded with the roar, the flutterings, the crowing, the gurgling, the mating cries. For a few weeks Father was lost to
view. He only rarely came down to the apartment and, when
he did, we noticed that he seemed to have shrunk, to have
become smaller and thinner. Occasionally, forgetting himself,
he would rise from his chair at table, wave his arms as if
they were wings, and emit a long-drawn-out bird's call while
his eyes misted over. Then, rather embarrassed, he would
join us in laughing it off and try to turn the whole incident
into a joke.

One day, during spring cleaning, Adela suddenly appeared
in Father's bird kingdom. Stopping in the doorway, she wrung
her hands at the fetid smell that filled the room, the heaps
of droppings covering the floor, the tables, and the chairs.
Without hesitation, she flung open a window and, with the
help of a long broom, she prodded the whole mass of birds
into life. A fiendish cloud of feathers and wings arose
screaming, and Adela, like a furious maenad protected by
the whirlwind of her thyrsus, danced the dance of destruction. My father, waving his arms in panic, tried to lift himself
into the air with his feathered cock. Slowly the winged cloud
thinned until at last Adela remained on the battlefield,
exhausted and out of breath, along with my father, who now,
adopting a worried hangdog expression, was ready to accept
complete defeat.

A moment later, my father came downstairs—a broken
man, an exiled king who had lost his throne and his kingdom.

(Translated by Celina Wieniewska)

Bruno Schulz

Tailors' Dummies

The affair of the birds was the last colourful and splendid
counteroffensive of fantasy which my father, that incor-
rigible improviser, that fencing master of imagination, had
led against the trenches and defence-works of a sterile and
empty winter. Only now do I understand the lonely hero
who alone had waged war against the fathomless, elemental
boredom that strangled the city. Without any support,
without recognition on our part, that strangest of men was
defending the lost cause of poetry. He was like a magic mill,
into the hoppers of which the bran of empty hours was
poured, to re-emerge flowering in all the colours and scents
of Oriental spices. But, used to the splendid showmanship of
that metaphysical conjurer, we were inclined to underrate
the value of his sovereign magic, which saved us from the
lethargy of empty days and nights.

Adela was not rebuked for her thoughtless and brutal
vandalism. On the contrary, we felt a vile satisfaction, a
disgraceful pleasure that Father's exuberance had been
curbed, for although we had enjoyed it to the full, we later
ignominiously denied all responsibility for it. Perhaps in our
treachery there was secret approval of the victorious Adela
to whom we simply ascribed some commission and assign-
ment from forces of a higher order. Betrayed by us all, Father
retreated without a fight from the scenes of his recent glory.
Without crossing swords, he surrendered to the enemy the
kingdom of his former splendour. A voluntary exile, he took

himself off to an empty room at the end of the passage and there immured himself in solitude.

We forgot him.

We were beset again from all sides by the mournful greyness of the city which crept through the windows with the dark rash of dawn, with the mushroom growth of dusk, developing into the shaggy fur of long winter nights. The wallpaper of the rooms, blissfully unconstrained in those former days and accessible to the multicoloured flights of the birds, closed in on itself and hardened, becoming engrossed in the monotony of bitter monologues.

The chandeliers blackened and wilted like old thistles; now they hung dejected and ill-tempered, their glass pendants ringing softly whenever anybody groped their way through the dimly lit room. In vain did Adela put coloured candles in all the holders; they were a poor substitute for, a pale reflection of, those splendid illuminations which had so recently enlivened these hanging gardens. Oh, what a twittering had been there, what swift and fantastic flights cutting the air into packs of magic cards, sprinkling thick flakes of azure, of peacock and parrot green, of metallic sparkle, drawing lines and flourishes in the air, displaying coloured fans which remained suspended, long after flight, in the shimmering atmosphere. Even now, in the depth of the greyness, echoes and memories of brightness were hidden but nobody caught them, no clarinet drilled the troubled air.

Those weeks passed under the sign of a strange drowsiness.

Beds unmade for days on end, piled high with bedding crumpled and disordered from the weight of dreams, stood like deep boats waiting to sail into the dank and confusing labyrinths of some dark starless Venice. In the bleakness of dawn, Adela brought us coffee. Lazily we started dressing in the cold rooms, in the light of a single candle reflected many times in black window-panes. The mornings were full of aimless bustle, of prolonged searches in endless drawers and cupboards. The clacking of Adela's slippers could be heard all over the apartment. The shop assistants lit the lanterns, took the large shop keys which mother handed them and went out into the thick swirling darkness. Mother could not come to terms with her dressing. The candles burned smaller in the candlesticks. Adela disappeared somewhere into the farthest rooms or into the attic where she hung the washing. She was deaf to our calling. A newly lit, dirty, bleak fire in the stove licked at the cold shiny growth of soot in the throat of the chimney. The candle died out, and the room filled with gloom. With our heads on the tablecloth, among the remains of breakfast, we fell asleep, still half-dressed. Lying face downwards on the furry lap of darkness, we sailed in its regular breathing into the starless nothingness. We were awakened by Adela's noisy tidying up. Mother could not cope with her dressing. Before she had finished doing her hair, the shop assistants were back for lunch. The half-light in the market place was now the colour of golden smoke. For a moment it looked as if out of that smoke-coloured honey, that opaque amber, a most beautiful afternoon would unfold. But the happy moment passed, the amalgam of dawn withered the swelling fermentation of the day, almost completed, receded again into a helpless greyness. We assembled again around the table, the shop assistants rubbed their hands, red from the cold, and the prose of their conversation suddenly revealed a full-grown day, a grey and empty Tuesday, a day without tradition and without a face. But it was only when a dish appeared on the table containing two large fish in jelly lying side by side, head-to-tail, like a sign of the zodiac, that we recognized in them the coat of arms of that day, the calendar emblem of the nameless Tuesday: we shared it out quickly among ourselves, thankful that the day had at last achieved an identity.

The shop assistants ate with unction, with the seriousness due to a calendar feast. The smell of pepper filled the room. And when they had used pieces of bread to wipe up the remains of the jelly from their plates, pondering in silence on the heraldry of the following days of the week, and nothing remained on the serving dish but the fishheads with their boiled-out eyes, we all felt that by a communal effort we had conquered the day and that what remained of it did not matter.

And, in fact, Adela made short work of the rest of the day, now surrendered to her mercies. Amid the clatter of saucepans and splashing of cold water, she was energetically liquidating the few hours remaining until dusk, while Mother slept on the sofa. Meanwhile, in the dining room the scene was being set for the evening. Polda and Pauline, the seam-stresses, spread themselves out there with the props of their trade. Carried on their shoulders, a silent immobile lady had entered the room, a lady of oakum and canvas, with a black wooden knob instead of a head. But when stood in the corner, between the door and the stove, that silent woman became mistress of the situation. Standing motionless in her corner, she supervised the girls' advances and wooings as they knelt before her, fittings fragments of a dress marked with white basting thread. They waited with attention and patience on the silent idol, which was difficult to please. That moloch was inexorable as only a female moloch can be, and sent them back to work again and again, and they, thin and spindly, like wooden spools from which thread is unwound and as mobile, manipulated with deft fingers the piles of silk and wool, cut with noisy scissors into its colourful mass, whirred the sewing machine, treading its pedal with one cheap patent-leathered foot, while around them there grew a heap of cuttings, of motley rags and pieces, like husks and chaff spat out by two fussy and prodigal parrots. The curved jaws of the scissors tapped open like the beaks of those exotic birds.

The girls trod absent mindedly on the bright shreds of material, wading carelessly in the rubbish of a possible car-nival, in the store room for some great unrealized masquerade. They disentangled themselves with nervous giggles from the trimmings, their eyes laughed into the mirrors. Their hearts, the quick magic of their fingers were not in the boring dresses which remained on the table, but in the thousand scraps, the frivolous and fickle trimmings, with the colourful fantastic snowstorm with which they could smother the whole city.

Suddenly they felt hot and opened the window to see, in the frustration of their solitude, in their hunger for new faces, at least one nameless face pressed against the pane. They fanned their flushed cheeks with the winter night air in which the curtains billowed—they uncovered their burning décolletés, full of hatred and rivalry for one another. ready to fight for any Pierrot whom the dark breezes of night might blow in through the window. Ah how little did they demand from reality! They had everything within themselves, they had a surfeit of everything in themselves. Ah! they would be content with a sawdust Pierrot with the long-awaited word to act as the cue for their well rehearsed roles, so that they could at last speak the lines, full of a sweet and terrible bitterness, that crowded to their lips exciting them violently, like some novel devoured at night, while the tears streamed down their cheeks.

During one of his nightly wanderings about the apartment, undertaken in Adela's absence, my father stumbled upon such a quiet evening sewing session. For a moment he stood in the dark door of the adjoining room, a lamp in his hand, enchanted by the scene of feverish activity, by the blushes— that synthesis of face powder, red tissue paper, and atropine—to which the winter night, breathing on the waving window curtains, acted as a significant backdrop. Putting on his glasses, he stepped quickly up to the girls and walked twice around them, letting fall on them the light of the lamp he was carrying. The draught from the open door lifted the curtains, the girls let themselves be admired, twisting their hips; the enamel of their eyes glinted like the shiny leather of their shoes and the buckles of their garters, showing from under their skirts lifted by the wind; the scraps began to scamper across the floor like rats towards the half-closed door of the dark room, and my father gazed attentively at the panting girls, whispering softly: '*Genus avium* . . . If I am not mistaken, Scansores or Psittacus . . . very remarkable, very remarkable indeed.'

This accidental encounter was the beginning of a whole series of meetings, in the course of which my father succeeded in charming both of the young ladies with the magnetism of his strange personality. In return for his witty and elegant conversation, which filled the emptiness of their evenings, the girls permitted the ardent ornithologist to study the structure of their thin and ordinary little bodies. This took place while the conversation was in progress and was done with a seriousness and grace which ensured that even the more risky points of these researches remained completely unequivocal. Pulling Pauline's stocking down from her knee and studying with enraptured eyes the precise and noble structure of the joint, my father would say:

'How delightful and happy is the form of existence which you ladies have chosen. How beautiful and simple is the truth which is revealed by your lives. And with what mastery, with what precision you are performing your task. If, forgetting the respect due to the Creator, I were to attempt a criticism of creation, I would say "Less matter, more form!" Ah, what relief it would be for the world to lose some of its contents. More modesty in aspirations, more sobriety in claims, Gentlemen Demiurges, and the world would be more perfect!' my father exclaimed, while his hands released Pauline's white calf from the prison of her stocking.

At that moment Adela appeared in the open door of the dining room, the supper tray in her hands. This was the first meeting of the two enemy powers since the great battle. All of us who witnessed it felt a moment of terrible fear. We felt extremely uneasy at being present at the further humiliation of the sorely tried man. My father rose from his knees very disturbed, blushing more and more deeply in wave after wave of shame. But Adela found herself unexpectedly equal to the situation. She walked up to Father with a smile and flipped him on the nose. At that, Polda and Pauline clapped their hands, stamped their feet, and each grabbing one of Father's arms, began to dance with him around the table. Thus, because of the girls' good nature, the cloud of unpleasantness dispersed in general hilarity.

That was the beginning of a series of most interesting and most unusual lectures which my father, inspired by the charm of that small and innocent audience, delivered during the subsequent weeks of that early winter.

It is worth noting how, in contact with that strange man, all things reverted, as it were, to the roots of their existence, rebuilt their outward appearance anew from their metaphysical core, returned to the primary idea, in order to betray it at some point and to turn into the doubtful, risky and equivocal regions which we shall call for short the Regions of the Great Heresy. Our Heresiarch walked meanwhile like a mesmerist, infecting everything with his dangerous charm. Am I to call Pauline his victim? She became in those days his pupil and disciple, and at the same time a guinea pig for his experiments.

Next I shall attempt to explain, with due care and without causing offence, this most heretical doctrine that held Father in its sway for many months to come and which during this time prompted all his actions.

Treatise on Tailors' Dummies, or The Second Book of Genesis

'The Demiurge,' said my father, 'has had no monopoly of creation, for creation is the privilege of all spirits. Matter has been given infinite fertility, inexhaustible vitality, and, at the same time, a seductive power of temptation which invites us to create as well. In the depth of matter, indistinct smiles are shaped, tensions build up, attempts at form appear. The whole of matter pulsates with infinite possibilities that send dull shivers through it. Waiting for the life-giving breath of the spirit, it is endlessly in motion. It entices us with a thousand sweet, soft, round shapes which it blindly dreams up within itself.

'Deprived of all initiative, indulgently acquiescent, pliable like a woman, submissive to every impulse, it is a territory outside any law, open to all kinds of charlatans and dilettanti, a domain of abuses and of dubious demiurgical manipulations. Matter is the most passive and most defenceless essence in cosmos. Anyone can mould it and shape it; it obeys everybody. All attempts at organizing matter are transient and temporary, easy to reverse and to dissolve. There is no evil in reducing life to other and newer forms. Homicide is not a sin. It is sometimes a necessary violence on resistant and ossified forms of existence which have ceased to be amusing. In the interests of an important and fascinating experiment, it can even become meritorious. Here is the starting point of a new apologia for sadism.'

My father never tired of glorifying this extraordinary element matter.

'There is no dead matter,' he taught us, 'lifelessness is only a disguise behind which hide unknown forms of life. The range of these forms is infinite and their shades and nuances limitless. The Demiurge was in possession of important and interesting creative recipes. Thanks to them, he created a multiplicity of species which renew themselves by their own devices. No one knows whether these recipes will ever be reconstructed. But this is unnecessary, because even if the classical methods of creation should prove inaccessible for evermore, there still remain some illegal methods, an infinity of heretical and criminal methods.'

As my father proceeded from these general principles of cosmogony to the more restricted sphere of his private interests, his voice sank to an impressive whisper, the lecture became more and more complicated and difficult to follow, and the conclusions which he reached became more dubious and dangerous. His gestures acquired an esoteric solemnity. He half-closed one eye, put two fingers to his forehead while a look of extraordinary slyness came over his face. He transfixed his listeners with these looks, violated with his cynical expression their most intimate and most private reserve, until he had reached them in the furthest corner whither they had retreated, pressed them against the wall, and tickled them with the finger of irony, finally producing a glimmer of understanding laughter, the laughter of agreement and admission, the visible sign of capitulation.

The girls sat perfectly still, the lamp smoked, the piece of material under the needle of the sewing machine had long since slipped to the floor, and the machine ran empty, stitching only the black, starless cloth unwinding from the bale of winter darkness outside the window.

'We have lived for too long under the terror of the matchless perfection of the Demiurge,' my father said. 'For too long the perfection of his creation has paralysed our own creative instinct. We don't wish to compete with him. We have no ambition to emulate him. We wish to be creators in our own, lower sphere; we want to have the privilege of creation, we want creative delights, we want—in one word—Demiurgy.' I don't know on whose behalf my father was proclaiming these demands, what community or corporation, sect or order supported him loyally and lent the necessary weight to his words. As for us, we did not share these demiurgical aspirations.

But Father had meanwhile developed the programme of this second Demiurgy, the picture of the second Genesis of creatures which was to stand in open opposition to the present era.

'We are not concerned,' he said, 'with long-winded creations, with long-term beings. Our creatures will not be heroes of romances in many volumes. Their roles will be short, concise; their characters—without a background. Sometimes, for one gesture, for one word alone, we shall make the effort to bring them to life. We openly admit: we shall not insist either on durability or solidity of workmanship; our creations will be temporary, to serve for a single occasion. If they be human beings, we shall give them, for example, only one profile, one hand, one leg, the one limb needed for their role. It would be pedantic to bother about the other, unnecessary, leg. Their backs can be made of canvas or simply whitewashed. We shall have this proud slogan as our aim: a different actor for every gesture. For each action, each word, we shall call to life a different human being. Such is our whim, and the world will be run according to our pleasure. The Demiurge was in love with consummate, superb and complicated materials; we shall give priority to trash. We are simply entranced and enchanted by the cheapness, shabbiness and inferiority of material.

'Can you understand,' asked my father, 'the deep meaning of that weakness, that passion for coloured tissue, for papier-mâché, for distemper, for oakum and sawdust? This is,' he continued with a pained smile, 'the proof of our love for matter as such, for its fluffiness or porosity, for its unique mystical consistency. Demiurge, that great master and artist, made matter invisible, made it disappear under the surface of life. We, on the contrary, love its creaking, its resistance, its clumsiness. We like to see behind each gesture, behind each move, its inertia, its heavy effort, its bearlike awkwardness.'

The girls sat motionless, with glazed eyes. Their faces were long and stultified by listening, their cheeks flushed, and it would have been difficult to decide at that moment whether they belonged to the first or the second Genesis of Creation.

'In one word,' Father concluded, 'we wish to create man a second time—in the shape and semblance of a tailors' dummy.'

Here, for reasons of accuracy, we must describe an insignificant small incident which occurred at that point of the lecture and to which we do not attach much importance. The incident, completely nonsensical and incomprehensible in the sequence of events, could probably be explained as vestigial automatism, without cause and effect, as an instance of the malice of inanimate objects transferred into the region of psychology. We advise the reader to treat it as lightly as we are doing. Here is what happened:

Just as my father pronounced the word 'dummy', Adela looked at her wristwatch and exchanged a knowing look with Polda. She then moved her chair forward and, without getting up from it, lifted her dress to reveal her foot tightly covered in black silk, and then stretched it out stiffly like a serpent's head.

She sat thus throughout that scene, upright, her large eyes shining from atropine, fluttering, while Polda and Pauline sat at her sides. All three looked at Father with wide-open eyes. My father coughed nervously, fell silent and suddenly became very red in the face. Within a minute the lines of his face, so expressive and vibrant a moment before, became still and his expression became humble.

He—the inspired Heresiarch, just emerging from the clouds of exaltation—suddenly collapsed and folded up. Or perhaps he had been exchanged for another man? That other man now sat stiffly, very flushed, with downcast eyes. Polda went up to him and bent over him. Patting him lightly on the back, she spoke in the tone of gentle encouragement: 'Jacob must be sensible. Jacob must obey. Jacob must not be obstinate. Please, Jacob . . . Please . . .'

Adela's outstretched slipper trembled slightly and shone like a serpent's tongue. My father rose slowly, still looking down, took a step forwards like an automaton, and fell to his knees. The lamp hissed in the silence of the room, eloquent looks ran up and down in the thicket of wallpaper patterns, whispers of venomous tongues floated in the air, zigzags of thought . . .

Treatise on Tailors' Dummies, continuation

The next evening Father reverted with renewed enthusiasm to his dark and complex subject. Each wrinkle of his deeply lined face expressed incredible cunning. In each fold of skin, a missile of irony lay hidden. But occasionally inspiration widened the spirals of his wrinkles and they swelled horribly and sank in silent whorls into the depths of the winter night.

'Figures in a waxwork museum,' he began, 'even fairground parodies of dummies, must not be treated lightly. Matter never makes jokes: it is always full of the tragically serious. Who dares to think that you can play with matter, that you can shape it for a joke, that the joke will not be built in, will not eat into it like fate, like destiny? Can you imagine the pain, the dull imprisoned suffering, hewn into the matter of that dummy which does not know why it must be what it is, why it must remain in that forcibly imposed form which is no more than a parody? Do you understand the power of form, of expression, of pretence, the arbitrary tyranny imposed on a helpless block, and ruling it like its own, tyrannical, despotic soul? You give a head of canvas and oakum an expression of anger and leave it with it, with the convulsion, the tension enclosed once and for all, with a blind fury for which there is no outlet. The crowd laughs at the parody. Weep, ladies, over your own fate, when you see the misery of imprisoned matter, of tortured matter which does not know what it is and why it is, nor where the gesture may lead that has been imposed on it for ever.

'The crowd laughs. Do you understand the terrible sadism, the exhilarating, demiurgical cruelty of that laughter? Yet we should weep, ladies, at our own fate, when we see that misery of violated matter, against which a terrible wrong has been committed. Hence the frightening sadness of all those jesting golems, of all effigies which brood tragically over their comic grimaces.

'Look at the anarchist Luccheni, the murderer of the Empress Elizabeth of Austria; look at Draga, the diabolical and unhappy Queen of Serbia; look at that youth of genius, the hope and pride of his ancient family, ruined by the unfortunate habit of masturbation. Oh, the irony of those names, of those pretensions!

'Is there anything left of Queen Draga in the wax figure's likeness, any similarity, even the most remote shadow of her being? But the resemblance, the pretence, the name, reassures us and stops us from asking what that unfortunate figure is in itself and by itself. And yet it must be somebody, somebody anonymous, menacing and unhappy, some being that in its dumb existence had never heard of Queen Draga...

'Have you heard at night the terrible howling of these wax figures, shut in the fairbooths; the pitiful chorus of those forms of wood or porcelain, banging their fists against the walls of their prisons?'

In my father's face, convulsed by the horror of the visions which he had conjured up from darkness, a spiral of wrinkles appeared, a maelstrom growing deeper and deeper, at the bottom of which there flared the terrible eye of a prophet. His beard bristled grotesquely, the tufts of hair growing from warts and moles and from his nostrils stood on end. He became rigid and stood with flaming eyes, trembling from an internal conflict like an automaton of which the mechanism has broken down.

Adela rose from her chair and asked us to avert our eyes from what was to follow. Then she went up to Father and, with her hands on her hips in a pose of great determination, she spoke very clearly.

The two other girls sat stiffly, with downcast eyes, strangely numb . . .

Treatise on Tailors' Dummies, conclusion

On one of the following evenings, my father continued his lecture thus: 'When I announced my talk about lay figures, I had not really wanted to speak about those incarnate misunderstandings, those sad parodies that are the fruits of a common and vulgar lack of restraint. I had something else in mind.'

Here my father began to set before our eyes the picture of that *generatio aequivoca* which he had dreamed up, a species of beings only half organic, a kind of pseudofauna and pseudoflora, the result of a fantastic fermentation of matter.

They were creations resembling, in appearance only, living creatures such as crustaceans, vertebrates, cephalopods. In reality the appearance was misleading—they were amorphous creatures, with no internal structure, products of the imitative tendency of matter which, equipped with memory, repeats from force of habit the forms already accepted. The morphological scope of matter is limited on the whole and a certain quota of forms is repeated over and over again on various levels of existence.

These creatures—mobile, sensitive to stimuli, and yet outside the pale of real life—could be brought forth by suspending certain complex colloids in solutions of kitchen salt. These colloids, after a number of days, would form and organize themselves in precipitations of substance resembling lower forms of fauna.

In creatures conceived in this way, one could observe the processes of respiration and metabolism, but chemical analysis revealed in them traces neither of albumen nor of carbon compounds.

Yet these primitive forms were unremarkable compared with the richness of shapes and the splendour of the pseudofauna and pseudoflora, which sometimes appeared in certain strictly defined environments, such as old apartments saturated with the emanations of numerous existences and events; used-up atmospheres, rich in the specific ingredients of human dreams; rubbish heaps, abounding in the humus of memories, of nostalgia, and of sterile boredom. On such a soil, this pseudo-vegetation sprouted abundantly yet ephemerally, brought forth short-lived generations which flourished suddenly and splendidly, only to wilt and perish.

In apartments of that kind, wallpapers must be very weary and bored with the incessant changes in all the cadenzas of rhythm; no wonder that they are susceptible to distant, dangerous dreams. The essence of furniture is unstable, degenerate, and receptive to abnormal temptations: it is then that on this sick, tired, and wasted soil colourful and exuberant mildew can flourish in a fantastic growth, like a beautiful rash.

'As you will no doubt know,' said my father, 'in old apartments there are rooms which are sometimes forgotten. Unvisited for months on end, they wilt neglected between the old walls and it happens that they close in on themselves, become overgrown with bricks and, lost once and for all to our memory, forfeit their only claim to existence. The doors, leading to them from some backstairs landing, have been overlooked by people living in the apartment for so long that they merge with the wall, grow into it, and all trace of them is obliterated in a complicated design of lines and cracks.

'Once, early in the morning towards the end of winter,' my father continued, 'after many months of absence, I entered such a forgotten passage, and I was amazed at the appearance of the rooms.

'From all the crevices in the floor, from all the mouldings, from every recess, there grew slim shoots filling the grey air with a scintillating filigree lace of leaves: a hothouse jungle, full of whispers and flicking lights—a false and blissful spring. Around the bed, under the lamp, along the wardrobes, grew clumps of delicate trees which, high above, spread their luminous crowns and fountains of lacy leaves, spraying chlorophyll, and thrusting up to the painted heaven of the ceiling. In the rapid process of blossoming, enormous white and pink flowers opened among the leaves, bursting from bud under your very eyes, displaying their pink pulp and spilling over to shed their petals and fall apart in quick decay.

'I was happy,' said my father, 'to see that unexpected flowering which filled the air with a soft rustle, a gentle murmur, falling like coloured confetti through the thin rods of the twigs.

'I could see the trembling of the air, the fermentation of too rich an atmosphere which provoked that precocious blossoming, luxuriation and wilting of the fantastic oleanders which had filled the room with a rare, lazy snowstorm of large pink clusters of flowers.

'Before nightfall,' concluded my father, 'there was no trace left of that splendid flowering. The whole elusive sight was a fata morgana, an example of the strange make believe of matter which had created a semblance of life.'

My father was strangely animated that day; the expression in his eyes—a sly, ironic expression—was vivid and humorous. Later he suddenly became more serious and again analysed the infinite diversity of forms which the multifarious matter could adopt. He was fascinated by doubtful and problematic forms, like the ectoplasm of a medium, by pseudomatter, the cataleptic emanations of the brain which in some instances spread from the mouth of the person in a trance over the whole table, filled the whole room, a floating, rarefied tissue, as astral dough, on the borderline between body and soul.

'Who knows,' he said, 'how many suffering, crippled, fragmentary forms of life there are, such as the artificially created life of chests and tables quickly nailed together, crucified timbers, silent martyrs to cruel human inventiveness? The terrible transplantation of incompatible and hostile races of wood, their merging into one misbegotten personality.

'How much ancient suffering is there in the varnished grain, in the veins and knots of our old familiar wardrobes? Who would recognize in them the old features, smiles and glances, almost planed and polished out of all recognition?'

My father's face, when he said that, dissolved into a thoughtful net of wrinkles, began to resemble an old plank full of knots and veins, from which all memories had been planed away. For a moment we thought that Father would fall into a state of apathy, which sometimes took hold of him, but all of a sudden he recovered himself and continued to speak:

'Ancient, mythical tribes used to embalm their dead. The walls of their houses were filled with bodies and heads immured in them: a father would stand in a corner of the living room—stuffed, the tanned skin of a deceased wife would serve as a mat under the table. I knew a certain sea captain who had in his cabin a lamp, made by Malayan embalmers from the body of his murdered mistress. On her head, she wore enormous antlers. In the stillness of the cabin, the face stretched between the antlers at the ceiling, slowly lifted its eyelids: on the half-opened lips a bubble of saliva would glint, then burst with the softest of whispers. Octopuses, tortoises and enormous crabs, hanging from the rafters in place of chandeliers, moving their legs endlessly in that stillness, walking, walking, walking without moving . . .'

My father's face suddenly assumed a worried, sad expression when his thoughts, stirred by who knows what associations, prompted him to new examples:

'Am I to conceal from you,' he said in a low tone, 'that my own brother, as a result of a long and incurable illness, has been gradually transformed into a bundle of rubber tubing, and that my poor cousin had to carry him day and night on his cushion, singing the luckless creature endless lullabies on winter nights? Can there be anything sadder than a human being changed into the rubber tube of an enema? What disappointment for his parents, what confusion for their feelings, what frustration of the hopes centred around the promising youth! And yet, the faithful love of my poor cousin was not denied him even during that transformation.'

'Oh, please, I cannot, I really cannot listen to this any longer!' groaned Polda leaning over her chair. 'Make him stop, Adela . . .'

The girls got up, Adela went up to my father with an outstretched finger made as if to tickle him. Father lost countenance, immediately stopped talking and, very frightened, began to back away from Adela's moving finger. She followed him, however, threatening him with her finger, driving him, step by step, out of the room. Pauline yawned and stretched herself. She and Polda, leaning against one another, exchanged a look and a smile.

(*Translated by Celina Wieniewska*)

Aleksander Wat

The History of the Last Revolution in England

Barely had the nervous, screaming Parisian stock-market sputtered 'Pound: 300' when a revolution broke out in England. Upon riding into what was usually a fairly empty street in the City, a clerk returning late from his relatives' cottage near London skidded and fell, smearing himself with something sticky and foul-smelling: blood. If he had not been late, if he had driven in twenty minutes earlier, he would most likely not be alive today: a fierce battle had raged in the streets of London. These were not crowds clashing with police, this was not a strike or even a general strike—it was a revolution! The first social revolution in England: armies of workers and the unemployed had poured in from the factory districts, from the industrial regions, from the provinces, a civil war, the red flag, blood. The heroically alert red eye of Moscow (red from sleeplessness as well) flickered with joy and hope: an international revolution! In Germany fear was stifled by the sweet hope of revenge. The franc—the powerless and defeated Carpentier got to his feet—would get stronger and return with a little extra punch. The mines of Upper Silesia and Dąbrowa thundered with a quickened pulse. Calm, phlegmatic Englishmen took to the streets in a stupor to examine the barricades, trenches, projectiles, and they understood nothing. And understanding nothing, they would die: in the rattle of machine-gun fire, in the onslaught of the front lines, in the strategy of street battles when the hissing projectiles—blasting holes, breaking windows, uprooting trees, lopping off treetops, toppling weak buildings, overturning buses, filling the air with gurgling, clatter, moans, commands, the internationale, and thunderclaps— sent the parchmentlike Anglo-Saxon souls of Englishmen who believed in the Bible, the King, and the Magna Carta into the afterworld.

On the morning of the third day the battle was concentrated on a narrow and insignificant street leading to the Parliament buildings. The success or failure of the revolution would be determined by the battle for this street. And a furious battle raged for two days. A mere few yards divided the enemies. The proles were attacking like lions. Police and army divisions defended themselves courageously. The vicissitudes of this battle will find historians who will not neglect to illuminate them exhaustively and universally, from all sides and positions. Even being aware of the involuntary distortions of the chroniclers in everything that concerns generalities, the amazingly absurd twisting of perspectives and false organization of facts into causes and effects, we feel obliged to objectively illuminate the mysterious finale of the last revolution in England (regardless of whether or not it will correspond to any ideology)—if not *ex visu et auditu* (as Swedenborg boasted in the subtitles of his works), then at least in the way we heard it from lips absolutely deserving of belief.

It happened thus. A freckled, lively Daniel Smith, while loading an ammunition belt into his outdated Maxim, suddenly saw a ball falling toward him from above—a bomb? shrapnel thrown from a plane or from a window by some fanatic enemy of the proletariat? This master of the forward line on the workers' team in Lexington, a man who worshipped three things—social revolution in England, soccer and large, healthy blondes—did not need long to think. He deflected the ball with an excellent manoeuvre in the direction of his opponents, in accordance with all the requirements of a good soccer game, of course. Must we go into detail except to say a certain Robin Smith, Police Officer No. 157 (who wore on his splendid torso, in between medals for courage, several medals for victory on the playing fields), claimed that he saw the bold and precise move of Daniel Smith? It is obvious that the cannonball, bomb or shrapnel flew, dashed and sailed from one army to the other, forgetting apparently where it was supposed to explode. It did not explode at all—it was not a cannonball or a bomb or shrapnel, but a normal soccer ball, which had wandered in no one knows how or where, sent by providence, as some claim; to illustrate the nonsense of historical chance, as others maintain; or simply thrown by some little tyke or crazy dreamer, who did not comprehend the enormous, almost cosmic weight of the contest for Great Britain, for the future of the world, for parliament, for MacDonald, for humanity, or for the king—as others would like.

The yelling of the furious trade unionists and the over-whelming lion's roar of British might continued. Missiles, bullets, projectiles fell, fighters fell, the cannonade boomed, salvos thundered, but a ball, an ordinary soccer ball, like so many others in sports shops, unremarkable in every way, a safe soccer ball threatening no one with anything sailed over the combatants, over the convolutions of battle, between the bloodied barricades, drawing more attention to itself, more passion and more heroic courage than deadly, dangerous bullets. Does it always have to be true in human history that the simple, safe, small, insignificant, worthless things excite more passion, kindle more courage, animosity and heroism; arouse more interest and encourage greater effort than the dangerous, harmful, great, dignified, deadly things? So be it—we will say with great solemnity. If that is how things really are, we should be happy; for there are so many harmful and explosive and annihilating things that one should wish that humanity devote as little attention to them as possible.

Leaving these superfluous digressions to sworn historians, then, let us return to our barricades, where death, reaped with carbines and cannons, is not neglecting the rational sports culture of its lower extremities, either.

First Fred Cook got off the barricade. The blood of a born soccer player took over in him as soon as he saw the shot the police officers had missed. Paying no heed to the bullets which, whistling like innocent flies, stung harder than the tsetse, and paying no heed to death, which in this instant knocked comrade Tom, Police Officer No. 530, naval officer Milton Black, a student from Oxford, and volunteer Bob Clay from the scaffolding, the combatants the people, and finally the soccer players began to climb down from the barricade smeared with red paste one by one and, as much as the narrowness of the street allowed, began to organize themselves into regular soccer teams. Harry Ball, a formidable speaker, the secretary of the union of leatherstitchers, the father of seven children, fell, without having had time to touch the ball with his raised leg. The ball was immediately picked up by a greater lover of whisky than soccer, Ball's compatriot, Samuels. Barely had Captain George Lloyd bounced the ball off his head than it (the head not the ball) was pierced by the bullet of a Russian communist, delegate Trofim Aibeshetz. It was he, Trofim Abramowicz Aibeshetz, the lumen of the Comintern, it was he alone who with madness, with despair, in his bulging, nearsighted eyes looked at the emotional *danse macabre* with the ball. In vain did he call to his comrades to come to their senses, to take advantage of the moment for a conclusive attack. Possessed by fury, he aimed at the accursed ball (and kept missing because of his extreme nearsightedness), until finally the mighty proletarian fist of comrade Daniel Smith brought him low and, in this way, with a truly English deed, documented the difference between a national and a nationalistic communism.

The shots were beginning to die down, the bullets were ceasing to cut the smoke-filled air, as if even they were becoming interested in the flight of the ordinary soccer ball. Hour after hour passed—the game continued with unflagging verve. The revolutionaries as well as the government side showed first-rate agility and skill, even more than earlier during the murdering. The advantage shifted from one side to the other, unable to make a decisive choice, due, perhaps, to the poor condition of the turf.

This lasted quite a while, until a certain (alas, nameless)

player from the camp of the revolutionaries shot the ball so badly that it fell in the middle of the road and got stuck among the fallen. What should they do? The first man to move out for the ball, the theoretician of small medieval revolutionary movements, Max Weller (with a true-believer, Marxist beard), a peerless dialectician and passionate hockey fan, fell right in front of the tangled ball after being shot by a corporal of the colonial armies who broke the ceasefire (and whose name, unfortunately, we are also unable to pass on to posterity). The next one who tried to get at the ball, a police officer, was felled by a proletarian bullet. Nine or ten boldhearted chaps lost their lives, their bodies lining both sides of the barricades right up to the ball. Once more, a penetrating historian might see some kind of symbol in this— but never mind what kind. It is enough that once again the cannons sounded, machine guns rattled and the life and death struggle, the harsh battle for prosperity, tradition, ideas, and revolution began anew.

In the meantime dusk had fallen; it was the evening of the second day. Throughout the entire night the thudding sounds continued, growing louder, then softer. The splendid courage of those fighting, itself worthy of a separate monograph, did not advance anyone's cause even an inch. The decisive moment of the fight was again put off to the next day and looked forward to impatiently by the tired, sleepless, famished combatants.

As soon as dawn broke and they saw—among the lifeless logs of corpses and the twisted bodies of the wounded, among hands stretched and frozen in movement—the ordinary, living rubber ball, whole and untouched, perfect in its round greyness—then, involuntarily, a joyous shout, a shout expressing an aroused instinct of self-preservation, the joy of life, a shout, which once must have greeted the sun after an eclipse, escaped from the breast of people weary with murdering, brutalized into a stubborn anger, hatred, deadly rancour, prejudice and the desire for blood—escaped from the breast of the police officers and communists alike.

Joyous white flags appeared over both sides of the barricades, almost simultaneously.

An hour later two divisions, formed from the best soccer players, were marching towards the nearest playing field. They had decided to settle the battle for the street with a proper match. The losing side was to surrender unconditionally. Only a guard remained on the barricades to maintain order.

We could not find out, in spite of scrupulously conducted research, what the course of the match was or how many goals were kicked on each side. After an undoubtedly fierce and heated game—for the stakes were the fate of the entire world—the government forces won a smashing victory. This does not mean that the proletarian team had worse players— this must be stated and underlined. As luck would have it, the players on the police team simply played better as a team, and why not—how was Red Bob from Loughborough supposed to get together with towheaded Harold from Blackwall, or with bearded Black Tom from the Liverpool docks? Luck, chance, or historical necessity? Seek your answer to this question from philosophers of history. I simply wanted to tell you how the first, and, God willing, last revolution in England came to an end.

(*Translated by Lilian Vallee*)

Witold Gombrowicz

Dinner at Countess Kotłubay's

I t's difficult to state with absolute certainty what my intimate acquaintance with Countess Kotłubay was founded
upon. Naturally, speaking of intimacy, I have in mind only
that fragile mode of closeness possible between a full-
blooded and to-the-bone aristocratic member of society, and
an individual from a sphere which is respectable and worthy
enough, but only middle-class. I flatter myself that on a good
day I possess in my demeanour a certain loftiness, a deeper
gaze and a sense of idealism, which allowed me to win the
discriminating sympathy of the countess. For since childhood
I have felt a close affinity with Pascal's 'thinking reed' and
have had an inclination towards the sublime; I often spend
long hours contemplating lofty and beautiful ideas.

Thus selfless inquiry—this nobility of thought, this
romantic, aristocratic, idealistic, slightly anachronistic attitude of mind—earned me, I suspect, access to the countess's
petits fours and to her incomparable Friday dinners. For the
countess belonged to that rare breed of women—at once
evangelic and renaissance—who preside over charity balls
and at the same time pay homage to the Muses. Her countless
acts of compassion aroused admiration. The fame of her
philanthropic 'teas' and artistic 'five o'clocks' at which she
performed like some Medici princess was widespread, while
the smaller salon, where the countess used to receive just a
handful of truly close and trustworthy guests, was tempting
in its exclusivity.

But most famous were the countess's vegetarian dinners.

Those dinners gave her, as she used to say, a breathing space in the continuous stream of philanthropy. They were something of a holiday, a new point of departure. 'I too want to have something for myself,' said the countess with a sad smile, inviting me for the first time to one of those dinners two months ago. 'Please come on Friday. A little singing and music, a small circle of my closest friends and you. And it's on Friday in order to avoid even a shadow of thought about, well . . . meat,' she recoiled slightly, 'about this eternal meat of yours and this blood . . . Too much carnivorousness, too many meaty smells. You see no happiness beyond a bloody beefsteak! You run away from fasts. You would gobble up disgusting scraps of meat all day long without a break! I am throwing down my gauntlet,' she added with a subtle wink of her eye, meaningful and symbolic as usual. 'I want to convince you that a fast is not a diet, but a feast for the spirit.'

What an honour! To be numbered among the ten people, fifteen at most, who gained access to the countess's meatless dinners!

The world of high society, let alone the world of those dinners, has always held a magnetic attraction for me. It seems that the countess's secret aim was to dig, as it were, new trenches of the Holy Alliance* against the barbarity of our days (after all the blood of the Krasińskis† ran in her veins), that she wanted to pay tribute to the deep conviction that blue-blooded aristocracy exists not only to adorn fêtes and parties but that also in other, spiritual and artistic areas, it is capable of self-sufficiency by virtue of the superiority of its race; that therefore a truly aspiring salon is an aristocratic

---

* The Holy Alliance: a league formed after the fall of Napoleon by the sovereigns of Austria, Russia and Prussia, professedly to regulate all national and international relations in accordance with the principles of Christian charity.
† An allusion to a masterpiece of Polish romantic literature, *The Un-Divine Comedy*, and its author, Count Zygmunt Krasiński, who, shaken by the waves of popular unrest sweeping post-Napoleonic Europe, depicted an apocalyptic vision of the collapse and destruction of European culture.

salon. It was an archaic, if somewhat unoriginal thought, but at any rate—in its venerable archaism—unbelievably brave and deep, such as could rightly be expected from the descendant of hetmans.* And indeed, at the table in the historic dining-room, away from corpses and murders, away from the billions of slaughtered cows and oxen, the representatives of the oldest families under the countess's leadership would resurrect Plato's symposia. It seemed that the spirit of poetry and philosophy rose from among the crystal and flowers and that the charmed words fell spontaneously into rhyme.

There was, for instance, one prince who at the countess's request took the role of intellectual and philosopher, and he acted it royally, delivering such beautiful and noble ideas that on hearing them Plato himself would have humbly consented to wait upon the prince, napkin in hand. There was a baroness who undertook to enliven the meetings with her singing, and although she had never been taught to sing I doubt whether even Ada Sari would have sung so well in such a situation. Something inexpressibly marvellous, wonderfully vegetarian, luxuriously vegetarian, I would say, was contained in the gastronomic frugality of those parties; and seeing those gigantic fortunes modestly bent over small portions of kohlrabi made an unforgettable impression, particularly in view of the horrific carnivorousness of our times. Even our teeth, the teeth of rodents, were losing their Cain-like stigma. As for the cuisine—undoubtedly the countess's had no equal. The extraordinarily rich, juicy taste of her tomatoes stuffed with rice, the firmness and aroma of her omelettes with asparagus were truly divine.

After a few months, on the Friday I'm going to speak about, I was honoured with another invitation, and with understandable nervousness I drove in a modest drozhka under the ancient fronton of the palace located near Warsaw.

---

* Hetman: one of the four highest commanders of the Polish army up to the eighteenth century; a position usually held by members of aristocratic families.

But instead of the greater number of people I had expected
I found only two guests, and even these were not in the least
distinguished: a toothless old marquise who made a virtue
of necessity by indulging in vegetables every day of the week,
and a baron, namely Baron de Apfelbaum of a somewhat
dubious family, who by means of his millions and his
mother—*née* Princess Pstryczyńska—had redeemed himself
from the number of his ancestors and his otherwise irredeem-
able nose. From the start I sensed a subtle dissonance, as if
something was out of tune. Moreover, the pumpkin soup—
spécialité de la maison—soup from a pumpkin cooked sweet
and tender, which was served as the first course, turned out
to be unexpectedly thin, watery and tasteless. However I
betrayed not the slightest sign of surprise or disappointment
(this kind of behaviour would be acceptable anywhere else
but not at Countess Kotłubay's); instead, with my face bright
and exalted I managed a compliment:

Can one praise this soup any further?
Cooked without a corpse or a murder.

As I mentioned before, at the countess's Friday dinners
poetic verses would form themselves on one's lips as a result
of the exceptional harmony and loftiness of these meetings;
it would be simply unbecoming not to weave rhymes into
stretches of prose. Suddenly—to my horror!—Baron de
Apfelbaum, who, as a poet of exceeding refinement and a
fastidious gourmand, was an ardent admirer of the hostess's
inspired gastronomy, leans towards me and whispers in my
ear with ill-concealed distaste and an anger which I never
would have suspected of him:

The soup could be good—agree without fuss
If only the cook weren't such an . . .

Surprised by this naughty aside I coughed. What did he mean
by that? Luckily the baron restrained himself. What on earth
had happened since my last visit? The dinner seemed to be

merely the phantom of a dinner, the food was mean, the faces were long... After the soup the second course was served—a platter of thin and peaky carrot in brown flour and butter. I admired the countess's spiritual strength. Pale, in a black *toilette* with family diamonds, she consumed the dubious dish with undaunted courage, thus forcing us to follow her, and with her usual skill she led the conversation towards celestial heights. She started off with charm, though not without melancholy, waving her napkin:

Let there flow some deeper thoughts, more fruity!
Tell me now, friends—what is Beauty?

I responded immediately, giving myself suitable airs and glittering along with the front of my evening suit:

No doubt it's Love in all its ways!
On us it shines and bestows its rays!
On us—the birds who don't sow but reap,
The dee-jayed birds on this earthly trip.

The countess thanked me with a smile for the immaculate beauty of this thought. The baron, like a thoroughbred seized by the spirit of noble rivalry, drumming his fingers, throwing sparks from the precious stones—and rhymes whose art he alone possessed—took off:

Beauty—rose,
Beauty—storm,
(and so on ...)
But more beautiful than those
is Charity. For look, behold!
Outside it's raining all the time.
Wind, rain and cold—
—like a punishment for a crime.
Oh! those unhappy and poor of mine!
Indeed, this little tear of sympathy,
This little shower of charity,

This is the secret of beauty and nobility.

'Beautifully expressed, dear sir,' lisped the toothless marquise ecstatically. 'Wonderful! Charity! St Francis of Assisi! I too have my poor little children suffering from the English disease to whom I have sacrificed my toothless old age. We ought to think constantly about the poor, unhappy ones.'

'About prisoners and cripples who can't afford artificial limbs,' added the baron.

'About old, skinny, emaciated ex-schoolmistresses,' said the countess compassionately.

'About hairdressers prostrated by swollen veins and starving miners suffering from ischaemia,' I added, deeply moved.

'Yes,' said the countess, as her eyes lit up and she gazed into the distance. 'Yes, Love, Charity, two flowers—*roses de thé*, tea roses of life . . . But one shouldn't forget about one's noble duty to oneself.' And having thought a little, she said, paraphrasing the famous dictum of Prince Poniatowski: 'God entrusted me with Maria Kotłubay and to Him alone shall I return her!'*

I need to stir inside me all the might
to keep ideals in my sight,
the everlasting light.

'Bravo! Excellent! What a thought! Deep! Wise! Proud! God entrusted me with Maria Kotłubay and to Him alone shall I return her!' everybody cried, while I, bearing in mind that Prince Józef had been mentioned, allowed myself to strike gently the note of patriotism: 'And remember always—Eagle White.'†

---

* Legend has it that Prince Józef Poniatowski, nephew of the last king of Poland, Stanisław August Poniatowski, threw himself into the river Elbe after the defeat of Napoleon in the 'Battle of the Nations'. This defeat dashed all hope the Poles had for the resurrection of an independent Poland under Napoleon's protectorate, with Prince Jósef as its head.
† White Eagle: Polish national emblem.

The servants brought in an enormous cauliflower swimming in fresh butter, glistening with gold, although on the basis of previous experience one could only assume that its colouring was as misleading as a consumptive's flush. That's what the conversation at the countess's was like. It was a feast even in such unfavourable gastronomic circumstances. I flatter myself that my statement that Love was the most beautiful virtue was by no means a shallow one; I'd even say it might be a jewel in the crown of any philosophical poem. And then another of the guests throws in an aphorism that Charity is even more beautiful than Love. Wonderful! And true! For indeed, when one thinks about it deeply Charity spreads its cloak wider and covers more than lofty Love. But that's not the end of it. This wise Amphitryon of ours, anxious that we should not be carried away by Love and Charity, mentions *en passant* the noble duties one owes to oneself; and then I, subtly taking advantage of the ending on '—ight', added just one thing, 'Eagle White'. And the form, the manners, the mastery of self-expression, the noble and elegant frugality of the feast, all competing with the content. 'Oh no!' I thought delightedly, 'someone who has never been to the countess's Friday dinner—he does not, properly speaking, know the aristocracy.'

'Excellent cauliflower,' all of a sudden muttered the baron, gastronome and poet, and in his voice one could detect a pleasant surprise.

'Indeed,' confirmed the countess, looking at the plate with suspicion.

As for myself I noticed nothing extraordinary in the taste of the cauliflower. It seemed to me as anaemic as the previous dishes.

'Could it be Philip?' asked the countess, her eyes firing sparks.

'We'd better check,' said the marquise mistrustfully.

'Call Philip!' ordered the countess.

'There is no reason to hide it from you, my dear fellow,' said Baron de Apfelbaum, and he explained to me in a low voice, with ill-concealed irritation, what was the matter. Thus, no more and no less, on the previous Friday the countess had caught the cook seasoning her idea of a vegetarian feast with bouillon. What a rascal! I couldn't believe it.

Indeed, only a cook could have done such a thing! What's worse the obstinate cook, as I heard, showed no repentance but had the cheek to contrive in his defence a peculiar argument: that he wanted their lordships to have their cake and eat it. What did he mean by that? (Allegedly, his previous employment was with a bishop.) Only when the countess threatened him with immediate dismissal did he swear to discontinue the practice. 'Fool!' the baron summed up his story. 'The fool, let himself be caught! And that's why, as you see, most people haven't come, and hm, if it hadn't been for the cauliflower I'm afraid they would be quite right.'

'No,' said the toothless marquise, chewing the vegetable with her gums, 'it's not a meaty taste ... Smack, smack ... It's not a meaty taste, rather ... *comment dirais-je*—exceptionally nourishing; must have masses of vitamins.'

'Something pepper-like,' remarked the baron, discreetly helping himself to another portion. 'Something delicately peppery ... smack, smack ... but meatless,' he added hastily. 'Clearly vegetarian, peppery-cauliflowery. You can rely on my palate, my dear Countess. In the matter of taste I'm another Pythia.' But the countess would not calm down until the cook appeared before her—a long, skinny, ginger-haired character with an oblique look—and swore on the grave of his dead wife that the cauliflower was pure beyond reproach.

'Cooks—they are all like that,' I said sympathetically and helped myself too to the dish which was enjoying such popularity (although I still couldn't find in it any outstanding quality). 'Oh yes, one needs to keep an eye on cooks.' (I'm not sure whether such remarks were sufficiently tactful but I was overcome by the excitement—light as champagne bubbles.) 'Cook—in that funny hat of his and an apron!'

'Philip looks so good-natured,' said the countess with a

tone of sadness and a mute reproach as she reached out for the butter-dish.

'Good-natured, good-natured...' I was insisting on my opinions perhaps too stubbornly. 'However, a cook... a cook—please consider this fact, ladies and gentlemen—is a common fellow, *homo vulgaris*, whose task it is to prepare elegant, exquisite dishes—there's a dangerous paradox. Churlishness preparing elegance! What's that supposed to mean?'

'Extraordinary aroma,' said the countess inhaling the bouquet of the cauliflower with her nostrils wide open (I couldn't smell it), and without putting down the fork which flickered constantly in her hand.

'Extraordinary,' repeated the banker, and in order not to spatter his shirt frills with the butter he tucked the napkin under his collar. 'Just a little more, if I may, dear Countess. I'm reviving indeed after that, hm, soup... Smack, smack... True, cooks cannot be trusted. I had a cook who cooked Italian macaroni like no one else. I would simply stuff myself! And one day, can you imagine, I come into the kitchen and see in the saucepan my macaroni swarming, literally swarming! And it was earth-worms—smack, smack—earth-worms which the rascal was serving as macaroni. Since then I never—smack, smack—look into saucepans.'

'There we are,' I said. 'Precisely.' And I went on saying something about cooks, that they are assassins, small-time murderers who don't care what or how as long as there is something to pepper, dress up or prepare. Not entirely proper remarks, and indeed wholly obnoxious, but I got carried away. 'You, dear Countess, who shudder at the idea of touching a cook's head—in soup—you eat his hair!' I could have gone on in that vein even longer, for in no time at all I was overwhelmed by a tide of treacherous eloquence—when suddenly I stopped. No one was listening to me. An extraordinary vista opened before me—that of the countess, an aristocratic patroness and dogaressa, devouring in silence and with such greed that her ears were quivering. It was a sight which both frightened and astonished me. The baron was seconding her bravely, bent over the plate, slurping and smacking with all his heart. The old marquise, too, was trying to keep up with them, chewing and swallowing enormous chunks, apparently afraid they would snatch up the best bits from under her nose.

This sudden and incredible picture of gluttony—I can't express it in any other way—such gluttony, in such a house, this dreadful transgression, this crashing discord, so shocked the foundation of my being that, unable to constrain myself, I sneezed. And because I had left my handkerchief in the pocket of my coat I was forced to excuse myself from the guests and leave the table. In the hall, having collapsed on a chair, I tried to calm my bewildered senses.

Only someone who, like me, had known the countess, the baron and the marquise for such a long time, the elegance of their movements, the delicacy, the frugality and subtlety of all their habits (especially their habits of eating), and the impeccable nobility of their features—only he could appreciate the impression they had made upon me. At that moment I glanced accidentally at a copy of the *Red Courier* sticking out from my coat pocket and my attention was drawn to a sensational headline:

MYSTERIOUS DISAPPEARANCE OF CAULIFLOWER!
Cauliflower Under Threat of Freezing to Death!

And below, the following note:

The farm-hand Walenty Cauliflower from the village of Rudka which belongs to the widely esteemed Countess Kotłubay has reported at the police station that his son Bolek, eight year old, round nose, blond hair, has run away from home. According to the police report the boy ran away because his father flogged him with a belt when drunk and his mother starved him (unfortunately a common occurrence in these days of crisis). There is a fear that the boy could freeze to death wandering about the fields in the bitter autumn weather.

'Tss,' I hissed to myself. 'Tss . . .' I looked through the window at the fields veiled by a thin screen of rain. I returned to the dining-room where the enormous silver platter gaped emptily with the remains of the cauliflower. The countess's stomach looked as if she were seven months pregnant, the baron was virtually drowning his head in the plate and the old marquise was chewing, tirelessly moving her jaws—indeed I'm forced to admit it—like a cow. 'Divine! Marvellous!' they kept repeating, 'Splendid, supreme!' Utterly confused I tried the cauliflower once more, giving it all my attention. But I tried in vain to find something that would even partially justify the astounding behaviour of the guests.

'What on earth can you see in it?' I mumbled shyly, a bit ashamed.

'Ha ha ha, he's asking!' cried out the baron as he stuffed himself, in excellent humour.

'Don't you really see, young man?' asked the marquise, without stopping her consumption even for a second.

'You are not a gastronome, sir,' remarked the baron as if with a shade of polite commiseration. 'And I . . . *Et moi, je ne suis pas gastronome, je suis gastrosophe!*'. And either my ears deceived me or, as he was pronouncing this French phrase, something swelled within him so that the last word '*gastrosophe*' was expelled from his puffed cheeks with an ostentatious superiority I had never seen him show before.

'Well cooked, certainly . . . very tasty, yes, very . . . but . . .' I stumbled.

'But? . . . What "but"? So you really cannot grasp the taste? The delicate freshness, the . . . smack . . . indefinable firmness, the particular pepperiness, the fragrance, the alcohol? Why, of course, dear sir is only pretending. He must be teasing us.' It was the first time since we had met that I had been addressed from such a height as 'dear sir'.

'Don't tell him!' the countess interrupted coquettishly,

rolling with laughter. 'Don't tell him! He won't understand anyway!'

'Good taste, young man, one sucks with one's mother's milk,' lisped the marquise good-naturedly, giving me, as it seemed, to understand that my mother—peace to her memory—must have fed me with a different kind of milk.

And then all of them, forgoing the rest of the dinner, carried their full stomachs over to the golden Louis XVI boudoir where, sprawling on all the softest armchairs, they began to laugh heartily, no doubt at me, as if I had indeed given them reason for such merriment. I have been rubbing shoulders with the aristocracy at teas and charitable concerts for a long time but on my word never have I seen such behaviour, never such a transformation, such an inexplicable metamorphosis. Not knowing whether to stand or sit down, whether to be serious or rather *faire bonne mine à mauvais jeu* and grin, I made a vague and shy attempt to return to Arcadia, that is to Beauty, that is to the pumpkin soup:

'Returning to what is Beauty . . .'

'Enough! Enough,' cried Baron de Apfelbaum, stopping his ears. 'What a bore! Now playtime! *S'encanailler!* I'll sing something better for you! An operetta piece!'

What a funny little twit!
Understands he not a bit.
Let me sharpen then his wit:
Nothing's beautiful in virtue of Beauty chaste.
What's beautiful is of Good Taste.
Taste! Taste! It's got to bear this sign!
That's how Beauty I define!

'Bravo!' exclaimed the countess, and the marquise repeated after her, revealing her gums in a senile giggle, 'Bravo! *Cocasse! Charmant!*'

'But it seems to me that . . . it's not like that . . .' I stuttered, my stupefied look ill becoming my evening dress.

'We, the aristocracy,' the marquise leaned towards me good-naturedly, 'we cultivate a great liberty of manners within our closest circles; but then, as you might have heard, sometimes we even use coarse expressions, sometimes we are frivolous and more often than not—in our own way— vulgar. But one doesn't need to be frightened. One needs to get used to us.'

'We are not so terrible,' added the baron patronisingly. 'Although our vulgarity is more difficult to comprehend than our elegance.'

'No, we are not terrible!' shrieked the countess. 'We don't eat people alive!'

'We don't eat anybody except ...'

'Apart from ...'

'*Fi donc*, ha ha ha!' They burst out laughing, throwing embroidered cushions in the air, and the countess sang:

Yes, yes,
Everything—good taste!
Everything—good taste!
To make lobsters for consumption fit
One must torture them a bit.
Even turkey won't be fat
At the drop of a hat,
Tease it slowly, without haste ...
Do you know how my lips taste?
Who has different taste, alas,
Cannot equal be to us.

'But why?' I whispered. 'Countess ... peas, carrots, celery, kohlrabi ...'

'Cauliflower,' added the baron, choking suspiciously.

'That's it,' I said in complete confusion. 'That's it! ... Cauliflower! . . . Cauliflower . . . Fasting . . . Vegetarian vegetables ...'

'And what about the cauliflower? Tasty, what? Good? I expect you've understood the taste of this cauliflower.' What a tone. How patronising. What a scarcely detectable but dangerous lordly impatience in his tone. I began to stutter, didn't know what to answer, how to deny, or confirm. And then (oh, I would never have believed that this noble, humane individual, this brother-poet, could let me feel to such an extent how their lordships change their manners), then, having spread himself comfortably in his armchair, caressing the thin leg he had inherited from Princess Pstryczyńska, he said to the ladies in a tone which virtually annihilated me: 'Truly, dear Countess, it's not worth inviting to dinner individuals whose taste has not yet passed the stage of a complete primitive.'

And no longer paying any attention to me they began, glasses in hand, to tell jokes among themselves, in such a way that all of a sudden I became superfluous, *quantité negligeable*: about Alice and her 'chimeras', about Gaba and Buba, about Princess Mary, about some 'pheasants' and about this one being 'intolerable' and the other 'impossible'. They gossiped and told anecdotes in a coded, higher language, using expressions such as 'maddening', 'fantastic', 'incredible', 'absolutely', and as often as not swearing—'damn it' or 'bloody hell', till it seemed almost possible that this kind of conversation was the peak of human abilities. And I, with my concept of Beauty, humanity and all the other topics of a thinking reed, not knowing why and how, annihilated and put aside like a useless tool, I couldn't find a word to say. They also swapped baffling aristocratic jokes which caused extraordinary mirth, but at which I, unable to understand them, could hardly raise a smile. Oh God! What had happened? What a sudden and cruel change! Why was their behaviour so different now? Were these the same people with whom, not so long ago, I had been sharing so harmoniously the milk of human kindness and the pumpkin soup? Why this sudden and inexplicable estrangement and coldness? Why so much irony, so much incomprehensible, painful derision, even in their appearance? And such distance, such forbidding remoteness! I couldn't explain to myself this metamorphosis, and the marquise's words about the 'closed circle' led me to think of all those horrible rumours which were spread among the middle classes, which I usually refused to believe, about the two faces of aristocracy and their double life. In the end, incapable of enduring my own silence, which with every second was pushing me into a terrible abyss, I addressed the countess without rhyme or reason, like a late echo from the past:

'Please forgive my interruption, Countess ... you promised to sign for me your triolets *Chit-chats of My Soul.*'

'Pardon me?' she asked, not hearing the question, playful and exhilarated. 'You were saying?'

'Do forgive me—you promised to sign for me your poems *Chit-chats of My Soul.*'

'Ah yes, true, true,' said the countess absent-mindedly but with her usual kindness (usual? or different? or new to such an extent that my cheeks flushed crimson without any conscious co-operation on my part?); and having taken from a little table a small book bound in white she casually scribbled a few kind words on the title page and signed it: 'Countess Kotuboy'. 'But Countess!' I cried out painfully, hurt seeing this historic name so twisted, 'Kotłubay!'

'What absent-mindedness!' exclaimed the countess amid general merriment, 'What absent-mindedness!' But I found nothing to laugh at in all this. Tss ... I almost hissed again. The countess laughed loudly and proudly, and at the same time her aristocratic foot performed various flourishes on the carpet in an immensely ticklish and enticing way, as if delighting itself with the slenderness of its own ankle—now to the left, now to the right, and in circles. The baron, tilted back in his armchair, seemed to be getting ready for an excellent *bon mot*—but his little ear, so typical of the Pstryczyńskis, was even smaller than usual, while his fingers pushed a grape between his lips. The marquise was sitting with her usual elegance, yet it was as if her long thin neck, the neck of a grand dame, grew even longer, and its withered skin seemed to be winking at me. And I should add a small but not irrelevant detail: that out there the rain, blown by the wind, was lashing against the window panes like a thin whip.

Perhaps I took my sudden and undeserved fall from grace too much to heart and, perhaps, this gave way to that persecution complex which preys on low-born individuals admitted to high society, while certain accidental associations, certain, say, analogies may have made me over-sensitive. I don't want to deny it, perhaps ... But suddenly I sensed an extraordinary change in them. And I'm not denying that their grandness, subtlety, elegance and politeness were still as grand, subtle, elegant and polite as they could possibly be—no doubt, but at the same time, and without reason, they were so suffocating that I was inclined to think that all those splendid and humanitarian virtues had gone berserk, as if bitten by a gadfly! What's more, it struck me suddenly (and it was undeniably the effect of that little foot, the ear and the neck), that without looking, and ignoring me in a lordly manner, they still saw my confusion and found it a constant source of delight. I was also touched with a premonition that 'Kotuboy' wasn't necessarily only a *lapsus linguae*, that in a word, if I'm to state it clearly—Kotuboy means 'kot-u-boy'. 'Caught you boy!' Yes, yes, the glittering noses of their patent-leather shoes confirmed my terrifying suspicion. It seemed that behind my back they were still splitting their sides with laughter because I hadn't caught on to the taste of the cauliflower, that for me this cauliflower was an ordinary vegetable, that I had thus proven my complete naivety and my lamentably bourgeois breed by failing to appreciate the cauliflower as I ought. They were secretly splitting their sides with laughter which would have burst forth had I given even the slightest inkling of the emotions raging within me. Yes, oh yes, they were ignoring me, pretending I was not there, but at the same time, slyly using those particular parts of their aristocratic bodies—that little foot, the ear, the neck—they were provoking and daring me to break off the seal on their secret.

No need to repeat again how this quiet tempting, this sly, unhealthy flirting shocked everything there was in me of the thinking reed. I remembered vaguely the 'secret' of aristocracy, this mystery of taste, this secret which no one will come to possess who is not of the chosen, even if, as Schopenhauer says, one were to memorize three hundred rules of *savoir vivre.* And if I were dazzled for a while with the hope that having discovered this secret I would be initiated into their circle, that I would be saying 'fantastic' and 'absolutely' just like them, even then, other things apart, the anxiety and the fear of—why not say it openly?—of being slapped in the face completely paralysed my burning curiosity. One is never sure of the aristocracy. With the aristocracy one needs to be more careful than with a tamed leopard. Once, someone from the bourgeoisie was asked by a Princess X about his mother's maiden name. Encouraged by the liberal manners reigning in that salon and by the tolerance with which his two previous jokes had been acknowledged, thinking he could take liberties, he answered, 'Excuse the expression—Piędzik.' And because of this 'Excuse . . .' (which turned out to be vulgar), he was immediately thrown out.

'Philip . . .' I was thinking carefully, 'but Philip swore . . .! A cook is nevertheless a cook. A cook is a cook, a cauliflower is a cauliflower and the countess a countess, and I wouldn't wish anyone to forget about the last! Yes, the countess is a countess, the baron is a baron, the gusts of wind and the rain outside—wind and rain. And the little hands groping in the darkness, the back bruised by a fatherly thong, now lashed by waves of rain, are just little hands and a bruised back, nothing more . . . And the countess is without any doubt a countess. The countess is a countess and, would to God, that she may not dish out a flick on the nose!'

Seeing that I remained in a complete, virtually paralysed state of passivity, they began to circle stealthily around me, closer and closer, growing more and more provocative and showing more openly their readiness to indulge in mockery and pranks. 'Look at his frightened face!' cried the countess suddenly and they all began to jeer and mock me: that, surely, I must be 'scandalized' and 'horrified' since no doubt in my sphere no one 'talks rhubarb' or plays pranks, that in my sphere manners are incomparably better, and not as barbaric as amongst them, the aristocracy. Pretending to be frightened by my seriousness they began to rebuke and admonish each other jokingly as if to show that above all they cared about my opinion.

'Don't talk nonsense, sir! You are awful!' cried out the countess (although in fact the baron wasn't awful; apart, that is, from his little ear which he was touching, not without pleasure, with the tips of his thin bony fingers).

'Behave yourselves, you lot!' shouted the baron. (The countess and the marquise were behaving quite properly.) 'Stop drivelling! Don't sprawl on the sofa! Stop fidgeting and don't put your feet on the table!' (God forbid! The countess was in no way going to do anything of the sort.) 'You are hurting the feelings of this unfortunate. Your little nose, Countess, is too aristocratic, really. Have pity!' (Who, I ask, was supposed to be pitied on account of that little nose?) The marquise shed silent tears of joy. However, the fact that I put my head in the sand like an ostrich excited them more and more: they looked as if they had thrown caution to the winds, insisting that I should understand; and, unable to restrain themselves, they made more and more transparent allusions. Allusions? To what? Oh, naturally, still to the same thing, and more clearly, circling closer and closer, with more and more daring . . .

'May I smoke?' asked the baron with affectation, taking out a gold cigarette-case. ('May I smoke?' As if he was unaware that out there the dampness and rain and the dreadful cold wind could freeze one stiff within minutes. 'May I smoke?')

'Can you hear the rain lashing down?' lisped the marquise naively. (Lashing?! Sure it's lashing! It must have lashed everything good and proper.) 'Ah, listen to that pitter-patter of single drops. Listen to the tap-tap-tap, listen, oh listen to the raindrops!'

'Oh, what foul weather, what awful wind,' said the countess. 'Ah, ha ha ha, what a terrific squall, hell to look at! The very sight makes me laugh and gives me goose-pimples!'

'Ha ha ha!' followed the baron. 'Look how everything is dripping so magnificently! Look at the arabesques the water is drawing on the window panes. Look at the squelchy mud, its greasy stickiness, how smudgy it is. Just like Cumberland sauce! And this little bit of rain, how it flays and flays, beautifully flays! And this little bit of wind, how it bites and bites! How it crushes, how it tenderizes, how it roasts! On my word, it makes my mouth water!'

'Truly, it's very tasty, very, very tasty.'

'Extremely elegant!'

'Just like *côtelette de volaille*!'

'Just like *fricassée à la Heine*!'

'Or like crabs in ragout!'

After these *bons mots*, thrown around with the liberty that only the full-blooded aristocracy can afford, there followed movements and gestures whose . . . whose meaning I wished, curled up in my chair, oh, how I wished I couldn't understand! I won't even mention here that the ear, the nose, the neck and the little foot were exceeding themselves and were reaching the stage of complete frenzy. What's more, the banker, having inhaled his cigarette smoke deeply, was puffing little blue circles into the air. Had it been one or two, by God! But he puffed and puffed one after another, his lips shaped into a little *moue*, while the countess and the marquise clapped their hands! And every circle soared up into the air, vanishing in a melodious haze. The long, white, serpent-like hand of the countess rested all the time on the variegated satin of the armchair while her nervy ankle twisted under the table, evil like a snake, black and baneful. It made me feel very uneasy! And that's not all (I swear I don't exaggerate): the baron went so far in his effrontery that having lifted his upper lip he took out his tooth-pick from his pocket and started to pick his teeth—yes, his teeth— rich, corrupt, abounding with gold, teeth!

Struck dumb, completely at a loss as to what to do and where to escape to, I turned imploringly to the marquise— who of all of them had been the most sympathetic, and who at the dining-table had extolled so movingly Charity and children suffering from the English disease—I turned to her and began to talk about Charity, almost begging for it myself!

'You, Madame,' I said, 'who with such sacrifice assist the unfortunate children. Madame?' For Christ's sake! Do you know what she said? Surprised, she looked at me with her faded eyes, wiped away the tears caused by the excess of hilarity and then, as if remembering, she said: 'Oh you mean my little ones suffering from the English disease? . . . Oh yes, indeed, when one sees how clumsily they move on those twisted pegs of theirs, how they stumble about and fall over, it makes one feel still vigorous! Old but vigorous! In the old days I used to ride in a black riding-hood and shiny boots, on English thoroughbreds, but now—*hélas, les beaux temps sont passés*—now that I'm not able to because of my age I ride cheerfully on my little twisted English cripples.' Her hand suddenly stretched down and I jumped away, for I swear she was going to show me her old but straight, healthy and vigorous leg!

'Christ the Lord!' I cried half alive. 'But Love, Charity, Beauty, prisoners, cripples, emaciated ex-schoolmistresses.'

'We remember them, we do,' said the countess, laughing, and cold sweat ran down my neck. 'Those poor, dear schoolmistresses.'

'We remember,' the old marquise reassured me.

'We remember,' repeated Baron de Apfelbaum. 'We remember' (I was petrified) 'those good old prisoners.'

They were looking not at me but somewhere at the ceiling, turning up their heads as if that were the only way they could constrain the violent spasms of their cheek muscles. Ha! I had no doubt left. I understood in the end where I was and my jaw started trembling uncontrollably. And the rain was still lashing against the window panes like a thin whip.

'But God, God does exist . . .' I stuttered in the end, my strength leaving me, desperately looking for some refuge. 'God exists,' I added in a lower voice, for the name of God sounded so out of place that in the ensuing silence I could see on their faces all the inauspicious signs confirming my *faux pas*. I was only waiting for the moment when they would show me the door.

'Gold?' responded Baron de Apfelbaum after a while, crushing me with his incomparable tact. 'Gold? Of course it exists. I deal in gold.'

Who could reply to this? Who wouldn't, as they say, forget the tongue in his mouth? I shut up. The marquise sat at the piano while the baron began dancing with the countess, and from their every move there flowed so much good taste and elegance that—oh—I wanted to escape. But how to leave without saying goodbye? And how to say goodbye while they were still dancing? I watched them from the corner and—on my word!—never, never had I dreamed of such wanton abandon. No, I can't go against my nature and describe what happened. No, no one can demand that from me. Suffice it to say that when the countess put forward her little foot the baron withdrew his, many, many times, and all the while their faces showed inexhaustible dignity, bearing an expression as if this dance were—phew!—an ordinary tango; with the marquise churning out trills and arpeggios on the piano! But I knew by then what it was; they had forced it down my throat—it was the dance of cannibals! The dance of cannibals! All done with daintiness, good taste and elegance. I was only looking around for a heathen god, a primeval monster with a square skull, turned-out lips, round cheeks and squashed nose, presiding over the bacchanalia from somewhere above. And turning my eyes towards the window I saw something just like that: a round, childish face, with a squashed nose, raised eyebrows, sticking-out ears, skinny and feverish, staring with the cosmic idiocy of a savage divinity, with such unearthly enchantment that for an hour or two I sat as if hypnotized, unable to tear my eyes away from the buttons of my waistcoat.

And when at dawn I finally sneaked out and ran down the slippery steps into the grey drizzle, in the flower bed under the window I saw a body among the dried irises. It was of course a corpse, the corpse of an eight-year-old boy, blond hair, round nose, wasted to such a degree that one could say it was completely devoured. Only here and there, under the dirty skin remained a little flesh. Ha, so poor Bolek Cauli-

flower had managed to wander as far as here, tempted by
the light of the windows, visible from the distant muddy
fields. And as I was running out of the gate the cook, Philip,
appeared from nowhere—white, in a round cap, with ginger
hair and squinting eyes, skinny but grand with the grandeur
of a master of the culinary art who first slaughters a chicken
in order to serve it later on the table in a ragout. Cringing,
bowing and wagging his tail he said in a servile voice:

'I hope your lordship enjoyed his lenten fare . . .'

(Translated by Wiesiek Powaga)

Tadeusz Borowski

This Way for the Gas, Ladies and Gentlemen

All of us walk around naked. The delousing is finally over, and our striped suits are back from the tanks of Cyclone B solution, an efficient killer of lice in clothing and of men in gas chambers. Only the inmates in the blocks cut off from ours by the 'Spanish goats'* still have nothing to wear. But all the same, all of us walk around naked: the heat is unbearable. The camp has been sealed off tight. Not a single prisoner, not one solitary louse, can sneak through the gate. The labour Kommandos have stopped working. All day, thousands of naked men shuffle up and down the roads, cluster around the squares, or lie against the walls and on top of the roofs. We have been sleeping on plain boards, since our mattresses and blankets are still being disinfected. From the rear blockhouses we have a view of the FKL—*Frauen Konzentration Lager*; there too the delousing is in full swing. Twenty-eight thousand women have been stripped naked and driven out of the barracks. Now they swarm around the large yard between the block-houses.

The heat rises, the hours are endless. We are without even our usual diversion: the wide roads leading to the crematoria are empty. For several days now, no new transports have come in. Part of 'Canada'† has been liquidated and detailed

---

* Crossed wooden beams wrapped in barbed wire.
† 'Canada' designated wealth and well-being in the camp. More specifically, it referred to the members of the labour gang, or Kommando, who helped to unload the incoming transports of people destined for the gas chambers.

to a labour Kommando—one of the very toughest—at
Harmenz. For there exists in the camp a special brand of
justice based on envy: when the rich and mighty fall, their
friends see to it that they fall to the very bottom. And
Canada, our Canada, which smells not of maple forests but
of French perfume, has amassed great fortunes in diamonds
and currency from all over Europe.

Several of us sit on the top bunk, our legs dangling over
the edge. We slice the neat loaves of crisp, crunchy bread. It
is a bit coarse to the taste, the kind that stays fresh for days.
Sent all the way from Warsaw—only a week ago my mother
held this white loaf in her hands . . . dear Lord, dear Lord . . .

We unwrap the bacon, the onion, we open a can of evapor-
ated milk. Henri, the fat Frenchman, dreams aloud of the
French wine brought by the transports from Strasbourg,
Paris, Marseille . . . Sweat streams down his body.

'Listen, *mon ami*, next time we go up on the loading ramp,
I'll bring you real champagne. You haven't tried it before,
eh?'

'No. But you'll never be able to smuggle it through the gate,
so stop teasing. Why not try and "organize" some shoes for
me instead—you know, the perforated kind, with a double
sole, and what about that shirt you promised me long ago?'

'*Patience, patience.* When the new transports come, I'll
bring all you want. We'll be going on the ramp again!'

'And what if there aren't any more "cremo" transports?'
I say spitefully. 'Can't you see how much easier life is
becoming around here: no limit on packages, no more beat-
ings? You even write letters home . . . One hears all kind of
talk, and, dammit, they'll run out of people!'

'Stop talking nonsense.' Henri's serious fat face moves
rhythmically, his mouth is full of sardines. We have been
friends for a long time, but I do not even know his last name.
'Stop talking nonsense,' he repeats, swallowing with effort.
'They can't run out of people, or we'll starve to death in this
blasted camp. All of us live on what they bring.'

'All? We have our packages . . .'

'Sure, you and your friend, and ten other friends of yours.

Some of you Poles get packages. But what about us, and the Jews, and the Russkis? And what if we had no food, no "organization" from the transports, do you think you'd be eating those packages of yours in peace? We wouldn't let you!'

'You would, or you'd starve to death like the Greeks. Around here, whoever has grub, has power.'

'Anyway, you have enough, we have enough, so why argue?'

Right, why argue? They have enough, I have enough, we eat together and we sleep on the same bunks. Henri slices the bread, he makes a tomato salad. It tastes good with the commissary mustard.

Below us, naked, sweat-drenched men crowd the narrow barracks aisles or lie packed in eights and tens in the lower bunks. Their nude, withered bodies stink of sweat and excrement; their cheeks are hollow. Directly beneath me, in the bottom bunk, lies a rabbi. He has covered his head with a piece of rag torn off a blanket and reads from a Hebrew prayer book (there is no shortage of this type of literature at the camp), wailing loudly, monotonously.

'Can't somebody shut him up? He's been raving as if he'd caught God himself by the feet.'

'I don't feel like moving. Let him rave. They'll take him to the oven that much sooner.'

'Religion is the opium of the people,' Henri, who is a communist and a *rentier*, says sententiously. 'If they didn't believe in God and eternal life, they'd have smashed the crematoria long ago.'

'Why haven't you done it then?'

The question is rhetorical; the Frenchman ignores it.

'Idiot,' he says simply, and stuffs a tomato in his mouth.

Just as we finish our snack, there is a sudden commotion at the door. The Muslims* scurry in fright to the safety of

* 'Muslim' was the camp name for a prisoner who had been destroyed physically and spiritually, and who had neither the strength nor the will to go on living—a man ripe for the gas chamber.

their bunks, a messenger runs into the Block Elder's shack. The Elder, his face solemn, steps out at once.

'Canada! *Antreten!* But fast! There's a transport coming!'

'Great God!' yells Henri, jumping off the bunk. He swallows the rest of his tomato, snatches his coat, screams '*Raus*' at the men below, and in a flash is at the door. We can hear a scramble in the other bunks. Canada is leaving for the ramp.

'Henri, the shoes!' I call after him.

'*Keine Angst!*' he shouts back, already outside.

I proceed to put away the food. I tie a piece of rope round the suitcase where the onions and the tomatoes from my father's garden in Warsaw mingle with Portuguese sardines, bacon from Lublin (that's from my brother), and authentic sweetmeats from Salonica. I tie it all up, pull on my trousers, and slide off the bunk.

'*Platz!*' I yell, pushing my way through the Greeks. They step aside. At the door I bump into Henri.

'*Was ist los?*'

'Want to come with us on the ramp?'

'Sure, why not?'

'Come along then, grab your coat! We're short of a few men. I've already told the Kapo.' And he shoves me out of the barracks door.

We line up. Someone has marked down our numbers, someone up ahead yells, 'March, march,' and now we are running towards the gate, accompanied by the shouts of a multilingual throng that is already being pushed back to the barracks. Not everybody is lucky enough to be going on the ramp ... We have almost reached the gate. *Links, zwei, drei, vier! Mützen ab!* Erect, arms stretched stiffly along our hips, we march past the gate briskly, smartly, almost gracefully. A sleepy SS man with a large pad in his hand checks us off, waving us ahead in groups of five.

'*Hundert!*' he calls after we have all passed.

'*Stimmt!*' comes a hoarse answer from out front.

We march fast, almost at a run. There are guards all around, young men with automatics. We pass camp II B, then some deserted barracks and a clump of unfamiliar green—apple and pear trees. We cross the circle of watch-towers and, running, burst on to the highway. We have arrived. Just a few more yards. There, surrounded by trees, is the ramp.

A cheerful little station, very much like any other provin-cial railway stop: a small square framed by tall chestnuts and paved with yellow gravel. Not far off, beside the road, squats a tiny wooden shed, uglier and more flimsy than the ugliest and flimsiest railway shack; farther along lie stacks of old rails, heaps of wooden beams, barracks parts, bricks, paving stones. This is where they load freight for Birkenau: supplies for the construction of the camp, and people for the gas chambers. Trucks drive around, load up lumber, cement, people—a regular daily routine.

And now the guards are being posted along the rails, across the beams, in the green shade of the Silesian chestnuts, to form a tight circle round the ramp. They wipe the sweat from their faces and sip out of their canteens. It is unbearably hot; the sun stands motionless at its zenith.

'Fall out!'

We sit down in the narrow streaks of shade along the stacked rails. The hungry Greeks (several of them managed to come along, God only knows how) rummage underneath the rails. One of them finds some pieces of mildewed bread, another a few half-rotten sardines. They eat.

'*Schweinedreck*,' spits a tall young guard with corn-col-oured hair and dreamy blue eyes. 'For God's sake, any minute you'll have so much food to stuff down your guts, you'll burst!' He adjusts his gun, wipes his face with a handkerchief.

'Hey you, fatso!' His boot lightly touches Henri's shoulder. '*Pass mal auf*, want a drink?'

'Sure, but I haven't got any marks,' replies the Frenchman with a professional air.

'*Schade*, too bad.'

'Come, come, Herr Posten, isn't my word good enough any more? Haven't we done business before? How much?'

'One hundred. *Gemacht?*'

'*Gemacht.*'

We drink the water, lukewarm and tasteless. It will be paid for by the people who have not yet arrived.

'Now you be careful,' says Henri, turning to me. He tosses away the empty bottle. It strikes the rails and bursts into tiny fragments. 'Don't take any money, they might be checking. Anyway, who the hell needs money? You've got enough to eat. Don't take suits, either, or they'll think you're planning to escape. Just get a shirt, silk only, with a collar. And a vest. And if you find something to drink, don't bother calling me. I know how to shift for myself, but you watch your step or they'll let you have it.'

'Do they beat you up here?'

'Naturally. You've got to have eyes in your ass. *Arschaugen.*'

Around us sit the Greeks, their jaws working greedily, like huge human insects. They munch on stale lumps of bread. They are restless, wondering what will happen next. The sight of the large beams and the stacks of rails has them worried. They dislike carrying heavy loads.

'*Was wir arbeiten?*' they ask.

'*Niks. Transport kommen, alles Krematorium, compris?*'

'*Alles verstehen,*' they answer in crematorium Esperanto. All is well—they will not have to move the heavy rails or carry the beams.

In the meantime, the ramp has become increasingly alive with activity, increasingly noisy. The crews are being divided into those who will open and unload the arriving cattle cars and those who will be posted by the wooden steps. They receive instructions on how to proceed most efficiently. Motor cycles drive up, delivering SS officers, bemedalled, glittering with brass, beefy men with highly polished boots and shiny, brutal faces. Some have brought their briefcases, others hold thin, flexible whips. This gives them an air of military readiness and agility. They walk in and out of the commissary—for the miserable little shack by the road serves as their commissary, where in the summer they drink mineral water, *Studentenquelle*, and where in winter they can warm up with a glass of hot wine. They greet each other in the state-approved way, raising an arm Roman fashion, then shake hands cordially, exchange warm smiles, discuss mail from home, their children, their families. Some stroll majestically on the ramp. The silver squares on their collars glitter, the gravel crunches under their boots, their bamboo whips snap impatiently.

We lie against the rails in the narrow streaks of shade, breathe unevenly, occasionally exchange a few words in our various tongues, and gaze listlessly at the majestic men in green uniforms, at the green trees, and at the church steeple of a distant village.

'The transport is coming,' somebody says. We spring to our feet, all eyes turn in one direction. Round the bend, one after another, the cattle cars begin rolling in. The train backs into the station, a conductor leans out, waves his hand, blows a whistle. The locomotive whistles back with a shrieking noise, puffs, the train rolls slowly alongside the ramp. In the tiny barred windows appear pale, wilted, exhausted human faces, terror-stricken women with tangled hair, unshaven men. They gaze at the station in silence. And then, suddenly, there is a stir inside the cars and a pounding against the wooden boards.

'Water! Air!'—weary, desperate cries.

Heads push through the windows, mouths gasp frantically for air. They draw a few breaths, then disappear; others come in their place, then also disappear. The cries and moans grow louder.

A man in a green uniform covered with more glitter than any of the others jerks his head impatiently, his lips twist in annoyance. He inhales deeply, then with a rapid gesture throws his cigarette away and signals to the guard. The guard removes the automatic from his shoulder, aims, sends a series of shots along the train. All is quiet now. Meanwhile, the trucks have arrived, steps are being drawn up, and the Canada men stand ready at their posts by the train doors. The SS officer with the briefcase raises his hand.

'Whoever takes gold, or anything at all besides food, will be shot for stealing Reich property. Understand? *Verstanden?*'

'*Jawohl!*' we answer eagerly.

'*Also los!* Begin!'

The bolts crack, the doors fall open. A wave of fresh air rushes inside the train. People ... inhumanly crammed, buried under incredible heaps of luggage, suitcases, trunks, packages, crates, bundles of every description (everything that had been their past and was to start their future). Monstrously squeezed together, they have fainted from heat, suffocated, crushed one another. Now they push towards the opened doors, breathing like fish cast out on the sand.

'Attention! Out, and take your luggage with you! Take out everything. Pile all your stuff near the exits. Yes, your coats too. It is summer. March to the left. Understand?'

'Sir, what's going to happen to us?' They jump from the train on to the gravel, anxious, worn out.

'Where are you people from?'

'Sosnowiec-Będzin. Sir, what's going to happen to us?' They repeat the question stubbornly, gazing into our tired eyes.

'I don't know, I don't understand Polish.'

It is the camp law: people going to their death must be deceived to the very end. This is the only permissible form of charity. The heat is tremendous. The sun hangs directly over our heads, the white, hot sky quivers, the air vibrates, an occasional breeze feels like a sizzling blast from a furnace. Our lips are parched, the mouth fills with the salty taste of blood, the body is weak and heavy from lying in the sun. Water!

A huge, multicoloured wave of people loaded down with luggage pours from the train like a blind, mad river trying to find a new bed. But before they have a chance to recover, before they can draw a breath of fresh air and look at the sky, bundles are snatched from their hands, coats ripped off their backs, their purses and umbrellas taken away.

'But please, sir, it's for the sun, I cannot ...'

'*Verboten!*' one of us barks through clenched teeth. There is an SS man standing behind your back, calm, efficient, watchful.

'*Meine Herrschaften*, this way, ladies and gentlemen, try not to throw your things around, please. Show some good-will,' he says courteously, his restless hands playing with the slender whip.

'Of course, of course,' they answer as they pass, and now they walk alongside the train somewhat more cheerfully. A woman reaches down quickly to pick up her handbag. The whip flies, the woman screams, stumbles, and falls under the feet of the surging crowd. Behind her, a child cries in a thin little voice '*Mamele!*'—a very small girl with tangled black curls.

The heaps grow. Suitcases, bundles, blankets, coats, hand-bags that open as they fall, spilling coins, gold, watches; mountains of bread pile up at the exits, heaps of marmalade, jams, masses of meat, sausages; sugar spills on the gravel. Trucks, loaded with people, start up with a deafening roar and drive off amidst the wailing and screaming of the women separated from their children, and the stupefied silence of the men left behind. They are the ones who had been ordered to step to the right—the healthy and the young who will go to the camp. In the end, they too will not escape death, but first they must work.

Trucks leave and return, without interruption, as on a monstrous conveyor belt. A Red Cross van drives back and forth, back and forth, incessantly: it transports the gas that will kill these people. The enormous cross on the hood, red as blood, seems to dissolve in the sun.

The Canada men at the trucks cannot stop for a single moment, even to catch their breath. They shove the people up the steps, pack them in tightly, sixty per truck, more or less. Near by stands a young, clean-shaven 'gentleman', an SS officer with a notebook in his hand. For each departing truck he enters a mark; sixteen gone means one thousand people, more or less. The gentleman is calm, precise. No truck can leave without a signal from him, or a mark in his notebook: *Ordnung muss sein*. The marks swell into thousands, the thousands into whole transports, which afterwards we shall simply call 'from Salonica', 'from Strasbourg', 'from Rotterdam'. This one will be called 'Sosnowiec-Będzin'. The new prisoners from Sosnowiec-Będzin will receive serial numbers 131–2—thousand, of course, though afterwards we shall simply say 131–2, for short.

The transports swell into weeks, months, years. When the war is over, they will count up the marks in their notebooks—all four and a half million of them. The bloodiest battle of the war, the greatest victory of the strong, united Germany. *Ein Reich, ein Volk, ein Führer*—and four crematoria.

The train has been emptied. A thin, pock-marked SS man peers inside, shakes his head in disgust and motions to our group, pointing his finger at the door.

'*Rein*. Clean it up!'

We climb inside. In the corners amid human excrement and abandoned wrist-watches lie squashed, trampled infants, naked little monsters with enormous heads and bloated bellies. We carry them out like chickens, holding several in each hand.

'Don't take them to the trucks, pass them on to the women,' says the SS man, lighting a cigarette. His cigarette lighter is not working properly; he examines it carefully.

'Take them, for God's sake!' I explode as the women run from me in horror, covering their eyes.

The name of God sounds strangely pointless, since the women and the infants will go on the trucks, every one of them, without exception. We all know what this means, and we look at each other with hate and horror.

'What, you don't want to take them?' asks the pock-marked SS man with a note of surprise and reproach in his voice, and reaches for his revolver.

'You mustn't shoot, I'll carry them.' A tall, grey-haired woman takes the little corpses out of my hands and for an instant gazes straight into my eyes.

'My poor boy,' she whispers and smiles at me. Then she

walks away, staggering along the path. I lean against the side of the train. I am terribly tired. Someone pulls at my sleeve.

'*En avant*, to the rails, come on!'

I look up, but the face swims before my eyes, dissolves, huge and transparent, melts into the motionless trees and the sea of people ... I blink rapidly: Henri.

'Listen, Henri, are we good people?'

'That's stupid. Why do you ask?'

'You see, my friend, you see, I don't know why, but I am furious, simply furious with these people—furious because I must be here because of them. I feel no pity. I am not sorry they're going to the gas chamber. Damn them all! I could throw myself at them, beat them with my fists. It must be pathological, I just can't understand ...'

'Ah, on the contrary, it is natural, predictable, calculated. The ramp exhausts you, you rebel—and the easiest way to relieve your hate is to turn against someone weaker. Why, I'd even call it healthy. It's simple logic, *compris*?' He props himself up comfortably against the heap of rails. 'Look at the Greeks, they know how to make the best of it! They stuff their bellies with anything they find. One of them has just devoured a full jar of marmalade.'

'Pigs! Tomorrow half of them will die of the shits.'

'Pigs? You've been hungry.'

'Pigs!' I repeat furiously. I close my eyes. The air is filled with ghastly cries, the earth trembles beneath me, I can feel sticky moisture on my eyelids. My throat is completely dry.

The morbid procession streams on and on—trucks growl like mad dogs. I shut my eyes tight, but I can still see corpses dragged from the train, trampled infants, cripples piled on top of the dead, wave after wave ... freight cars roll in, the heaps of clothing, suitcases and bundles grow, people climb out, look at the sun, take a few breaths, beg for water, get into the trucks, drive away. And again freight cars roll in, again people ... The scenes become confused in my mind— I am not sure if all of this is actually happening, or if I am dreaming. There is a humming inside my head; I feel that I must vomit.

Henri tugs at my arm.

'Don't sleep, we're off to load up the loot.'

All the people are gone. In the distance, the last few trucks roll along the road in clouds of dust, the train has left, several SS officers promenade up and down the ramp. The silver glitters on their collars. Their boots shine, their red, beefy faces shine. Among them there is a woman—only now I realize she has been here all along—withered, flat-chested, bony, her thin, colourless hair pulled back and tied in a 'Nordic' knot; her hands are in the pockets of her wide skirt. With a rat-like, resolute smile glued on her thin lips she sniffs around the corners of the ramp. She detests feminine beauty with the hatred of a woman who is herself repulsive, and knows it. Yes, I have seen her many times before and I know her well: she is the commandant of the FKL. She has come to look over the new crop of women, for some of them, instead of going on the trucks, will go on foot—to the concentration camp. There our boys, the barbers from Zauna, will shave their heads and will have a good laugh at their 'outside world' modesty.

We proceed to load the loot. We lift huge trunks, heave them on to the trucks. There they are arranged in stacks, packed tightly. Occasionally somebody slashes one open with a knife, for pleasure or in search of vodka and perfume. One of the crates falls open; suits, shirts, books drop out on the ground . . . I pick up a small, heavy package. I unwrap it— gold, about two handfuls, bracelets, rings, brooches, diamonds . . .

'*Gib hier*,' an SS man says calmly, holding up his briefcase already full of gold and colourful foreign currency. He locks the case, hands it to an officer, takes another, an empty one, and stands by the next truck, waiting. The gold will go to the Reich.

It is hot, terribly hot. Our throats are dry, each word hurts. Anything for a sip of water! Faster, faster, so that it is over, so that we may rest. At last we are done, all the trucks have gone. Now we swiftly clean up the remaining dirt: there must be 'no trace left of the *Schweinerei*'. But just as the last truck disappears behind the trees and we walk, finally, to rest in the shade, a shrill whistle sounds around the bend. Slowly, terribly slowly, a train rolls in, the engine whistles back with a deafening shriek. Again weary, pale faces at the windows, flat as though cut out of paper, with huge, feverishly burning eyes. Already trucks are pulling up, already the composed gentleman with the notebook is at his post, and the SS men emerge from the commissary carrying briefcases for the gold and money. We unseal the train doors.

It is impossible to control oneself any longer. Brutally we tear suitcases from their hands, impatiently pull off their coats. Go on, go on, vanish! They go, they vanish. Men, women, children. Some of them know.

Here is a woman—she walks quickly, but tries to appear calm. A small child with a pink cherub's face runs after her and, unable to keep up, stretches out his little arms and cries: 'Mama! Mama!'

'Pick up your child, woman!'

'It's not mine, sir, not mine!' she shouts hysterically and runs on, covering her face with her hands. She wants to hide, she wants to reach those who will not ride the trucks, those who will go on foot, those who will stay alive. She is young, healthy, good-looking, she wants to live.

But the child runs after her, wailing loudly: 'Mama, Mama, don't leave me!'

'It's not mine, not mine, no!'

Andrei, a sailor from Sevastopol, grabs hold of her. His eyes are glassy from vodka and the heat. With one powerful blow he knocks her off her feet, then, as she falls, takes her by the hair and pulls her up again. His face twitches with rage.

'Ah, you bloody Jewess! So you're running from your own child! I'll show you, you whore!' His huge hand chokes her, he lifts her in the air and heaves her on to the truck like a heavy sack of grain.

'Here! And take this with you, bitch!' and he throws the child at her feet.

'*Gut gemacht*, good work. That's the way to deal with

degenerate mothers,' says the SS man standing at the foot of the truck. '*Gut, gut, Russki.*'

'Shut your mouth,' growls Andrei through clenched teeth, and walks away. From under a pile of rags he pulls out a canteen, unscrews the cork, takes a few deep swallows, passes it to me. The strong vodka burns the throat. My head swims, my legs are shaky, again I feel like throwing up.

And suddenly, above the teeming crowd pushing forward like a river driven by an unseen power, a girl appears. She descends lightly from the train, hops on to the gravel, looks around inquiringly, as if somewhat surprised. Her soft, blonde hair has fallen on her shoulders in a torrent, she throws it back impatiently. With a natural gesture she runs her hands down her blouse, casually straightens her skirt. She stands like this for an instant, gazing at the crowd, then turns and with a gliding look examines our faces, as though searching for someone. Unknowingly, I continue to stare at her, until our eyes meet.

'Listen, tell me, where are they taking us?'

I look at her without saying a word. Here, standing before me, is a girl, a girl with enchanting blonde hair, with beautiful breasts, wearing a little cotton blouse, a girl with a wise, mature look in her eyes. Here she stands, gazing straight into my face, waiting. And over there is the gas chamber: communal death, disgusting and ugly. And over in the other direction is the concentration camp: the shaved head, the heavy Soviet trousers in sweltering heat, the sickening, stale odour of dirty, damp female bodies, the animal hunger, the inhuman labour, and later the same gas chamber, only an even more hideous, more terrible death . . .

Why did she bring it? I think to myself, noticing a lovely gold watch on her delicate wrist. They'll take it away from her anyway.

'Listen, tell me,' she repeats.

I remain silent. Her lips tighten.

'I know,' she says with a shade of proud contempt in her voice, tossing her head. She walks off resolutely in the direction of the trucks. Someone tries to stop her; she boldly pushes him aside and runs up the steps. In the distance I can only catch a glimpse of her blonde hair flying in the breeze.

I go back inside the train; I carry out dead infants; I unload luggage. I touch corpses, but I cannot overcome the mounting, uncontrollable terror. I try to escape from the corpses, but they are everywhere: lined up on the gravel, on the cement edge of the ramp, inside the cattle cars. Babies, hideous naked women, men twisted by convulsions. I run off as far as I can go, but immediately a whip slashes across my back. Out of the corner of my eye I see an SS man, swearing profusely. I stagger forward and run, lose myself in the Canada group. Now, at last, I can once more rest against the stack of rails. The sun has leaned low over the horizon and illuminates the ramp with a reddish glow; the shadows of the trees have become elongated, ghostlike. In the silence that settles over nature at this time of day, the human cries seem to rise all the way to the sky.

Only from this distance does one have a full view of the inferno on the teeming ramp. I see a pair of human beings who have fallen to the ground locked in a last desperate embrace. The man has dug his fingers into the woman's flesh and has caught her clothing with his teeth. She screams hysterically, swears, cries, until at last a large boot comes down over her throat and she is silent. They are pulled apart and dragged like cattle to the truck. I see four Canada men lugging a corpse: a huge, swollen female corpse. Cursing, dripping wet from the strain, they kick out of their way some stray children who have been running all over the ramp, howling like dogs. The men pick them up by the collars, heads, arms, and toss them inside the trucks, on top of the heaps. The four men have trouble lifting the fat corpse on to the car, they call others for help, and all together they hoist up the mound of meat. Big, swollen, puffed-up corpses are being collected from all over the ramp; on top of them are piled the invalids, the smothered, the sick, the unconscious. The heap seethes, howls, groans. The driver starts the motor, the truck begins rolling.

'Halt! Halt!' an SS man yells after them. 'Stop, damn you!'

They are dragging to the truck an old man wearing tails and a band around his arm. His head knocks against the gravel and pavement; he moans and wails in an uninterrupted monotone, '*Ich will mit dem Herrn Kommandanten sprechen*—I wish to speak with the commandant...' With senile stubbornness he keeps repeating these words all the way. Thrown on the truck, trampled by others, choked, he still wails: '*Ich will mit dem* ...'

'Look here, old man!' a young SS man calls, laughing jovially. 'In half an hour you'll be talking with the top commandant! Only don't forget to greet him with a *Heil Hitler!*'

Several other men are carrying a small girl with only one leg. They hold her by the arms and the one leg. Tears are running down her face and she whispers faintly, 'Sir, it hurts, it hurts...' They throw her on the truck on top of the corpses. She will burn alive along with them.

The evening has come, cool and clear. The stars are out. We lie against the rails. It is incredibly quiet. Anaemic bulbs hang from the top of the high lamp-posts; beyond the circle of light stretches an impenetrable darkness. Just one step, and a man could vanish for ever. But the guards are watching, their automatics ready.

'Did you get the shoes?' asks Henri.

'No.'

'Why?'

'My God, man, I am finished, absolutely finished!'

'So soon? After only two transports? Just look at me, I ... since Christmas, at least a million people have passed through my hands. The worst of all are the transports from around Paris—one is always bumping into friends.'

'And what do you say to them?'

'That first they will have a bath, and later we'll meet at the camp. What would you say?'

I do not answer. We drink coffee with vodka; somebody opens a tin of cocoa and mixes it with sugar. We scoop it up by the handful, the cocoa sticks to the lips. Again coffee, again vodka.

'Henri, what are we waiting for?'

'There'll be another transport.'

'I'm not going to unload it! I can't take any more.'

'So, it's got you down? Canada is nice, eh?' Henri grins indulgently and disappears into the darkness. In a moment he is back again.

'All right. Just sit here quietly and don't let an SS man see you. I'll try to find you your shoes.'

'Just leave me alone. Never mind the shoes.' I want to sleep. It is very late.

Another whistle, another transport. Freight cars emerge out of the darkness, pass under the lamp-posts, and again vanish in the night. The ramp is small, but the circle of lights is smaller. The unloading will have to be done gradually. Somewhere the trucks are growling. They back up against the steps, black, ghostlike, their searchlights flash across the trees. *Wasser! Luft!* The same all over again, like a late showing of the same film: a volley of shots, the train falls silent. Only this time a little girl pushes herself halfway through the small window and, losing her balance, falls out on to the gravel. Stunned, she lies still for a moment, then stands up and begins walking round in a circle, faster and faster, waving her rigid arms in the air, breathing loudly and spasmodically, whining in a faint voice. Her mind has given way in the inferno inside the train. The whining is hard on the nerves: an SS man approaches calmly, his heavy boot strikes between her shoulders. She falls. Holding her down with his foot, he draws his revolver, fires once, then again. She remains face down, kicking the gravel with her feet, until she stiffens. They proceed to unseal the train.

I am back on the ramp, standing by the doors. A warm, sickening smell gushes from inside. The mountain of people filling the car almost halfway up to the ceiling is motionless, horribly tangled, but still steaming.

'*Ausladen!*' comes the command. An SS man steps out from the darkness. Across his chest hangs a portable searchlight. He throws a stream of light inside.

'Why are you standing about like sheep? Start unloading!' His whip flies and falls across our backs. I seize a corpse by the hand; the fingers close tightly around mine. I pull back with a shriek and stagger away. My heart pounds, jumps up to my throat. I can no longer control the nausea. Hunched under the train I begin to vomit. Then, like a drunk, I weave over to the stack of rails.

I lie against the cool, kind metal and dream about returning to the camp, about my bunk, on which there is no mattress, about sleep among comrades who are not going to the gas tonight. Suddenly I see the camp as a haven of peace. It is true, others may be dying, but one is somehow still alive, one has enough food, enough strength to work . . .

The lights on the ramp flicker with a spectral glow, the wave of people—feverish, agitated, stupefied people—flows on and on, endlessly. They think that now they will have to face a new life in the camp, and they prepare themselves emotionally for the hard struggle ahead. They do not know that in just a few moments they will die, that the gold, money and diamonds which they have so prudently hidden in their clothing and on their bodies are now useless to them. Experienced professionals will probe into every recess of their flesh, will pull the gold from under the tongue and the diamonds from the uterus and the colon. They will rip out gold teeth. In tightly sealed crates they will ship them to Berlin.

The SS men's black figures move about, dignified, businesslike. The gentleman with the notebook puts down his final marks, rounds out the figures: fifteen thousand.

Many, very many, trucks have been driven to the crematoria today.

It is almost over. The dead are being cleared off the ramp and piled into the last truck. The Canada men, weighed down under a load of bread, marmalade and sugar, and smelling of perfume and fresh linen, line up to go. For several days the entire camp will live off this transport. For several days the entire camp will talk about 'Sosnowiec-Będzin'. 'Sosnowiec-Będzin' was a good, rich transport.

The stars are already beginning to pale as we walk back to the camp. The sky grows translucent and opens high above our heads—it is getting light.

Great columns of smoke rise from the crematoria and merge up above into a huge black river which very slowly floats across the sky over Birkenau and disappears beyond the forests in the direction of Trzebinia. The 'Sosnowiec-Będzin' transport is already burning.

We pass a heavily armed SS detachment on its way to change guard. The men march briskly, in step, shoulder to shoulder, one mass, one will.

'*Und morgen die ganze Welt . . .*' they sing at the top of their lungs.

'*Rechts ran*! To the right, march!' snaps a command from up front. We move out of their way.

(*Translated by Barbara Vedder*)

Marek Hłasko

Searching for the Stars

The boy was ten years old, in love, and he knew he was in love for life. He said as much to his father, asking him first not to tell anyone. Only later, convinced by his father, he agreed to let mother in on the secret, though he doubted she would be able to understand him. The little girl he loved was called Ewa and she was younger than him by one month and twelve days. She lived with her parents in the house next door and used to come to see the boy in the evenings.

'Can't you come earlier?' he asked her one day.

'No,' she said.

'Why?'

'Father doesn't let me. I can leave the house only after dark.'

'I shall talk to your father,' said the boy.

'He won't let me, anyway.'

'We shall see.'

They were sitting in a shed in which the boy used to keep rabbits until some stranger broke in and stole them. After that he didn't want to keep rabbits any more; he only asked his father if he could furnish the shed and keep it for himself, and that nobody should come in. His father agreed, asking in return if in the autumn the boy would let him store the firewood which they were to saw up together. And so it stayed. He was sitting now next to the girl on the heap of dry, light and fragrant sawdust. It was evening, quiet; he could hear the beating of his own heart and heard the beating

of her heart. When one is nine years old one doesn't know
what desire is, for then desire means curiosity and surprise
offered by another's body, and it is then that the throat dries
out, the heart beats fast and the hair bristles up as on a dog.
But that this curiosity is stronger than desire—that the boy
didn't know. He was sitting on the heap of sawdust next to
the girl, stroking her body with his hands and the only thing
he knew was that he was in love for life.

'Come early tomorrow,' he said.

'I'll try.'

'You really don't want me to speak to your father?'

'Father is ill,' she said. 'Perhaps some other time.'

'Tomorrow I will know,' he said.

'From whom?'

'From someone. He used to go to school with me,' he said.
'We'll meet tomorrow. I'm to give him the cages for it.' The
boy sighed. 'He wouldn't tell me anything until he saw the
cages.'

'Do you think he knows?'

'He knows for sure,' he said. 'Shall I tell you who he is?
It's Nadera.'

'Nadera,' repeated the girl.

'Yes,' he whispered. 'He's a brother of this other Nadera,
you know. His father is a railwayman. When the old man
goes out he locks the other one in the cellar, or chains him
by the leg. He is already seventeen, this bigger Nadera. And
this one is his brother. And he will tell me.'

'Do you think we will be able to do it?'

'If only he will tell us how. And he will certainly tell us.
You see these cages? I made them with my father. All you
need to do is pull a string and they open up.' He turned
suddenly and looked at her but couldn't see her face; in the
darkness he could see only the glistening saw-blade in
the corner. 'Will you be scared?' he asked.

'I don't know,' she said.

'If you have a baby they will have to let you out during
the day,' he said. 'Your folk . . . they'll have nothing to say.

You will be a grown-up and you'll be able to do what you want.'

'I've got to go now,' she said.

'Yes,' he said. 'I'll walk you home.'

The next day, he waited, impatient, angry, but Nadera didn't show up. It was evening again and he was sitting with Ewa in the dark on the heap of sawdust, which was warm from the warmth of their bodies. And then he heard a whistle. He got up and went out into the yard.

'Why so late?' he asked.

'I couldn't come earlier,' said the other boy. 'My father got drunk and kicked up a racket. He's asleep now. Where are the cages?'

'Come,' said the boy.

They went into the shed.

'This is Nadera's brother,' said the boy to Ewa, 'the one whose father chains him by the leg. He's come for the cages.'

'But I've got to go now,' said the girl.

'Don't you want to wait?'

She shook her head.

'I'm sorry,' said the boy to the other one. 'We've got a secret. It won't take a moment.'

'I'll 'ave a look at them cages,' said Nadera's brother.

'OK.'

He went with the girl into the corner.

'Why don't you want to wait?' he asked. 'Now that he's come specially to tell us.'

'If I don't go home now, tomorrow they won't let me out at all,' she whispered. 'You don't know my father.'

He squeezed her hand.

'All right,' he said. 'Go. In the meantime I'll sort out everything here. But come early tomorrow.'

'Will it take us a long time?' she asked.

'I don't know,' he said. 'I've never done it before, have I? But a child is a child. It isn't just one-two-three, you know.'

The girl left. Young Nadera's eyes followed her until she went into the house and closed the door.

'Who's that chick?'

'Just a girl . . .' said the boy.

'From Warsaw?'

'Yes.'

'Dark,' said Nadera thoughtfully. 'Her hair is black, and her eyes are black.'

The boy put his left foot forward, chin close to his chest.

'Don't you like her?' he asked. 'Just say you don't like her.'

The other suddenly hit him with his head in the stomach, but the boy knew him well and was prepared. Father had taught him how to fight. He jumped at Nadera, punched him twice and jumped back, remembering about the even footwork and that the foot should follow the hand.

'I'll tell me brother,' sobbed Nadera.

'I'm not afraid of your brother,' shouted the boy; he believed what he was saying now. He got hold of the other by the lapels of the jacket and shook him. 'I'm afraid of nobody, nobody!' He pushed him and Nadera ran away across the yard.

He went into the house, looking at his bleeding hands.

'Did you fall?' his father asked.

'No,' he said. 'I had a fight with Nadera's brother.'

'What about?'

'Pardon?'

'You know very well. I'm asking what were you fighting about?'

'I can't tell you,' said the boy quietly.

'You can't tell me?'

He pointed pleadingly at the mother.

'I can't,' he said.

'I understand,' said the father. 'Go to bed.' Later, when the boy was already lying in bed he sat at the bedside and bent over the boy. 'Have you told him where Ewa lives?' he asked.

'He knows,' said the boy.

'And you, do you know?'

'What, Dad?'

'Do you know who Ewa is?'

'Ewa?' repeated the boy. 'What do you mean, Dad?'

'Well, nothing,' said the father. 'Good. But this Nadera . . . I think he works for the Germans. At least people say so.' He stood up suddenly, went over to the wardrobe, pulled out a rucksack, a sheepskin and a skiing hat. 'You'll be all right,' he said to the mother. 'But I prefer to make myself scarce for a couple of days.' And he added, 'Go there and tell them that it will be better if they themselves disappear from here for a few days. I'm afraid of these Naderas. Maybe I'm wrong, but we'd better make sure.'

The mother left.

'Do you know, Dad,' said the boy, falling asleep, 'that this Nadera's father chains him before he goes out? Once he even locked him up in the cellar and he sat there for three days?' And then he forgot all about Nadera. He only regretted that he hadn't found out what he wanted to know, and that Ewa would have to wait before her parents let her out during daytime. He didn't hear when his mother returned.

'And what?' asked the father.

'They don't want to go,' she said. 'They say they haven't got anywhere to go. And that it's bound to happen sooner or later.' She was looking at his big, dark hands struggling with the straps of the rucksack. 'And you want to go now?' she said.

'I wouldn't be able to protect you anyway,' he said. 'But they won't hurt you. I believe that. But them, they'll finish them off.'

'Can anything be done?'

'It's too early to talk about it,' he said. 'We'll think about it when the war's over. Perhaps God will spare the Germans, and He certainly will. I think that of all the nations God needs them most and that's why he will spare them. So that everybody can know and feel what evil is like. Only for this reason, so that we can choose goodness.'

'You shouldn't say things like this,' she said. 'If you ever teach again it won't be this, will it?'

'I was a bad teacher,' he said. 'But I think I've learned

something. When the war is over I shall talk about it. But now I have to go killing them, and pray to God to spare them. I'll keep in touch.'

He threw the rucksack over his shoulder, walked to the bed and kissed the boy. Then he walked up to the stove, carefully removed one of the tiles and look out a gun wrapped up in a greasy rug. 'Tomorrow take some grout and replace this tile,' he said.

'Go, and may God be with you.'

'God be with you,' he said. 'And tell him to watch closely when they will be killing them. Let him watch and learn. And let him remember it for the rest of his life.'

The father left, closing the door quietly behind him. But the boy slept soundly and didn't hear his father leaving. He didn't even hear them as they pulled up in front of the house at four o'clock in the morning. He didn't even hear their voices or the pounding on the door, or the barking of the dog. He slept on, oblivious of their presence and of the noise they brought in. He only woke up when his mother shook him. He sat up in the bed, rested and alert like a young animal.

'Get dressed,' said the mother.

'But it's Sunday,' said the boy.

'I know,' said the mother. 'You'll go back to bed later, but now get dressed.'

He put on his clothes and went out of the house. He wanted to run up to the car but the mother caught his hand. She stood on the porch of an old, wooden house, breathing loudly, and he felt the warmth of her hand.

'What's going on?' he asked. 'Has something happened, Mum?' She didn't answer so he repeated the question: 'Has something happened?'

He was looking at the car's bonnet glistening with the dew, at the dog lying with its tongue hanging out, and at the barrels of the guns. Then he whistled quietly; the dog readily pricked its ears. The policeman, who was standing on the side, now stepped forward and said. 'Follow us.'

'Where are you taking us?' asked the boy's mother.

'It's not far,' said the policeman. 'You'll only watch for a while and go back home.'

'I'll go alone,' said the mother. 'There's no need for the child to watch things like that. You do understand, officer, don't you?'

The policeman hesitated for a moment.

'It's an order,' he said without enthusiasm. 'It says that everybody's got to watch. As an example.'

They followed the policeman and the Germans. The mother still held his hand and the boy was embarrassed. He tried to free himself but his mother's grip was strong. He regretted that his father wasn't there. Father would never do a thing like that. At most he would place his hand on the boy's shoulder and then they'd simply look like two mates returning home after work.

Later, they stood and watched as Ewa's father and the farmer, at whose house they lived, were digging the hole, working fast and in silence. He saw Ewa, whose mother held her by the hand, just like his mother held him, and then he pulled sharply towards her but his mother was stronger. So he stood and watched. He saw as one of the Germans came up to the crying Ewa and stroked her hair.

'Don't cry little one,' he said. 'Do you know who we are?'

'No . . .?' said Ewa.

'We are hunters,' he said. 'We look for yellow stars.'

'Bring her a doll,' he said to the policeman.

'A doll?' the policeman was surprised.

'Yes,' said the German. 'Something to play with.'

The policeman went into the house and came out after a minute holding a teddy bear.

'How old is she?' the German asked Ewa's mother.

'Eight.'

The German handed the toy to Ewa; she stood, holding the teddy bear by its hand.

'Well,' he said, 'don't be afraid. Do you know this tale about the wolf and seven little goats? No? Once upon a time Mummy Goat said to her children, "Don't open the door to anybody when I'm out," and she left. Then the wolf came up to the house and with his paw knocked on the door. "Who's there?" asked the little goats. And he said, "It's me, your grandma." "And why do you have such a deep voice, granny?" asked the little goats . . .'

The policeman came up to him and said, 'It's ready. Shall I tell them to strip?'

'No,' said the German.

The policeman stretched his hand towards Ewa.

'Give me the teddy, little one,' he said.

'Why are you taking it away from her?' asked the German.

'I wanted it for my child,' said the policeman.

'But you can see she's a child, too,' said the German. 'You're a strange man. You should be ashamed of yourself.'

Later, they were returning home and the boy was glad it was the mother who was with him and not the father. For with his father he would have been too embarrassed to cry. And cry he did. He had to; he couldn't help it. In the course of the next few days the partisans killed Nadera and his eldest son, some young man killed the German in broad daylight on the station platform, and a Jewish family committed suicide one night, lying down on a railway track. The boy knew it all, heard people talk about it, and was slowly forgetting. But he cried from time to time. It was when he remembered that he would never be able to have a wife and children for he had sworn to be faithful; and that he was in love for life.

(Translated by Wiesiek Powaga)

Sławomir Mrożek

The Elephant

The director of the Zoological Gardens has shown himself to be an upstart. He regarded his animals simply as stepping stones on the road of his own career. He was indifferent to the educational importance of his establishment. In his Zoo the giraffe had a short neck, the badger had no burrow and the whistlers, having lost all interest, whistled rarely and with some reluctance. These shortcomings should not have been allowed, especially as the Zoo was often visited by parties of schoolchildren.

The Zoo was in a provincial town, and it was short of some of the most important animals, among them the elephant. Three thousand rabbits were a poor substitute for the noble giant. However, as our country developed, the gaps were being filled in a well-planned manner. On the occasion of the anniversary of the liberation, on 22nd July, the Zoo was notified that it had at long last been allocated an elephant. All the staff, who were devoted to their work, rejoiced at this news. All the greater was their surprise when they learnt that the director had sent a letter to Warsaw, renouncing the allocation and putting forward a plan for obtaining an elephant by more economic means.

'I, and all the staff,' he had written, 'are fully aware how heavy a burden falls upon the shoulders of Polish miners and foundry men because of the elephant. Desirous of reducing our costs, I suggest that the elephant mentioned in your communication should be replaced by one of our own procurement. We can make an elephant out of rubber, of the correct size, fill it with air and place it behind railings. It will be carefully painted the correct colour and even on close inspection will be indistinguishable from the real animal. It is well known that the elephant is a sluggish animal and it does not run and jump about. In the notice on the railings we can state that this particular elephant is exceptionally sluggish. The money saved in this way can be turned to the purchase of a jet plane or the conservation of some church monument.

'Kindly note that both the idea and its execution are my modest contribution to the common task and struggle.

'I am, etc.'

This communication must have reached a soulless official, who regarded his duties in a purely bureaucratic manner and did not examine the heart of the matter but, following only the directive about reduction of expenditure, accepted the director's plan. On hearing the Ministry's approval, the director issued instructions for the making of the rubber elephant.

The carcase was to have been filled with air by two keepers blowing into it from opposite ends. To keep the operation secret the work was to be completed during the night because the people of the town, having heard that an elephant was joining the Zoo, were anxious to see it. The director insisted on haste also because he expected a bonus, should his idea turn out to be a success.

The two keepers locked themselves in a shed normally housing a workshop, and began to blow. After two hours of hard blowing they discovered that the rubber skin had risen only a few inches above the floor and its bulge in no way resembled an elephant. The night progressed. Outside, human voices were stilled and only the cry of the jackass interrupted the silence. Exhausted, the keepers stopped blowing and made sure that the air already inside the elephant should not escape. They were not young and were unaccustomed to this kind of work.

'If we go on at this rate,' said one of them, 'we shan't finish before the morning. And what am I to tell my Missus?

She'll never believe me if I say that I spent the night blowing up an elephant.'

'Quite right,' agreed the second keeper. 'Blowing up an elephant is not an everyday job. And it's all because our director is a leftist.'

They resumed their blowing, but after another half-an-hour they felt too tired to continue. The bulge on the floor was larger but still nothing like the shape of an elephant.

'It's getting harder all the time,' said the first keeper.

'It's an uphill job, all right,' agreed the second. 'Let's have a little rest.'

While they were resting, one of them noticed a gas pipe ending in a valve. Could they not fill the elephant with gas? He suggested it to his mate.

They decided to try. They connected the elephant to the gas pipe, turned the valve, and to their joy in a few minutes there was a full-sized beast standing in the shed. It looked real: the enormous body, legs like columns, huge ears and the inevitable trunk. Driven by ambition the director had made sure of having in his Zoo a very large elephant indeed.

'First class,' declared the keeper who had the idea of using gas. 'Now we can go home.'

In the morning the elephant was moved to a special run in a central position, next to the monkey cage. Placed in front of a large real rock it looked fierce and magnificent. A big notice proclaimed: 'Particularly sluggish. Hardly moves.'

Among the first visitors that morning was a party of children from the local school. The teacher in charge of them was planning to give them an object-lesson about the elephant. He halted the group in front of the animal and began:

'The elephant is a herbivorous mammal. By means of its trunk it pulls out young trees and eats their leaves.'

The children were looking at the elephant with enraptured admiration. They were waiting for it to pull out a young tree, but the beast stood still behind its railings.

' . . . The elephant is a direct descendant of the now extinct mammoth. It's not surprising, therefore, that it's the largest living land animal.'

The more conscientious pupils were making notes.

' . . . Only the whale is heavier than the elephant, but then the whale lives in the sea. We can safely say that on land the elephant reigns supreme.'

A slight breeze moved the branches of the trees in the Zoo.

' . . . The weight of a fully grown elephant is between nine and thirteen thousand pounds.'

At that moment the elephant shuddered and rose in the air. For a few seconds it swayed just above the ground but a gust of wind blew it upwards until its mighty silhouette was against the sky. For a short while people on the ground could still see the four circles of its feet, its bulging belly and the trunk, but soon, propelled by the wind, the elephant sailed above the fence and disappeared above the tree-tops. Astonished monkeys in the cage continued staring into the sky.

They found the elephant in the neighbouring botanical gardens. It had landed on a cactus and punctured its rubber hide.

The schoolchildren who had witnessed the scene in the Zoo soon started neglecting their studies and turned into hooligans. It is reported that they drink liquor and break windows. And they no longer believe in elephants.

(*Translated by Konrad Syrop*)

Sławomir Mrożek

Spring in Poland

That year April was exceptionally warm. Early in the month, just before noon one day, the crowds milling on the pavements of the main Warsaw thoroughfares witnessed a most unusual happening. Floating above the rooftops like a bird was a man. He was dressed in an ordinary grey raincoat and hat; under his arm a brief-case. He was not using any mechanical aids but slight movements of his hands and arms were enough to keep him flying.

The man circled above the building of the International Press Club and then, as if having noticed something in the road, he dived. Astonished passers-by stopped dead. He was now flying so low that they could see the glint of the ring on his finger and examine the condition of the soles of his shoes. With a loud and penetrating wail the man soared again, circled majestically above the city centre, and flew away in a southerly direction.

It is fully understandable that the event gave rise to a great deal of talk. The news was withheld from the press and radio because the political attitude of the bird-man was not known, but all the same the whole country was soon aware of the strange occurrence. There can be no doubt that this happening would have been long remembered were its memory not erased by further and even stranger developments which took place a few days later: two other men, also with brief-cases, were observed flying through the clouds above the centre of Warsaw. They too disappeared in a southerly direction.

The advance of the spring brought in its wake even warmer weather. Above Warsaw, later also above the provincial cities and even above the smaller district towns, the sight of men with brief-cases flying in twos and threes, but more often singly, became a daily occurrence. They all floated gracefully and performed aerobatics, but in the end they always flew away towards the south.

The nation demanded to be told the truth. There seemed to be no point in trying to hush it all up, and a communiqué was issued, announcing that, as the result of rising temperatures during the mild spring weather and the opening of windows in Government offices, many civil servants, yielding to their eagle nature, had been leaving their desks and flying out of the windows. The communiqué ended with an appeal to civil servants and all other Government employees to remember the lofty aims of the five-year plan, to conquer the urge of their blood and to remain at their posts. During the following days mass meetings of civil servants were held at which they gave pledges to fight their nature and not to fly away. This led to tragic conflicts. In spite of their will to stay, the numbers flying above the capital and other cities did not diminish. They could be observed diving in and out of white cumulus clouds, turning somersaults in the blue skies, wallowing in sunsets and, drunk with the power of flying, racing ahead of spring storms. Sometimes they would come down almost to ground level only to soar again to a height which made them invisible. In the streets passers-by found spectacles, spats and scarves raining from the sky, lost in the mad flight. In the emptying offices work was grinding to a halt.

From the Tatra mountains in the south came alarming reports. The mountain guards had observed masses of civil servants settling on crests and peaks, flying about and causing damage to the wild life of the national park. Complaints from the population started coming in thick and fast. In the Nowy Targ district twenty-eight lambs disappeared without trace, and at Muszyna an eagle, which was later identified as the deputy director of a Government department, made a

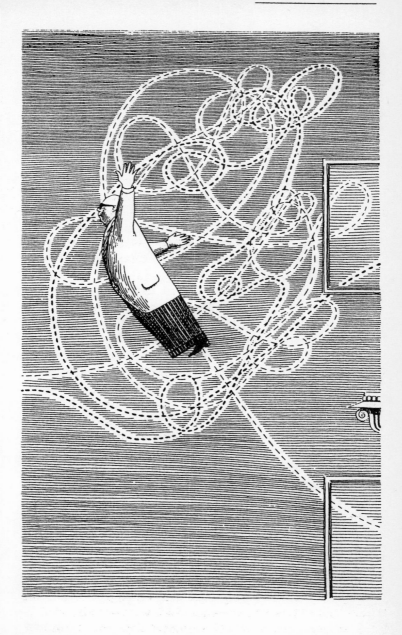

particularly daring raid and flew away with a pig. They descended from the skies like lightning.

May was on the way, and in all the offices windows were wide open. The situation was made even more serious by the fact that most cases of reversal to eagles took place among the central authorities. In fact, the higher the authority the larger the percentage of officials turning into birds of prey. All this adversely affected the reputation of the State, especially that again and again people saw high officials, known to them only from photographs and public appearances, floating above their heads, waving their legs and turning like balloons.

A decree was issued ordering windows in all public offices and institutions to be kept shut—in vain. The windows remained closed, but a true eagle can escape even through a small skylight.

Various other measures were tried. Lead weights attached to the shoes of civil servants proved of no avail—they escaped in their socks. Those suspected of wanting to fly away were tied to their desks with ropes but they always managed to undo the knots. And so, now and again, a civil servant would sigh, struggle for a few minutes with his sense of duty, allow his true nature to assert itself, climb the window-sill, give an embarrassed cough and fly away, often finishing his sandwiches and tea while already airborne.

In these circumstances the execution of any form of official business became very complicated indeed. The escaping civil servants usually took with them all the papers on which they were working. I managed to get one matter settled only because a friendly forester had informed me that he had seen the official concerned fighting with a mountain goat near a well-known lake in the Tatras. Some people organized expeditions into the mountain regions where they expected to find the nests or hunting grounds of the officials dealing with their applications. In this way mountaineering flourished, but the administration of the country was disorganized.

The foresters and mountain guards were issued with new

orders: they were to catch the fugitive officials. But who can catch a bird that flies like an arrow! Only one method produced surprisingly good results: nets around the offices of cashiers on pay day. On that day whole flocks of flying civil servants, driven by an instinct stronger than their will, circled above the pay offices, pressing against each other and issuing excited shrieks. But pay day over, they disappeared again, and those who had been caught either wasted away or escaped once more.

In this manner the spring passed, followed by a hot summer, bursting with freedom, soaring with frequent flight. Then imperceptibly, like a sickness, autumn appeared and damped down the fire of the sun. Finding food in the mountains became difficult. The day came when a party of schoolchildren on an excursion to a mountain peak saw in a crevasse a senior civil servant who did not fly away on their approach, but stood there dejectedly looking at them. His beard was hidden under the collar of his tattered coat in which he had flown away in the spring. Only when the children were almost next to him did he clumsily run a few steps and with a hoarse cry fly heavily away into the mist.

The first snow came. Its damp flakes fell silently on peasant roofs up and down the country. Under those roofs a folk song could be heard, a song full of wonder. A song about various officials, those leaders of ours—true eagles.

(*Translated by Konrad Syrop*)

Jarosław Iwaszkiewicz

Fame

On 21 May 1952, at 10.23 in the morning, the statue of
Fame, which had come from Warsaw Castle, and was
now to be found in the Great Hall of the National Museum,
sounded its trumpet three times. At the moment in question,
there were four people in the vicinity of the statue: Franciszek Monument, the museum porter, aged fifty-four;
Professor Stanisław Wolski, the famous art historian, aged
seventy-six; Tosiek Tralka, known as 'Hercules', a student at
the Drama School, aged nineteen; and Miss Hollander, a
composer, aged forty-two.

Monument, making his way down to the gents from the
upper floor, was right next to the object guilty of indulging
in such unusual behaviour; and he saw as clearly as may be
that Fame moved her hand, applied the trumpet to her lips,
and sounded a penetrating trumpet-call. She repeated this
movement three times, as Franciszek observed, stupefied,
with his own eyes.

The professor had passed into the Gothic Room, and was
bent over the Altarpiece of the Visitation: the professor
was writing a scholarly work on the influence of Polish Lower
Pomeranian and Szczecin sculpture on the art of Leonardo
da Vinci, and this very altarpiece, which came, to be sure,
from the Holy Cross Mountains, but revealed the influence
of Master Jan, the court sculptor of Prince Kazio of Szczecin,
the grandson of Kasimir the Great, was one of the corner-
stones of his thesis. The professor, despite the fact that he
was utterly engrossed in his contemplation of the lower pleat

of St Elizabeth's gown, which formed the fundamental refer-
ence point of all his arguments, nevertheless heard the weird,
piercing, yet melodious call of the trumpet, and with all the
sprightliness he could command at his age, made haste into
the hall, so as to check up on the source of this unusual
music. He just managed to catch the moment when Fame
had raised her trumpet to her lips for the third time; the
sound of the instrument, 'at close quarters', shook him to
the core.

Tosiek Tralka was on the first floor, looking down from
time to time towards the door to the hall, because he was
waiting for Basia Gorska, a friend from another school who
had arranged a date with him in the museum at quarter past
ten. Basia hadn't come. Tosiek kept on looking over the
balustrade, but at the same time he drew back apprehen-
sively every now and then, because he did not want Basia
to find out how impatient he was, and get God knows what
ideas into her head. When Fame started to sound her
trumpet, he couldn't make out at first what was going on,
and kept on looking down. But then a slight cry, or rather a
sort of choking hiss, uttered by the museum porter, caught
his attention. Just then he looked at the statue, and froze in
stupefaction.

Miss Hollander had only just entered the museum; she
had also made her way to the Gothic Sculpture hall; Polish
Radio had commissioned her to compose a work that would
show clearly what the Realist sculptors of Lower and Upper
Silesia and of Lower and Upper Pomerania, especially those
from Szczecin, had had in mind when they made their altar-
pieces not characters from the Christian stories at all, but
contemporary peasants and workers, carving them in the
attitudes of folk-dances of the age, Polish dances, of course,
which have been lost nowadays, the only remaining trace
being precisely these sculptures. Miss Hollander was to
reconstruct these dances in her compositions and by doing
so forge a link with the realism of medieval Polish art. This
wasn't a hard nut to crack for our realist lady composer, the
creator of enormously popular songs for the masses like

'Duty Calls', 'The Shock Worker and his Mate', 'The Heart of Sokorski' and so on. Nevertheless, she went into the museum in quite a thoughtful mood, weighing up the difficulties of her task, and so paid little attention to what was going on in there. The trumpet sounding roused her from these reveries, but she might have paid no attention to this either if it had not been for the fact that to her ears the trumpet-call did not ring true. Miss Hollander, who had perfect pitch, distinctly heard C sharp, C sharp, A flat, A flat, A flat. She shivered at these false notes; and here they came again: C sharp, C sharp, A flat, A flat, A flat! When she looked up, she became aware of the fact that the statue was raising the trumpet to its lips for the third time, with Monument standing gaping up at it.

—What are you gawping at?—she shouted.—Grab her, put a stop to it! This is a scandal, really!

—Grab her yourself—sighed the museum porter reflectively, when the last A flat had already sounded.

At this moment all four witnesses found themselves in front of the rococo statue, which was just calmly standing there.

—This is scandalous—repeated Miss Hollander, in a slightly fainter voice.

—This will have to be studied scientifically—said the professor, after a moment's silence.

—The newspapers will have to be told—Tosiek interjected.

—And the Party—said Miss Hollander.

—All in good time—protested Franciszek, the museum porter—It's the director first and foremost who answers for what goes on in the museum. Maybe the director has actually inserted a little mechanical spring into her? The director knows everything.

—So let's go to the director—said the composer, in her super-correct Polish.

They set off. They could see that in the long vestibule, where there were a lot of porters, cloakroom attendants, and a couple of visitors, everything was going on as usual. Nobody had noticed a thing.

Miss Hollander exchanged glances with her comrades.

—Colleagues—she said, rather grandly—for the time being, no one utters a word!—Everyone nodded agreement.

Even Tosiek inflated his Herculean chest and rolled his eyes. Despite being extremely short, he was still taller than Miss Hollander.

They were soon in the director's office. The latter, who had grown accustomed to receiving quite a lot of delegations, wasn't at all put out by the motley composition of the group standing in front of his desk. He asked them to sit down, and made as if to offer them cigarettes. Miss Hollander refused, but added,—I'd rather have a glass of water.

—Are you tired?—asked the director.—It's pretty cold today.

—I am simply beside myself with agitation—the composer suddenly burst out, and she wanted to go on but Porter Monument wouldn't let her get the words out. He thumped the desk with his fist under the director's nose, so that the latter stared at him in amazement, and expostulated:

—Mr Director, sir, she's trumpeting! Fame is blowing her trumpet!

The director cast a look of dread in the direction of the professor. The tall, distinguished-looking old man with the long grey beard just nodded affirmatively.

—That's right, Mr Director—he added after a moment, as if in sadness.—We all heard it: Fame is blowing her trumpet.

—This is outrageous, outrageous—spat out the fat little composer in a state of nervous excitation.—This is simply unacceptable. The Directorate must see to this at once in every way it knows how to, according to its own lights.

The director shrugged his shoulders and still hadn't unshrugged them when Tosiek said soberly—Mr Director, the statue of Fame in the hall of the National Museum is trumpeting on its trumpet.

—Have you all gone mad?—hissed the director.

And all four of them said as one man—We saw it, we all heard it.

And one after the other they gave the director their

accounts of the episode, which we see no reason to repeat. We already know how the event occurred, and how the members of this presumptive delegation reacted to it.

The director, who listened dumbfounded to these accounts until they all fell silent, did not know what to say.

He tried to speak, but started stammering, which shut him up.

—Wh . . . wn . . . what?—he said, then looked helplessly at each of them in turn. He gazed at the whole of this bizarre portrait gallery installed in front of his desk: the old professor, the museum porter with the purple nose, the little fair-haired chap who was training to be an actor, and the plump lady composer. Despite looking into their faces, he found nothing to say. Silence reigned for a moment.

Finally, Tosiek spoke up again, sounding very sober.

—Mr Director, sir, we won't tell anybody about this.

—Not a word—Miss Hollander said, turning in his direction.—No one makes so bold as to know anything at all about this.—Upon which she directed a frosty stare at the director.

—I dare say that these events will not repeat themselves— she added.

The director spread his hands.

Up to now he hadn't uttered a single word. Taking in this bizarre information had deprived him of the power of speech. At the prompting of Miss Hollander, Tosiek handed his address to the director; the addresses of the other witnesses of the unusual incident were already known to the administrators of the museum. Making one more request for complete silence, the group dispersed, expressing their hope that this bizarre event would not repeat itself.

These hopes, alas, turned out to be vain. The following day Fame trumpeted twice. Once at 6.18 in the morning, when only Franciszek Monument the porter was in the vicinity; and again after the museum had closed, when the director and his assistant were still in the upstairs study. On this occasion the sound of the trumpet was so resonant that the director immediately recognized the nature of the echo that reverberated through the empty halls of the museum. His assistant got quite upset, wondering where the noise was coming from, but the director quickly distracted him:

—That must be the fire engine on its way to Praga—he said.

—It can't be. The fire engine has a quite different-sounding siren—the assistant assured him, going to the window.—It's like something making a noise right here in the museum!

—That's just the way it sounded to you—the director explained authoritatively, and the confused assistant fell silent, and just smiled into his moustache.

On the third day Fame held her peace. However, the director summoned the initiates into his office at 11.00 and gave them an account of things from the previous day.

—Yesterday the statue trumpeted twice, and I'm afraid this could happen again—the director concluded his story—and I've called you to a consultation so that we can decide what on earth to do. If the Ministry of Culture and Art got wind of this trumpeting, who knows how all this might end.

—It trumpets so loudly, devil take it, you can hear it in the street—the museum porter said mournfully.

—Do you think they can hear it in the building next door?—Miss Hollander asked in alarm.

The director of the museum gave her a searching look.

—Which building are you thinking of?—he asked, with a meangful air.

Miss Hollander did not reply.

All the members of the 'Committee' were in a very bad mood today. Each of them, we should add in parentheses, had experienced some personal setback the day before. Tosiek had had enough of Basia, and besides he had a lot of things to worry about at college; the professor had had an attack of kidney-stones; Franciszek had quarrelled with Miss Bernhard, and Miss Hollander had heard that in the Ministry of Culture she had been censured for left-wing deviationism.

Professor Wolski spoke out at once with a certain

impatience.—Why did you summon us, Mr Director, sir? What help do you suppose we can give you in this business?

The director had no time to answer this question; at that very same moment the whole museum building was filled with the mighty echo of a silver trumpet. The sounds did not cease for a single moment, and gradually got louder. The window-panes shook.

—That's her!—shouted Franciszek, and everyone broke into a run.

From the director's office you had to run right along the corridor, than go down three floors. Tosiek, of course, led the way, followed by the director of the museum. Glancing at the clock, he said,—Eleven twenty-two, this time it's eleven twenty-two . . .

Miss Hollander was spinning along after him like a ball; every bit of her plump frame was shaking away rhythmically on the staircase . . .

—A flat, A flat, A flat, A flat! she howled, leaping from step to step—A flat, A flat, A flat, A flat—she counted the notes of the trumpet. And suddenly she summoned up her Lwów accent and shouted:—And what can that mean? C! Today it's playing C, not C sharp!

This expostulation brought them to the cloakroom of the hall.—Shut the doors!—the director shouted in mid-stride.—Nobody comes in or goes out.

The cloakroom attendants fell over one another in their haste to carry out this order, and the director's assistant flew to him from the depths of the other wing in horror, waving his arms:

—Bloody hell!—! Tosiek swore.

Quite impossible to get at Fame. A dense throng of children surrounded her.

—What's that? What is it?—shouted the breathless Miss Hollander.

A terrified little lady in a grey mac and a mauve veil emerged from the serried ranks of children.

—We are an excursion of schoolchildren from the elementary school in Klimontow—she burst out.

—Class dismiss, class dismiss!—Franciszek shouted on the run.

And the statue trumpeted like good-oh.

An hour later, in the director's office, the same group of people thronged together, augmented by the director's assistant, and the teacher from Klimontow, who was in tears. Despite her entreaties, the children had not been allowed to leave, and the museum was locked up tight on all sides.

The group that had gathered sat around the director's round table, which stood in the corner of his office, and held their peace for a while. Finally the director looked round helplessly at everyone, and, wringing his hands, said:

—What is to be done?

—The insurance people could help—Miss Hollander hissed authoritatively.

—The last thing in the world—answered the director.

—Quite impossible—added his assistant importantly.—We really have to keep the whole thing hidden as assiduously as possible.

—Get someone here from the Ministry of Culture and Art—Professor Wolski suggested.

—Right!—The Director seemed pleased.—I'll ring straight away.

And without waiting for general consent he lifted the receiver and dialled the number. He was soon deep in conversation.

—Hello! Is that the secretary? Yes, that's right, it's me . . . I have to speak to the minister at once. An unfortunate episode in the museum, very unfortunate. Someone has to come at once . . . Yes? . . . Yes? . . . Yes . . . Yes . . . I see . . . Yes . . . In an hour? Fine, an hour, then . . .

He put the phone down and looked glumly at his companions in distress.—The minister is in Łomza, the vice-minister is in Chodziez, the department manager is at a meeting, Director Lisek is unable to leave the Ministry . . . They've told us to ring in an hour.

—Mr Director, sir—said his assistant patiently—that's not the way to do it. Haven't you learned yet?

Upon which he picked up the receiver and dialled the same number.

—Hello—he said—deputy director of the National Museum speaking. I wanted to ask you whether you have received invitations to our meeting today? They were sent out a week ago. You didn't know that? But people have already gathered here, they're waiting, and your representative hasn't turned up yet. What's it about? What's it about? . . . It's about planning the subjects of paintings for 1956. Yes, yes, right after the six-year plan . . . Well, yes, you have to think of the future. Who's here? Professor Wolski, Miss Hollander . . . Yes, Miss Hollander, some of the subjects will be musical. Painters love musical instruments, we have to make concessions to their passion for such subjects, yes, yes . . .

—Director Lisek? Fine. He'll be here right away? Good, we'll hold up the beginning of the meeting. No, really, it's no problem . . . We've got quite used to that.

—Director Lisek will be along in a moment—he added, putting down the phone.

—That's fine—Miss Hollander remarked.—I've got something to talk to him about.

About half an hour later Director Lisek appeared. He looked fresh and absolutely *compos mentis*. He did not notice that the museum was closed and that he had been admitted specially. He formed no special impression of the people gathered there, though the teacher from Klimontow was weeping silently.

At this moment there was a summons for the janitor, Franciszek. His wife had come for him.

Miss Hollander thrust herself upon Director Lisek's attention.

—What do you mean, 'left-wing deviationism'? What sort of deviation? What's this supposed to mean? Why do you say this?

Director Lisek, unruffled, smiled.—Miss Henryka, my dear colleague, listen for a moment! Your 'Kurpiowski Tango' for piano has the melody in the left hand. Why? What for? If the melody is progressive enough, the listener will get it, even if it's in the right hand. You don't have to underline it . . .

—Right—interjected Tosiek Tralka suddenly, in his low, affected bass voice—and when I began playing Bolesław the Bold at a school performance . . .

—Yes, yes—The director, who was losing patience, interrupted him in mid-sentence—because if Bolesław is shorter than the bishop, people will feel sympathy for the bishop . . .

—But I played it like that—Tosiek raised his Herculean elbow to the height of his ear—and then Motykowska wrote in the paper . . .

—My friends—the director interjected, his voice betraying distress—we are gathered here today in connection with a very different matter.

Upon which he told the flabbergasted representative of the Ministry of Culture and Art the whole history of the trumpet-call. Lisek managed to control his amazement, and tried to rise to the occasion.

—Have you taken precautions that nobody should be let out of the museum?

—But of course.

At this point, overcoming her shyness, the schoolteacher in the mauve veil broke in:

—Mr Director, the children are hungry, and I have a train to catch . . .—and tears once again began to choke her.

—Right, we'll arrange for the children to have their canteen lunch here. We only have to ring the Catering Centre . . . How many children are there?

—Sixty—stammered the teacher.

—Right, we must provide sixty place settings, sixty bowls of soup . . .

—And what about us?—asked Tosiek, who was already very hungry.

—OK, eighty.

—Yes, but the people who bring lunch won't be able to leave the museum again, because they'll know that Fame has sounded her trumpet—interjected the director's assistant.

—Can't be helped.

—And what about supper?—asked Tosiek, who always took a lively interest in questions of food.

—Other people will bring that.

—But if this goes on the museum will fill up to the rafters—the director said, more and more upset.

—Maybe, but there's nothing else to be done—Director Lisek asserted, implacably.

—Until Fame stops blowing her trumpet?—asked Professor Wolski.

—And if this Fame of yours never stops trumpeting? Till Judgment Day? said the pedagogue, tearfully.

—A teacher in People's Poland has no business believing in Judgment Day—Miss Hollander observed.

—One moment, one moment—Director Lisek interrupted, knotting the fingers of both hands under his nose.—We must work out how many calories the children need. Are fifteen grams of meat per child enough? We'll have to lodge an estimate for food with the Ministry of Home Trade.

—Right!—cried the director.—But then we'll have to tell people why we have shut the children in the museum.

—And then what, when they find out?—sighed Miss Hollander.

At that moment Franciszek dropped in.

—Mr Director, sir—he shouted from the doorway—help! The children are running wild! They've been running round the whole museum. The little girls are playing at housekeeping with the porcelain collections, and the boys are playing at cops and robbers. The cops have Grecian vases on their heads instead of helmets, and the robbers are all got up in gold sashes . . . and the little ones have peed all over the toilet floor.

Everyone made their way downstairs. It was hard work collecting up the children from the various rooms, and taking the valuable exhibits away from them, and making a pile of them in the hall. The caretaker made a cordon on the stairs so that the children couldn't get through to the upper floors. Shouts, babble, an incredible uproar. This lasted an hour.

Fame blew her trumpet a couple of times during all this, but nobody paid any attention. Only the children split their sides laughing.

In the end everything grew calm again. The children fell silent and sat on the marble floor. They looked like a confused flock of partridges. A few were beginning to fall asleep.

Meanwhile, Director Lisek had done a bunk. He'd been summoned to another meeting. The other members of the 'Committee for the Salvation of Polish Art' no longer had the strength to go upstairs. They all sat down by the cloakroom, next to the felt slippers, and looked helplessly at one another.

The lady teacher from Klimontow, handing out to the sickliest-looking children buns from her huge handbag, which she heaved in the air with her hand, also sat down on the sofa, with an expression of resignation on her face. There was no more talk about communal catering for the children who had been detained in the museum.

At that moment one pupil broke away from the group of the oldest boys, who were waiting on the steps in front of the janitorial cordon, and went up to the teacher:

—Please, Miss! Please, Miss!—he lisped soundlessly.—I have something to say to you.

—My dear boy—the teacher suddenly brightened up and her face became radiant, like the sun peeping from behind clouds—not me, not me. Tell it to the director.

And as she said this she propelled the youngster towards the director of the museum, who was sitting with his head bowed, plunged in gloomy thoughts. Moreover, he had moved his chair to a position from which he could peep nervously from time to time through the entrance door in the direction of the lifeless statue.

—Mr Director, Mr Director—exclaimed the teacher—he has something to say to you. This is our 'productivity expert', Gabrys Ponowa. He can do anything, he's the leader of our 'Beat the Maybug' campaign in Klimontow, he sweeps chimneys, he's reorganized our fire brigade ... I know him well, he has a way . . . go on, young 'un . . .—and she pushed the young man closer to the gloomy official.

The eyes of all were turned on Gabrys with curiosity and disbelief.

He was a lad of about twelve, tall and thin, with reddish hair and freckles, and with a crew-cut. He had big blue eyes with reddened eyelids, a retroussé nose, which he used to pull before he spoke, and thick, puffy cheeks. He was dressed in very short trousers, from which thick, stick-like, very sun-burned legs poked out, and a sweater of a grassy-green colour and a discoloured old-fashioned calico shirt.

He stood in front of the director, and with a bit of a lisp said:

—As I understand it, Mr Director, you're having a problem with that figure that trumpets. Does she trumpet quite independently of you?

The director directed his gaze in great amazement towards the stick-like figure.

—Absolutely independently—he answered, with a sigh.

—And you don't know where to start in on this?—Gabrys went on to ask.

Everyone present heard the tone of these questions with amazement. They, too, turned their chairs round, to face in the same direction, so that Gabrys found himself, after a while, in the middle of a circle of curious spectators. The teacher from Klimontow again shed a tear, but this time a tear of pride.

—Meaning that you don't want the world to find out that mystical and irrational things are going on in your museum?—Gabrys reeled off in one breath.

—Well, yes!—everyone answered this time in a single chorus.

—Fine, I'm certainly sure I know the way—said Gabrys, giving a special lisp to both S's in the words 'certain' and 'sure'.

—My lad, are you quite sure you are not deceiving your-self?—Professor Wolski asked sadly.—There are some things that just don't have a way.

But Gabrys wasn't listening to the professor. Like some unquenchable stream, he went on as if he was giving some splendidly learned but imperfectly understood lecture.

—According to the third principle of dialectical thinking, if it is not possible to master a particular phenomenon confronting us, we must assimilate its power, make use of it for our own ends, like a water turbine. Comrade Stopczyk said, in his speech on 10 February 1950 in Opatow, that 'If a phenomenon does not fall into line with our objectives, it must be transformed to the point where it can co-operate with us.' I propose to transform the phenomenon located in the National Museum, and, if I may say so, rationalize it.

Gabrys stopped for a moment, and everyone was silent, plunged into sheep-like stupefaction.

—What is the third principle of the dialectic?—Tosiek asked Miss Hollander in a whisper.

—I don't know—the composer answered, even more quietly.

Professor Wolski broke the silence.—This youngster expresses it well: you have to transform it. We have just the same problem. Like old Feigenfeld, good painter, but what a peasant, straight from the plough, understands nothing, just says you have to paint the way you feel—old Feigenfeld exhibited his picture *Clouds in Loing-sur-Marne*, it's a good picture what's more, got a gold medal in Paris, so we called it *Bricklayers on Scaffolding*, and everyone liked it, got the fourth prize at the show, and Sokorski praised it, and *Ogonyok* reproduced it. But it was the same picture . . .

At this very instant Fame started rumbling. But everyone was so taken up with Gabrys that they couldn't have cared less. Only the children, who were already half asleep, turned their heads reluctantly towards her.

—OK, fine—said the director's assistant in a down-to-earth manner, when the trumpet had ceased braying and its last echo had resounded from somewhere up in the glass roof of the building—and what are you transforming?

Gabrys didn't hesitate for an instant.—I would give it the

following caption: 'Even statues thunder in honour of socialist realist art', and let it trumpet.

—My boy, you're a genius—exclaimed the director.

—Maybe you're trying to become a minister?—asked Miss Hollander.

—No, I want to be an actor—said Gabrys with conviction.

—Sure he does—said Tosiek to himself.—You can tell by the way he lisps.

In less than no time Franciszek had brought a piece of red cloth, left over from a May Day banner. Everyone, even the teacher from Klimontow, cut out white paper letters, drawn in haste by Professor Wolski. In less than three-quarters of an hour the banner was ready. It was carried in triumph to the hall and placed on the statue. To reinforce it, the director handed over the last drawing pins in the museum; which were also the last drawing pins in Warsaw.

—Mr Director—Franciszek Monument volunteered self-effacingly—what are we going to use instead, for fastening things?

—Prehistoric nails—the director's assistant answered in his practical way.

Just as the inscription was being fixed to the figure, Fame raised the hand with the trumpet to her lips, but she didn't trumpet. Her hand fell slowly back again and remained motionless in its habitual position.

—This is a realistic figure—said Gabrys.—The breasts are formed just like real ones. It's just a bit narrow in the waist, but that's because of the girdle. Our women aren't like that any more. That sculpture is historically determined.

Tosiek, making his deep voice all velvety, read out the inscription one more time: 'Even statues thunder in honour of socialist realist art.'

—What a feeling of verisimilitude—said Miss Hollander.

—Now the doors of the museum can be opened as wide as you like, let them come, let them look—declared the director of the Warsaw National Museum, who had been infected with strong emotions.

—What a splendid idea—Professor Wolski ejaculated.

And so it was. The idea was splendid. From the time they hung the inscription on her, Fame stopped trumpeting.

(*Translated by George Hyde*)

Stanisław Lem

The Use of a Dragon

So far, I have kept my trip to the planet Abrazia in the Whale constellation a secret. The civilization of that planet seemed to have based its economy on a dragon but unfortunately, not being an economist myself, I could not fathom this system of theirs, even though the Abrazians were very forthcoming with explanations. Perhaps someone more familiar with dragons will understand it better than I do.

For some time, the radiotelescope in Arecibo had been receiving signals which no one was able to decode, until, that is, Assistant Professor Dr Katzenfanger had a crack at it. He was puzzling over this riddle while suffering from an acute attack of catarrh. His blocked and dripping nose was such a nuisance and distraction that it led him to the idea that the inhabitants of the unknown planet were not visiles, as we are, but olfactives. And indeed, it turned out that they operated a code composed not of letters of the alphabet but of symbols representing various smells. Nevertheless, the translation table drawn up by Dr Katzenfanger still yielded rather baffling results. The messages seemed to indicate that, apart from sentient beings, the planet was also inhabited by a creature which was as big as a mountain, at once extremely voracious and shy. But what surprised the scientists was not this phenomenon of cosmic zoology but the fact that, apparently through its excessive greed, the Abrazian monster was bringing the local economy all kinds of benefits. The beast was dangerous, and the more dangerous it grew the greater were the profits derived from it. As I have a weakness for mysteries I decided on immediate departure for Abrazia.

Once there, I noted that the Abrazians were quite anthropoidal, the only difference being that where we have ears they have noses, and vice versa. They too are descendants of apes except that our ancestors were narrow- and broad-nosed apes, while theirs divided into uni- and bi-nasals. Later, the uni-nasals died of starvation. The reason is that the planet is surrounded by many moons, which makes for frequent and lengthy eclipses of the sun plunging the globe into Cimmerian darkness. Those who relied on their eyes in search of food could not find it. Those who used their sense of smell were in a better position, but, naturally, those who had two widely spaced noses fared best, as the stereo-olfaction gave them the same advantages we enjoy with two eyes and two ears.

Then the Abrazians invented artificial light, and bi-nasality was no longer necessary for survival, becoming merely an anatomical curiosity. In winter the Abrazians have to wear special hats with flaps designed to protect their noses from frostbite. I may be wrong, but my impression was that they were not particularly happy with their noses, which reminded them of their difficult past. Their fair sex tried to hide them under all sorts of jewellery, sometimes as big as plates. But I didn't pay much attention to it. My experience as an astronaut has taught me that anatomical differences are of little significance. The important, difficult problems lie somewhere else, usually hidden. For the Abrazian civilization, such a problem was the local dragon.

The planet has only one huge continent, containing some eighty states. The land is surrounded on all sides by an ocean. The dragon occupies the far north, bordering directly on three states—Klaustria, Lelipia and Laulalia. Seeing the dragon both in the photographs taken by a satellite and as a 1:1 000 000 scale model, I thought it a loathsome beast. Besides, it does not resemble the dragons known from the legends and stories popular on Earth. Their dragon doesn't have seven heads, in fact it has no head at all, and presumably no brain either. What's more, it doesn't have wings, so it cannot fly. As for the legs, there is an uncertainty here, but it seems completely limbless. It's a mountain of a beast, covered by a thick, jelly-like substance resembling aspic. That it is actually a live creature can be ascertained only after long and patient observation. It moves extremely slowly, by way of peristalsis, not infrequently violating the borders of Klaustria and Lelipia. The beast consumes about eighty thousand tons of food each day. It likes gruel, barley and all kinds of cereals, but it's not herbivorous. The food is supplied by the states of the Union for Economic Co-operation, or the UEC. Most of the food is transported by train to a special unloading station; soups and syrups are pumped through a pipeline. In winter, during general shortage of vitamins, big transporter planes air-drop extra supplies; there is no need to aim for the mouth as the monster can swallow with any part of its massive body.

When I arrived in Klaustria and learned all these facts, the first question that sprang to my mind was: Why do they, with so much effort and so eagerly, feed this monstrous creature instead of waiting for a bit till it starves to death? But I held my tongue when I heard about an attempted assassination of the dragon. One Lelipian, who wanted to gain fame as the deliverer of Abrazia, set up a paramilitary organization whose aim it was to bump off the greedy giant. The assassination was to be carried out by lacing the dragon's vitamin-enriched nutrients with a chemical causing unquenchable thirst, so that the monster would start drinking the ocean waters till it burst. I immediately remembered the story, well known to a certain nation on Earth, about a brave youngster who killed a dragon which fed mainly on virgins, by tempting it with a lambskin stuffed with sulphur. But that is where the similarities between the legend from Earth and the reality of Abrazia ended. The Abrazian monster is under protection of international law. Moreover, the treaty of co-operation with the dragon, signed by forty-nine states, guarantees the beast regular supplies of tasty nourishment.

My computerized translator—I never leave home without

it—enabled me to undertake a thorough study of the local press. The news of the failed assassination caused a great outcry of public opinion, which demanded a severe punishment for the conspirators. This struck me as rather odd, as nobody I'd heard had a good word to say about the dragon. Neither the journalists nor the members of the public writing to newspapers tried to hide the fact that it was a very nasty beast indeed. At first I thought they regarded it as a kind of divine dispensation, or an evil deity, and it was only because of a quirk of their religious vernacular that they called a sacrifice 'an export'. On Earth, we can speak ill of the devil, though it would be a mistake to take him lightly. But the devil can lead us into temptation and whoever sells his soul to him will receive a lot of worldly pleasures in return, while the dragon—as far as I could tell—didn't promise anything and wasn't in the least bit tempting. From time to time it would swell and flood its neighbours' borders with the remnants of its undigested food; in bad weather the stench would carry for a thousand miles. None the less, the Abrazians insisted the dragon needed to be looked after and that the odour was symptomatic of bad digestion, which required the administration of medicine to regulate its metabolism. As for the assassination itself, if, God forbid, it had been successful, it would have resulted in some disaster of unimaginable proportions. I carried on reading the newspapers but I couldn't find out what kind of disaster that would have been. Utterly confused, I visited one library after another, checking encyclopedias and the volumes of *The History of Abrazia*, until finally I decided to pay a visit to the Dragon Friendship Society. I didn't learn anything there either. Apart from a few office clerks there was nobody there. They were keen, however, to issue me with a membership card, encouraging me to pay a year's fee in advance, which I declined as this was not exactly the reason for my visit.

The states sharing borders with the dragon are all liberal democracies and anybody can say anything he wants. It was only after a long search, however, that I found a publication condemning the dragon. Yet the authors were still of the opinion that in dealing with the dragon one should adopt a position of reasonable compromise; the use of force or any undercover activities might prove fatal.

Meanwhile the failed assassins were locked up awaiting trial. Although they admitted to having intended to kill the dragon, they pleaded not guilty. The pro-government press branded them irresponsible terrorists, the opposition called them harmless cranks who needed their heads examined, while a Klaustrian illustrated magazine put forward a theory that they were *agents provocateurs*. According to this theory, the provocation was the work of a certain neighbouring country which considered its quota of dragon exports, allocated by the UEC, too small and wanted to create a situation whereby the fixed export quotas would have to be revised.

I asked the reporter who came to interview me for his paper, why, rather than let the assassins finish the beast off, they were putting them in the dock?

The journalist answered that it would be nothing short of cruel murder. The dragon, he said, is basically a good-natured creature, but the difficult conditions in which it has to live in the icy north prevent it from showing its naturally sweet disposition. Anybody who is constantly hungry—dragon or not—is angry. The dragon needs to be fed properly and then it will calm down and stop pushing south.

'How can you be so sure?' I asked. 'I have collected some press cuttings from the last few days. Here are the headlines: POPULATION OF NORTHERN KLAUSTRIA AND LELIPIA ABANDON HOMES, THE MASS EXODUS CONTINUES. Or look at this one: THE DRAGON HAS AGAIN SWALLOWED A GROUP OF TOURISTS. HOW LONG WILL IRRESPONSIBLE TRAVEL AGENTS GO ON ORGANIZING DANGEROUS TRIPS? Or this one: THIS YEAR THE DRAGON HAS INCREASED ITS DOMAINS BY 900,000 ACRES. What do you say to that?'

'It only confirms what I've just said,' he said. 'We still don't give it enough food! As for the tourists, I admit there have been incidents, very unpleasant, but then the dragon should not be provoked. It cannot stand tourists, especially those taking photographs. It's particularly sensitive to camera flashes. And what do you expect—for three-quarters of the year it lives in total darkness ... Besides, the industry producing the high-calorie nutrients for the dragon alone creates 146,000 jobs. OK, so a handful of tourists died, but think how many people would have died of starvation losing their work?'

'Wait a minute, wait a minute,' I interrupted him. 'You deliver the food, which doesn't get produced all by itself. Who pays for it?'

'Our parliaments vote special export credits.'

'So, the dragon is fed from the tax-payer's pocket?'

'In a way, yes. But it's worth it.'

'Wouldn't it be worth more to finish off the monster?'

'You are talking sheer madness! During the last thirty years we have invested over 400 billions in the dragon-food industry ...'

'Wouldn't it be better to turn the money into something that would bring you direct benefits?'

'You are repeating the arguments of our most reactionary conservatives!' The irritated reporter raised his voice. 'They are accomplices in a murder! They want to turn the dragon into canned meat. Life is sacred! It's wrong to kill!'

Seeing that the discussion was leading nowhere, he got up and left. Then I went to the Record Office to dig through the old and dusty annals of the press and legal archives, hoping at least to find out where the dragon had come from in the first place. It was hard work, but I did find something very curious indeed.

Fifty years before, when the dragon was occupying a mere two million acres, nobody took it seriously. I found a number of articles advocating rooting it out or freezing it to death by flooding it with water via specially constructed canals. This was countered by the economists arguing that the operation would be too costly. However, when the dragon, which at that time was feeding only on moss and lichen, doubled in size and the population of the neighbouring countries began to complain about its unbearable smell, particularly in spring and summer when warm winds blew south, various self-help organizations embarked on a programme of 'perfumization' of the dragon, and the collection of stale bread.

At first, these actions were ridiculed, but with time they gained in momentum and popularity. In the later annals I could not find a word about getting rid of the dragon. Instead, there was more and more about the benefits which could be derived from helping it. So, I did learn something, but, still dissatisfied, I decided to visit the local university and its Institute of General and Practical Dragonology. Its director greeted me with obliging kindness.

'Your questions are, shall we say, anachronistic in character,' he said with an indulgent smile, after my initial queries. 'The dragon is an objective, integral part of our reality, I'd even say the central one, and as such deserves to be studied as a very important problem of international dimensions.'

'Could you be more specific?' I asked. 'Where did it come from, this dragon?'

'God knows,' said the dragonologist phlegmatically. 'Archaeology, the pre-dragonian era, dragonogenetics—all these subjects lie outside my sphere of interest. Dragogenesis is not my speciality either. As long as the dragon was small it posed no problem, just like everything else here, my friend.'

'Somone told me it grew out of mutating snails.'

'I doubt it. Anyway, it doesn't matter how it came into existence since it exists, and very much so. If the dragon suddenly disappeared it would be a disaster. I doubt we would be able to deal with the consequences.'

'Really? But why?'

'As a result of computerization we had growing unemployment; among intellectuals as well.'

'And what? The dragon put a stop to it?'

'Of course. We had a gigantic surplus of food, a whole mountain of spaghetti, lakes of vegetable oil, there was over-production of sweets. Now we can export the surplus north. And the food also needs to be processed—it won't eat any old grub.'

'The dragon?'

'The dragon. In order to come up with an optimal programme of nutrition we had to set up a number of research
centres, like for instance the Dragon's Pasturage Centre and
the Higher Institute of Dragonian Hygiene, and at every
university there is at least one department of dragonology.
We have an entirely new food industry producing new kinds
of foods and special nutrition. The Ministry of Propaganda of
each country set up information networks explaining the
benefits of trade exchange with the dragon.'

'Exchange? Does it give you anything in exchange? I don't
believe it.'

'Of course it does. First of all it gives us dragogel, the
dragon's secretion.'

'That slimy stuff? I saw it on the photographs. Does it
have any use?'

'When condensed, it is suitable for the production of plasticine, though there are still certain problems. Its odour is
difficult to eliminate.'

'It stinks?'

'In a sense, even badly. In order to deodorize it there are
special fragrant agents added to it. At the moment however,
'dragosticine' is eight times more expensive than normal
plasticine.'

'And what do you feel about the assassination, Professor?'

The scientist scratched his ear, which flapped loosely over
his mouth.

'If this assassination were successful, firstly there would
be an outbreak of diseases of epidemic proportions. Can you
imagine the amount of unwholesome gases produced by a
rotting corpse of this size? Secondly, the banks would go
bust, followed by a crash of the monetary system. It would
be a disaster, dear friend, total disaster.'

'But the dragon's presence is a bit of a nuisance, isn't it?
Or, to put it bluntly, it's downright unpleasant?'

'Unpleasant? What isn't?' answered the dragonologist
philosophically. 'The post-dragonian crisis would be even
more unpleasant. Please consider that we not only feed it

but also deal with other aspects besides its gastronomy. We try to soothe it, control its temper. We call it the 'domestication and pacification' programme. Recently, we started giving the dragon a lot of sweets. It has a very sweet tooth.'

'I doubt it's going to make it any more sweet-tempered,' I remarked under my breath.

'But the export of sweets has risen 400 per cent. And we mustn't forget the CCCP.'

'What's that?'

'The Controlling Consequences of Co-existence Programme. It provides jobs for graduates. The dragon has to be studied, researched, and from time to time treated. Before, we had a surplus of health-service workers; not all young doctors have their jobs guaranteed.'

'Well, all right,' I said, unconvinced. 'But you are simply exporting your charity. Doesn't charity begin at home?'

'How do you mean?'

'You are sinking billions into this dragon!'

'Why, do you think we should hand out money as gifts to our citizens? It breaks the basic rules of economics! I see you don't know much about it. The credits for exports stimulate our economies, they increase our turnovers . . .'

'But they also increase the dragon's size,' I interrupted him. 'The more you feed it, the bigger it grows, the bigger it grows, the bigger its appetite. What sort of calculation is this? That beast will finally gobble you all up!'

'Nonsense.' The professor was indignant. The banks treat the credits as investment assets.'

'You mean you expect a return on the money? In what? Plasticine?'

'Please don't be so narrow-minded. If it weren't for the dragon, who else would we construct the dragogel pipelines for? Just think—the pipelines mean steelworks, plate mills, welding machines, transport, and so on. The dragon has real needs. Do you understand that or don't you? And production needs cannot be plucked from thin air. The producers won't produce anything if they are just going to throw the produce into the ocean. They have to have a specific consumer in mind. The dragon represents a huge, all-absorbing foreign market with a massive demand . . .'

'That I do not doubt,' I said, seeing that this discussion too was leading nowhere.

'So, have I convinced you then?'

'No.'

'That's because you come from a different civilization from ours. Besides, the dragon has long since ceased to be just a trading partner importing our produce.'

'And what has it become instead?'

'An idea, dear sir. A historical necessity, a *raison d'état*. It has become a powerful factor unifying our efforts into a common cause. If you look at it from this angle, you will see what fundamental questions lie buried in an otherwise disgusting beast when it reaches global dimensions.'

PS: They say that the dragon has since fallen apart and divided into little dragons, but their appetites are just as big.

(*Translated by Wiesiek Powaga*)

Leszek Kołakowski

Cain, or an Interpretation of the Rule: To Each According to His Deserts

We know that Cain was a tiller of the soil, while Abel was a herdsman. So it would seem quite natural that Cain should offer God a sacrifice of sweet corn, flax, beetroot, and other such fruits, while Abel offered meat, dripping, skins and saddles of mutton. Unfortunately, it was equally natural that from the point of view of market price Abel's sacrifice would be seen as an incomparably greater gift. It was this gift that interested God, whilst at Cain's offering He waved His hand contemptuously. He may even have said something not very polite. For there is no reason to think He was a vegetarian. In that case the affair might have turned out quite differently. Still, what happened, happened, and we know the outcome.

It is clear that God's reaction to the brothers' sacrifices is an excellent interpretation of the rule: To Each according to his Deserts. For this rule has been inaccurately formulated and therefore falsely interpreted. The word 'deserts' suggests mistakenly that in the division of reward one considers only a man's efforts, the amount of work put in and his good intentions. By this system, of course, the sacrifices of the two brothers would have been equal, since each of them gave what he possessed according to the established division of labour—one gave corn, the other meat. But it was precisely here that God revealed the essence of justice. Justice in the division of reward is unable to distinguish the objective conditions under which work, or even 'deserts', are carried out. It cannot take into consideration the fact that fate made one man a tiller of the soil and another a cattle herdsman. It considers only the objective result of the work. In the last resort Cain could perhaps have tried for something better. At worst he could have stolen from his brother and offered the booty to God as a sacrifice. This would not have been very admirable, but it would have been far more pleasant than what in fact happened. We can assume that God would have winked at such a small transgression from which He was Himself deriving benefit. But no, Cain wanted to be honest and he brought what he had. He was then unable to bear what, he was convinced, was injustice. In this he was either inconsistent, or else ignorant and naïve. If he already knew what constituted justice but still decided to act honestly, he should have kept up this rôle to the end and not let himself become angry in the face of facts which could quite easily have been foreseen. If he did not know, he showed a naïvety so extreme that it is not really worthwhile feeling sorry for him.

The moral: we should count on receiving a reward according to the market price, and not according to how much work and effort we have put into the business. This fact is supported by many learned men (among them Karl Marx) not to mention the experience of everyday life. Our friend or brother may take into consideration our good will, our attempts, efforts and honest desires. But it is not our friend or brother who will make judgement upon us. This function belongs to society or to God. And it depends on the consequences of our actions, not on our intentions. By observing this rule we can probably achieve a certain happiness. Every unexpected penny over and above the market price we shall accept as a most extraordinary gift of fortune. But so long as, ignoring the character of true justice, we reckon in advance that we are going to receive it, we shall live in a permanent state of bitterness. We shall nurse a grudge against the whole world, and finally, out of malice, we may kill our own brother.

Sarah, or the Conflict between the General and the Individual in Morality

Sarah finally decided to tell her husband that as a result of certain inborn defects she was unable to give him children. Abraham sat there grim and gloomy, and they fell into a tense silence, filled with the expectation of words they both knew, but which for a long time neither dared say aloud. In the end it was Sarah who spoke, both because, as a woman, she was blessed with greater courage, and also because in this matter it was clearly her duty to carry out the act of renunciation. She said, 'You must have a child by my servant, Hagar.' Abraham breathed a deep sigh of relief. He was not a man of great courage, and was glad the proposition had not had to come from him. If he had been less pusillanimous, he should have suggested this solution himself. He should have asked his wife's permission, but not exposed her to the humiliation of speaking first. He should not have run like a coward from the accusation of selfishness. At least, he should have allowed his wife the privilege of knowing she had become the victim of his brutal lust, for she had been aware for a long time now of how much he desired Hagar, and not left her thinking she had absolved him in advance by her own initiative and had pushed him into the sin of seduction. For Hagar the Egyptian was the most beautiful young girl in all the valleys of the Euphrates.

Sarah's decision was not a completely spontaneous reaction, nor was it a result of her generosity. It came entirely from the modest knowledge she possessed about the concept of a family. Sarah knew there existed a general rule laid down by God by which it is a man's duty to prolong his existence in children. If this rule is not carried out, the family is no family and does not realize its essence. It was thus a question of co-ordinating essence and existence, the general idea of a family with the individual concrete thing consisting in the couple Abraham and Sarah. Sarah knew also that a childless Abraham would become a laughing stock amongst his friends and an object of public scorn, that his social position might be shaken by such an abnormal situation. But it was not fear of her husband's being ridiculed which really motivated her. She was guided by her knowledge of general duty, a pure need to satisfy a general norm, and a feeling of anxiety at the fact that existence does not provide essence, and that her family was not carrying out the general function of a family: procreation. It was in this way that the general triumphed over the individual.

Motionless and without a single tear of regret, Sarah lay on the grass through the cold night, gazing at the stars, not far from the tent where her husband, beside himself with ecstasy, was taking possession of the incomparable body of Hagar. The night was long, endless. Abraham did not feel its passing, while Sarah grew old before her time.

And so the foreseeable occurred. Hagar was a good girl, but naïve and a trifle vain. She did not understand the task which fate had assigned to her. The night she had spent with Abraham, already several times repeated, had been for her simply a night of pleasure, not a night of duty, as it had been for Sarah. (Abraham maintained a dual position. He carried out his duty, but since he had the chance, why not enjoy his proper share of the pleasure?) As regards fulfilling the law, Hagar was only a passive tool, entirely ignorant of her rôle. She was ignorant of the *general* situation. She made use of the law so as to taste sheer delight. Her motives were individual and tied to the present moment.

Hagar knew it was good to have children. This was why, instead of fulfilling her rôle modestly, she carried her growing belly around proudly, and revealed her condition wherever she could for all to see. By subtle allusions and gestures she expressed her feeling of superiority over the unfortunate lady whose dedication was being ever more strongly put to the test. In the beginning Abraham walked about proudly, as if he had accomplished some very difficult act, but soon the domestic atmosphere became intolerable, and he began to spend his time away from home, so as not to get involved in women's quarrels.

In the end Sarah's anger and bitterness burst into the open. Giving way to her long-restrained rage and desire for revenge, she demanded satisfaction from Abraham.

Abraham, like all those who have a reputation as 'real men', was an unmitigated coward. His bravery consisted only in brandishing a sword about when surrounded by a fanatical crowd of warriors. He was never able to face the conflicts of life. He avoided taking any initiative, and always tried to act in such a way that someone else would make difficult decisions for him. In this case he behaved exactly according to character. To the pained cries of his wife, to the fury of her aggravated hatred he gave the speedy answer, 'But Hagar is your servant. You can do what you like with her. I have no intention of interfering. It's nothing to do with me what happens to her.'

Sarah was only waiting for this licence. That evening Hagar, great with child, pelted with a mass of cruel insults, bruised and disgraced, fled weeping loudly from her employers' house. It was thus that impulse finally gained the upper hand over the law, existence rebelled against essence, the individual won a victory over the general. Abraham returned home after it was all over, quite content with the way things had turned out. The slight pangs of conscience he felt at the thought of his banished mistress were soon drowned in his satisfaction and relief that the whole affair was finally over and that his slate, at least, was clean since he had not laid a finger on anybody and had taken no decision. Like all cowards he was sure that if he did nothing he was not responsible for anything and so the best thing was not to get involved. He had made Hagar pregnant on his wife's instructions, he had taken no part in their women's quarrels, and in the end all he had said was that Hagar was Sarah's servant and could be treated just as Sarah wished. This was no more than a simple statement of fact. And so a tiresome situation had been resolved of its own accord.

The last part of this story is not so interesting.

The first moral: Sarah's situation. If the law turns out truly intolerable and is an excessive violation of our nature, it is no fault not to fulfil it, but to fulfil it is a virtue. In other words, '*Naturam expelles furca . . .*' etc.

The second moral: Sarah's situation. If we *do* take on ourselves the burden of fulfilling the law, it is wrong not to persevere to the end, because otherwise someone else will have to pay for our inconsistency.

The third moral: Hagar's situation. Undeserved advantages bring deserved punishments.

The fourth moral: Abraham's situation. Cowardice may sometimes work itself out profitably under the stress of the most powerful emotions.

The fifth moral: Abraham's situation. We should not delude ourselves that we do not take decisions if all we do is to state the facts.

The sixth moral: the triangle situation. What a monstrous story—to take a lover for the purpose of having children! But each man must work out his own system of priorities.

God, or Relative Mercy

This little story is quite short and compact. It contains only a plot, a question, and a moral.

Plot: The psalmist writes about God (Ps. 136:10, 15): 'He hath smitten Egypt with her firstborn; for His mercy endureth for ever.

'And He hath cast Pharaoh with his horde into the Red Sea; for His mercy endureth for ever.'

Question: What do Egypt and Pharaoh think about the mercy of God?

Moral: Mercy and benevolence cannot exist for everyone. When using these words, we should always say whom they are for. And when we confer benevolence upon whole nations, we should first of all ask them what they think of our benevolence. For example, Egypt.

(*Translated by Nicholas Bethell*)

Janusz Anderman

Poland Still?

Bells ring above the bulk of the church; swifts swish, black glints against the pargetted wall. Down below, the square expands as a massive crowd pours from the church, then overflows in all directions and stops dead, help-less, sapped of all energy. Darkness rises in the warm breaths, swallows the walls and climbs slowly toward the towers, till the muffled bell dies away.

The crowd is alone.

The crowd is alone and doesn't know what to do with itself, which way to turn, whom to bawl at or what demands to make. It is tired, crumpled and undecided. It's not the crowd it was, and people eye one another with distrust.

A handful of people like specks of dust break away from the crowd; furtively they unpin the coloured badges on their coats, crowned eagles that could gouge out alien eyes. Compliantly they clench their fingers and nimbly pick their way between the serried ranks of silent militiamen; they dart off to the nearby bus-stops; they want to lie low at home and forget.

The crowd remains rooted.

People scrutinize one another; not to fall apart, not to disperse, to stay put, stay put; there is after all a chance, a settlement could be reached . . .

—Settle what . . .

—Well, try and settle all the issues . . .

—What issues do you mean . . .

—Well, to discuss . . .

—Discuss what . . .

—Well, formulate . . .

—Formulate what . . .

—Well, decide everything . . .

—Decide what . . .

—Well, coordinate everything . . .

—But with whom . . .

—Well, with them . . .

—With them . . .

—Not with them . . . With the others . . .

—It's high time to coordinate . . .

—And definitely postulate . . .

—Absolutely, absolutely . . .

A husky amplified voice floats out from an undefined point in the dark towards the crowd—Disperse peacefully, go home, don't form groups, disperse, otherwise we shall have to resort to . . .—There's a riot on the way, a man whispers, a riot . . .

—Time to start?

—Start what?

—'Poland Still'?*

—'Poland Still'?

—Well . . .

—Not yet, not yet . . .

At a safe distance from here a hunched silhouette cowers behind a windowpane—Meduz calling, Meduz calling; it'll probably move, a crowd's formed and now it's waiting, it'll probably move; the blues've lined the square, they're in control; no curses or abuse for the time being, no shouting; right now it's singing 'Give us back, o Lord' or something like that, but in patches, in patches; the situation calls for water cannon; when it moves give 'em water cannon for a scare; some of 'em are laughing and gaping, hey, some are already giving the salute and there's our little eye recording it all, and now I can hear 'We'll not desert the land' and 'You sovietized our kids'; I can see old women and young-

---

* The Polish national anthem begins, 'Poland still has not perished/As long as we are alive.'

sters making the V-sign to one another and laughing; I can
see one fellow with a lens recording it all, but it's not one
of ours, it's coloured, gaudy as a parrot, he'll be recorded by
our lens and he'll have to be checked outside the precincts;
the blues are standing quietly by waiting for the kick-off,
and then there'll be water for a scare . . .

Voices rage more and more distinctly above the crowd,
beads of mist settle on bare heads, a helicopter hovers in the
darkness and coarsely grinds the dense air.—Grandpa, a ten-
year-old boy asks, say Grandpa, what was it like in Wałęsa's
time? In Wałęsa's time, to be perfectly honest—the old man
strains his eyes—to tell you the truth it wasn't that simple.
There's more than one way. It varied, like. One way and the
other. That's what. Something like.

And standing aside, the faceless reporter formulates his
version for tomorrow morning's news bulletin and asks
himself who drove this handful of disoriented youngsters, kids
really, to demonstrate; who are the bosses cowering behind
the youngsters' backs; who wanted to plant this arsenal of
dirty tricks on Polish soil; who lined Geremek's and Michnik's
pockets with fat wads of Bonn marks, London pounds, Wash-
ington dollars and other foreign currencies; we all know only
too well the answers to these and other problems that spring
inevitably to the minds of the broad masses of indignant
citizens, who in their overwhelming majority daily voice their
support. To the disrupters of dialogue and partisans of Star
Wars, the spokesmen of national reconciliation resolutely say
no. The reporter peers cautiously about him and sees loathsome faces that disgust him. Not long ago he had to repent
in sackcloth and ashes before these people, making tearful
promises, and he'll never forget his humiliation, never get
over that stifling hatred. He fears the crowd and the future.

The collective silence is ominous, and the foreign reporter
is also afraid of the crowd; she looks at the crowd, no longer
knowing if those faces staring white in the darkness are wild
and Asiatic or gentle and wisely European; she is fascinated
by the crowd, and excited by it; she is in its midst, and at
the same time embraces the thousands; she sees two, then

four, five and ten thousand; she would hug them to her breast; she ignores the hostile blue lane, for she is a Western reporter; she is untouchable and besides, the communists in Nicaragua did her no harm, she wasn't trampled during the carnival in Havana, so she must get to the bottom of this lot too; thoughts scurry through her brain without her being able to fix on any; a defeat that's not a defeat, a victory that's not a victory, a defeat that'll be a victory, a victory that'll be a victory; she sees an old woman being shunted along by an equally ancient and jaded old boy and hears the woman shouting some words in that strange withered-ivy language that rustles warmly on her parched lips, and the reporter gives the old woman a friendly smile, nods vivaciously and stabs the air with her forked fingers—Listen, the woman shouts out, listen; you think you're badly off, do you? What more do you want? Two televisions each? Three? Did you have those TVs before the war? No, you didn't. Bloody hell!

—Hold it! You right bitch—the man says.—You ain't got a pennyworth of shame . . .

—Bitch. Bitch. That's all you can say. How many TVs can a man have, when all's said and done?

The edge of the crowd is lined by church guardians in tall caps that look like Uhlan shakos from a distance; the guardians penetrate the crowd; some of them stand motionless and stare at the ZOMO men without a word; and without a word the ZOMO men return the stare.

—Maybe now's the time for Poland Still?

—What?

—'Poland Still'?

—'Poland Still', 'Poland Still'! Not yet . . .

Voices are borne from end to end of the crowd, which stays put, waiting, not budging an inch; helmets gleam dangerously close, for the time being they hold, stock still as the paving stones; the waiting goes on until from somewhere among the treetops or the church roof muffled words break loose and ripple amid the crowd—What's he saying, what's he saying, that voice; it's the underground speaking on tape, it's a tape; but what's he saying, what's that voice—

we shall   we celebrate   not lay down   festival
we remember   solemnly   as always
the August   we must   festival   the December
we'll give   festival   inflexibly   our reply
achievements   festival   we pledge
ceremony   our communal   we'll clench
festival   we persist   we reject
we recall
festival   sign our pacts   and postulate
standing   festival   festive   festival
celebrat   celebrat   celeb

—Well, are we getting on with it, or aren't we; what're we supposed to—people ask the voice, but the voice can't hear; words float through the crowd, the echo lifts them back into the air, into the dark and the mist; the words bounce off the poet; the poet isn't listening, because he's doing his level best to compose a poem that will bear witness, the poet remembers; today the bells are ringing, sounding the alarm, the crowd outside the church, hope kindled in its hearts, while the red dragon in the sky, flaps its real tail in vain, in vain it sends its cohorts in; and the poet pauses awhile as the rhyme for cohorts eludes him, what rhymes with cohorts; cohorts reports; janissaries, mercenaries; but Poland still has to be fitted in, phalanx black hundreds tatars mortars, there's still nothing to rhyme with Poland . . . so the poet leaves the rhyme for later, and for the time being constructs a couplet, repeating the words with emphasis for fear they give him the slip—Rejoice not, vicious dragon red; the day we fight you'll soon be dead . . .

—Well folks, what are we doing—someone asks in an unnaturally loud voice—seeing as we're doing nothing, we'd better be snappy. The guardians in the chef's-hat helmets stalk the crowd with their eyes; people retreat respectfully just in case; they exchange swift glances and slight motions of the head; the man over there is silent beyond recall and someone else, wanting to smooth over the situation, explains coaxingly:—I might even get the truncheon. Better still. Let

England know. Then we'll see. England must say stop. Either there's some justice in the world, or there isn't.

A woman squeezes her way deftly through the crowd; she is wearing trousers and a blue sweater and a too-small cap with a pompom on a thread that bobs about like a yoyo; she peers into the bystanders' eyes and whispers—Hungar fruit drops, Hungar bubblegum, what, fruit drops, fruit drops . . .

—Wouldn't mind some of the bubble stuff, but it depends how much—someone mutters mechanically, but he makes no move and the woman's voice drifts into the distance and a child tugs hopefully at its mother's sleeve, and she says without looking in a tone of torment, get off my sleeve, get off my sleeve, or I'll knock you off.

—So what's up?

—How d'you mean what's up?

—When's the speech?

—It's already been.

—How come? When?

—Why ask? Ought've listened . . .

—When was the speech?

—Wakey wakey—the man unexpectedly replies, and looking round in triumph, he breaks out into prolonged uncontrollable laughter that blocks his windpipe.

—Must be time for 'Poland Still'?

—What?

—How about 'Poland Still'?

—'Poland Still' . . . not yet . . .

The foreign television team probes the crowd with its lens. A correspondent swathed in a coloured scarf adopts a professional air and hustles the cameraman for good measure. Make sure you show the church helping Solidarity. It's a must.

—I know my job.

—It must be made clear. When you did the prison, you were meant to show the political prisoners. And all you could see was walls, bare walls. Nothing to show it was political. Just bars and rooftops.

—I did it myself—says the cameraman, offended.

—There's nothing to get uptight about—the correspondent says.—If you did it, then that's OK. Can you see how the church is being supportive?

—Clear as day.

—Well then, we'll be off.

—Couldn't we perhaps wait for the bloodshed?

—Bloodshed, ah, bloodshed. The trouble with bloodshed...

The crowd waits patiently; shouts and scraps of songs sparkle in the darkness; words reverberate against the plastic shields of the impenetrable militia.

Again the loudspeaker is heard from the roof of a car slowly driving round the posts and cordons—I appeal to you to disperse.

—By the church they can't touch us.

—They won't enter the precincts. We're immune.

—Not here they won't. Out there it's different.

—Out there they would.

The crowd is rooted but will probably soon move under the batons, it has no other way out.

Here and there banners open like flowers.

The crowd stirs, no one asks where, it won't get far anyway.

The crowd knows it will be routed and will achieve nothing. But it sallies forth because it has no other way of honouring today's anniversary. So the crowd celebrates the way it knows best.

A stone's throw from here asylum ends at the black asphalt and the rasping loudspeaker on the car roof. There's a cordon ahead waiting to receive the crowd.

Faces are now turned in the opposite direction, rage and despair and fear swell in the helpless people, mouths are rent by more and more cries.

—Flunkeys!

—Gestapo!

—Bandits!

—Scroungers!

—Fascists!

—Anti-Poles!

—Red plague!

—Butchers!

—Renegades!

The disciplined ranks give a faint shudder, but do not stir from their posts. The transparent visors drop with a clatter and a glass wall of shields rears up.

The crowd waves, sways, swells.

And suddenly the first drops fall, followed by an abundant rain of coins; the crowd chucks fistfuls of small change at the motionless ranks; the coins glitter in the lamplight like a shoal of fish on the move.

The ranks withdraw not a step; the rain slowly abates, the crowd soon discards its loose change; people breathe helplessly and watch . . .

Single huddled silhouettes break away from the crowd; their numbers increase as people watch speechless; they stoop dutifully before the cordon; they are within the batons' reach; they crouch low and eagerly scoop up the coins and stuff them into their pockets; elderly fingers fumble feverishly in the mud.

—Disperse singly to your homes!—cries the loudspeaker on the car roof.

Brightened by the falling coins, the darkness slowly fades.

—Friends, look friends, how could you . . .

—Why ask, why ask . . . You'll be old too one day. And you'll just have a pension to live on. Then you'll see. Just you wait . . .

—You have to make ends meet somehow . . .

Pockets stuffed, indifferent, the pensioners carry their booty into the crowd.

—Now?

—What now?

—'Poland Still'?

—'Poland Still'? Any minute now.

The crowd stirs.

(*Translated by Nina Taylor*)

Paweł Huelle

The Table

'Oh, that table!' my mother would shriek 'I just can't stand it a moment longer! Other people have decent furniture.' She'd point at the round table where we ate our dinner everyday. 'Do you really call that a table?' she'd ask.

My father would never rise to her goading; he'd withdraw into himself, and the room would fill with a heavy silence. Actually, the table wasn't all that bad. Its short leg was propped up with a wedge, and the gnarled surface could be covered with a tablecloth. My father had acquired the table in 1946 from Mr Polaske of Zaspa, when Mr Polaske packed his bags and took the last train west to Germany. In exchange, my father gave Mr Polaske a pair of army boots he'd got from a Soviet sergeant, who'd done a swap with him for a second-hand watch, but since the boots were not in mint condition, my father threw in some butter as well. Moved by this gesture, Mr Polaske gave my father a photograph from his family album. It showed two elegant men in suits, standing on what was then called Lange Brücke. I liked to look at this photograph, not out of interest in Mr Polaske and his brother, of whom I knew very little, but because in the background stretched a view that I'd sought in vain to rediscover on our own 'Long Harbour'. Dozens of fishing boats were moored at the Fish Market quay, the jetty was crowded with people buying and selling, and barges and steamships were sailing by on the Motława River, their funnels as tall as masts. The place was full of bustle and life.

Lange Brücke looked like a real port, and although the signs above hotels, bars and tradesmen's counting houses were all in German, it was an attractive scene. It bore no resemblance to our own Long Harbour, rebuilt after the bombardment, the main features of which were a wasteland of administrative offices with red banners hanging on the walls, and the green thread of the Motława, constantly patrolled by a militia motorboat.

'It's a German table,' my mother would say adamantly. 'You should have hacked it to bits years ago. When I stop to think,' she'd go on, a little calmer now, 'that a Gestapo man used to sit at it and eat his eels after work, it makes me feel quite sick.'

My father would shrug his shoulders and hold out the photograph of Mr Polaske.

'Look,' he'd say to my mother, 'is that a Gestapo man?' And then he'd tell the story of Mr Polaske, who was a Social Democrat and spent three years in Stutthof concentration camp because he didn't agree with Hitler. When our city was incorporated into the Reich in 1939 and changed its name from Gdańsk to Danzig, Mr Polaske made a point of not hanging a flag out of his window. It was after that they took him away.

'Well, his brother was a Gestapo man.' And with that my mother went into the kitchen, while my father, distressed that his audience had been reduced by half, told me the story of the other Mr Polaske, the brother, who immediately after the war had gone to Warsaw on behalf of the Gdańsk Germans to ask President Bierut if they could stay provided they signed a declaration of loyalty.

'And then,' my father tale went on, 'President Bierut's moustache began to bristle, and he told Mr Polaske that the German Social Democrats had never erred on the side of good judgement, and that they had long since betrayed their class instinct—of which Comrade Stalin had written so wisely and comprehensively. "And any kind of request whatsoever"—President Bierut said, striking the desk top with his worker's fist—"is anti-state activity."' Mr Polaske's brother returned to Gdańsk and hanged himself in the attic of their home in Zaspa. 'And why do you think he did that?' my father asked loudly. 'After all, he could have gone back to Germany, like his brother.'

'He hanged himself,' my mother said as she came into the room with a steaming dish, 'because he was finally trouble by his conscience. If all Germans examined their consciences, they'd do just the same,' she added as she set the jacket potatoes on the table. 'They should all hang themselves, after what they've done.'

'And what about the Soviets?' my father exclaimed, shoving potato skins to the edge of his plate, 'what about them?'

I knew that the bickering was about to start. My mother had a deep-rooted and ineradicable fear of Germans, while my father reserved his venom for the compatriots of Fyodor Dostoevsky. An invisible borderline now ran across Mr Polaske's table, and it separated the two of them, just like in 1939, when the land of their childhood, scented with apples, halva and a wooden pencil-case with crayons rattling in it, was ripped in half like a piece of canvas, with the silver thread of the River Bug glittering down the middle.

'I saw them,' my father said, as he gulped down the white potato flesh. 'I saw them . . .' What he meant, of course, was the march-past in the little town where the two armies met. 'They raised the dust to the very heavens,' my father said, helping himself to more crackling, 'and they marched abreast in step, taking turns to sing in German and then in Russian, but you could hear the Russian louder because the Soviets had sent a whole regiment—the Germans sent only two companies.'

'The Germans were worse,' my mother interrupted, 'because they had no human feelings.'

I didn't like these conversations; the strong flavour of broth or the fragrant aroma of horseradish sauce would be infused with the thunder of cannon-fire or the clatter of a train carrying people off to a slow or instant death. I didn't like it when they argued about such things. I used to think, as I forced down my jacket potatoes or cheese-filled *pirozhki*, that if it weren't for Mr Polaske and his table, my parents would be chatting about a Marilyn Monroe film. or this year's strawberry crop, or the latest launching at the Lenin shipyard which Premier Cyrankiewicz had attended. Mr Polaske's table was like a persistent toothache. Whenever the pain eased, they'd be seized by an irresistible urge to touch the sore spot and provoke the throbbing agony again.

Then, in addition to its lame leg and blistered veneer came woodworm. It gave my mother sleepless nights. In the morning she'd be tired and bad-tempered.

'Do something,' she'd say to my father. 'I just can't stand it any longer! Those are German weevils. Soon they'll attack the dresser and the cupboard, because they are insatiable, like everything German.'

Often I imagined Mr Polaske rubbing his hands together, laughing to himself somewhere in Hamburg or Munich. He'd have eaten the butter and thrown out the Soviet boots yet we were still suffering with his table; it was like an alien member of the household, always getting in everybody's way, impossible to get rid of. Why should Mr Polaske want revenge on us? We'd done him no harm. We weren't even living in his house, which was now occupied by some high-up Party official. Could he have wished us ill simply because we were Polish? For hours I'd gaze at the photograph, in which Long Harbour looked like a real port, and I'd count the funnels of the steamships winding their way along the Motława River. The table, meanwhile, seemed to get bigger, swelling to impossible dimensions within the small confines of the room.

At last the inevitable happened. As my mother set down a tureen full of soup, the wedge came loose from beneath the short leg, and the table staggered like a wounded beast. Beetroot soup splashed across my father's shirt and trousers.

'Oh!' exclaimed my mother and clasped her hands

together in rapture. 'Didn't I say this would happen? Didn't I predict a catastrophe?'

My father didn't say a single word. He replaced the wedge, ate his second course, sat out the cherry blancmange in silence, and only after dessert, with a cigarette between his teeth, did he go down to the cellar for his saw and tape-measure. Soon he was leaning over the table, squinting first with one eye, then the other, like a surgeon preparing to operate. My father, who was handy at repairs, was having trouble coping with Mr Polaske's table. Or rather with the table's uneven legs. After each pruning it would turn out that one of them—each time it was a different one—was just a fraction shorter than the rest. My father refused to admit defeat: possessed by the Fury of perfection, or maybe of German pedantry, he went on and on, shortening the table legs, until at last on the floor, beside heaps of wood and sawdust, lay the top of Mr Polaske's table, like a great brown shield. My mother's eyes glittered with emotion. Nothing could restrain my father from completing the task. The snarling saw ripped into the table-top; my mother held her breath, and then cried:

'Well, at last!'

Mr Polaske's table was only good for burning now.

My father took the bits of wood down to the cellar, my mother swept up the sawdust, and I had a feeling in my bones that this wasn't the end of the matter: our real troubles were only just beginning.

Next day we ate dinner in the kitchen. It was cramped and uncomfortable and smelled of fried herrings.

'We'll have to buy a new table,' said my mother, 'a bit smaller than the old one perhaps, though it should still be round. And then some new chairs,' she added, drifting into the realms of fantasy, 'with plush covers!'

My father was silent.

After dinner we took the tram to the furniture shop. The salesman threw his arms wide in a gesture of helplessness, smiled tellingly and said all they had, we could see before us: nothing but triangular tables.

'It's the latest model,' he said, pointing out the geometric shape. 'Experimental, it is.'

'What about round ones?' asked my mother. 'Aren't there any round ones?'

The salesman explained that this year's central plan had already been fulfilled, and that while of course there would be some more round tables, they would not arrive until January or February. My father gave an acid smile, since we were bang in the middle of May. My mother, meanwhile, walked about among the triangular tables, touching their surfaces in disbelief and horror. Light streamed into the shop through the dust-caked window, illuminating her chestnut hair with a soft halo, giving her a melancholy allure.

Once outside, she insisted we go to another shop. But the blind Fate of the central plan hovered over all the furniture shops in town. The only non-triangular table, brought out at her express demand from a murky storeroom, turned out to be rectangular, very long and narrow, and utterly unsuitable for our room. I wondered if Mr Polaske could imagine this scene. After a few hours, we got home exhausted, while his table went on hanging in our midst, like a spectral cloud of sawdust.

'At the end of the day,' my father commented, 'we could always order a table. It'll be dearer, but'—here he paused meaningfully and raised his finger aloft like a preacher—'in view of the central plan there is no other way out.'

This made sense. But we soon found out that of the five carpenter's workshops in the neighbourhood, three had closed down long ago. Their owners, ruined by high taxes, now worked at the state factory, fulfilling the central plan. The fourth, which belonged to a Mrs Rupiejek, the window of a carpenter from Wilno, was in the process of liquidation. And the fifth had been turned into a private business, making very fine coffins which—for now, at least—were exempt from central planning.

We still had no table.

My father's ephemeral, poetic improvisations were doomed to failure. He balanced the ironing board on twin chests, then knocked something resembling a table-top together in the cellar. Finally he had the idea of placing an advertisement in the morning paper—'Wanted: second-hand table. If it's round, I'll buy it.' This notion seemed particularly awful to my mother. It was a second-hand table which had caused all this trouble in the first place! And so our final hope lay with Mr Gorzki, who without shop sign or permit, did a bit of carpentry on the side, using materials pilfered from the shipyard. He also drank, as if he were a sailor, not a carpenter. Anyway, he took a large deposit from my father and promised to make the table within a week. A first-rate round table. My mother was very pleased, although my law-abiding father was a little uncomfortable.

'If I'm aware,' he'd ask loudly each evening, 'that he's going to make us a table out of stolen wood, can that be right? Is that really honest?'

My mother was a pragmatist.

'Who's it stealing from? It all belongs to the state. Every last bit of it,' she said, describing a vast circle in the air, like destiny itself.

However, destiny spoke even more conclusively through Mr Gorzki. The carpenter did not complete his drinking on the previous Sunday evening, but prolonged it through the whole of Monday. He resumed it on Tuesday, sustained it on Wednesday, and expertly added impetus on Thursday, until at last he'd pulled through to Friday, where, after midnight, Saturday and Sunday lay in thirsty anticipation. On Monday my father and I reached Mr Gorzki's shed, where he received us sitting on the earthen floor amid bottles and scattered tools. His face shone with a mixture of gloom and ecstasy. He raised his head, guffawed throatily and croaked out the same old sentence over and over: 'I know! I know!'

My father went purple.

'Where's my money?' he shouted. 'Where's our table? Give me back my deposit!' His voice cracked. 'Give it back this instant!'

But even I could see that my father's shouting was purely for the sake of form. It no longer had anything to do with Mr Gorzki who, right now, before our very eyes, was cutting the threads that tied him to the world of cause and effect.

From then on Mr Polaske began to visit our flat. He'd knock very gently at the door, greet my father with a nod and then silently walk round his table, which was by now entirely invisible. He'd put down gifts on it—a packet of coffee. some chocolate, a box of English tea—and then he'd slip away quietly, to avoid encountering my mother. The presents looked odd hanging in mid-air, and whenever I reached out to touch them they vanished, just like Mr Polaske. I never discussed these visits with my father, who was growing more and more distracted. It was possible that he hadn't even noticed the fleeting presence of our guest. But I wondered what, for instance, would be the result of an encounter between my mother and Mr Polaske? And what if he made an unexpected appearance at the kitchen table? But nothing like that happened.

One day my father came home from work particularly excited.

'I've got it!' He cried from the doorway. 'I've got us a table at last!'

My mother looked out of the window.

'I don't see the van,' she noted drily.

My father took a slip of paper from his pocket and announced that what we had to do was go to Mr Kasper, who makes the kind of table they used to make before the war—good and solid and round, or oval, or elliptical, whatever the customer's order. And this was the secret of the enterprise: Mr Kasper accepted commissions only from reliable people, on a personal recommendation. My father flourished the note in the air like a winning lottery ticket and added that Kasper the carpenter lived in Żuławy, on the other side of the Vistula.

The carpenter's house looked like a little wooden box with a small porch and fancy attic windows. It was submerged in the greenery of ancient willow trees and shrubs. We stood in the deserted yard, looking around us uncertainly. Eventually a wrinkle-faced woman of indeterminate age came out towards us from the garden which extended behind the house.

'Who is it you want?' she asked.

'Mr Kasper,' said my father, smiling. 'We have business to do with him.'

'It's not Kasper, it's Kaspar,' said the woman.

She looked at us with suspicion, or maybe just indifference; anyway she didn't say anything else, and we went on standing there, in the close, motionless mid-day air.

'Is he at home?' my father asked after a long pause.

'At home?' the woman said indignantly. 'You'll have to go down the path till you get to the cattle round-up. That's where he is!' And she swiftly turned away, the hem of her apron flapping, and disappeared among the bushes.

'Come on then,' I heard my father sigh. 'We'll find him.'

We followed the cobblestones, and then a sandy path, which threw up a thick dust that stung our throats, made our eyes smart and felt gritty between our teeth. We were guided along by hoofmarks.

'It can't be far now,' said my father.

The path was covered with animal dung, and we had to be careful not to sink our feet into cow shit. It was blazing hot, and if it hadn't been for my father, I'd have turned back. Even the sight of a windmill, with useless stumps for blades, did not arouse my curiosity.

At last we reached an open space. A bunker-like building stood in the middle, its walls made of cement. It had no proper windows, only a strip of small skylights running just beneath a flat, board-like roof. A shabby yellow inn sign announced that we were standing before the Boar's Head. Inside, several men were sitting at wobbly little tables.

'There's no beer left,' the portly barman cried. 'They've swilled the lot already.'

The strong smell of tobacco smoke, urine, sweat and soured alcohol engulfed us like a mist. My father explained to the barman who we were looking for, while I scrutinized the customers' faces. They were tanned and deep-furrowed, all wearing the same expression, as if staring into space.

Mr Kaspar was in the corner, almost invisible in the semi-darkness, smoking the stump of a cigar. There was no empty tankard on his table. Leaning forward, my father took the note out of his pocket, placed it down like a visiting card and whispered the story of the table to Mr Kaspar, who listened in silence, smoking the last of this cigar.

Mr Kaspar rose and we followed him out of the bar. He had a piglet on a bit of rope. He mentioned that official inspectors had been round today, which was why he hadn't sold his pig, and had sat waiting in the bar. God knows what he was waiting for—the end of the world, perhaps, or maybe better days. A few days before he'd dreamed that a grown-up man and a little boy had knocked at his door with good news. The dream had put him in an excellent mood. My father glanced discreetly at his watch; the last narrow-gauge railway train was leaving in an hour's time.

'Doesn't life disturb you?' said the carpenter, suddenly gripping my father's arm, 'What is it beside eternity? A brief moment, nothing but a speck of dust! Where are we going? And where have we come from?'

'Yes, indeed,' said my father, 'but,' and he hesitated, 'will you make the table? It's extremely important to us.'

We had reached the house. Between the blackcurrant bushes and some thick clumps of peonies, an uncommon bustle was underway. The wrinkle-faced woman had brought out plates and cutlery, while Mr Kaspar, as if he hadn't heard my father, set out wicker chairs round a small stone table. Before my father had a chance to say anything further, we were sitting down to soup with the large golden eyes of egg yolks floating in it, followed by a joint of meat. After our meal, Mr Kaspar brought a jug up from the cellar; from it he filled chunky glasses with dark, aromatic juniper beer.

'The real art of it,' he said, raising his glass to eye level, 'relies on not adding too many of these little berries—and on picking them at the right time of day, early in the afternoon, when they've been warmed up by the sun and are giving off their juice.'

I watched my father as he took long draughts of the cloudy liquid. His face gradually brightened, taking on an unusual shine, and the two gentlemen began to spin the yarn of reminiscences. My father related how in 1945 he'd paddled across the Vistula to Gdańsk in an old canoe, because he didn't have any documents and was afraid of railway stations and places frequented by Soviet patrols. Mr Kaspar spoke of a long train journey which had ended abruptly when German saboteurs blew up the tracks not far from here. He'd had to find a place to stay and walked through one village after another—the only sound the occasional creak of shutters—unable to stop because nothing he saw matched the city he had left behind him, the most beautiful city in the world, a city of churches and synagogues, near gentle hills and pine forests, the city of his childhood, youth and war, which was now under Bolshevik power.

'And that's the power of Satan,' said Mr Kaspar pensively. 'The land of darkness and cruel oppression.'

Mr Kaspar poured more juniper-scented beer into the glasses. A light early-evening mist floated on the air, shrilly whistling swallows were swooping under the eaves, and my father, as if he'd forgotten all about the narrow-gauge railway and the table, said that the Lord God must long since have lost interest in us, for a world like this one to be possible.

'Oh, no!' Mr Kaspar snorted. 'We can never be sure what lies ahead. And anyway, has the world really deserved a better fate?'

The leaves began to rustle and a light breeze blew across the garden from the river. Mr Kaspar began to tell my father about a storm which one spring had broken down the dams and demolished the floodgates. The sea had invaded all the way up to here, to the foot of Mr Kaspar's house.

'Just imagine,' he said, leaning over my father, 'I cast my rod out of the window and reeled in a . . . Can you guess?'

'A catfish!' cried my father. 'There must be enormous catfish in these canals!'

'It was a seven-kilo cod!' recalled Mr Kaspar delightedly. 'And when the water had been standing there a bit longer, I could draw in netfuls of herrings!'

I'd been given a couple of mouthfuls of beer and could feel the little bubbles of juniper starting to spin in my head. Without being noticed, I left the veranda and plunged into the undergrowth, walking along paths overgrown with burdock, the strong scent of peonies swirling in the air.

'We're the men of the First Brigade!' my father's voice soared high above the trees.

'With a rifle fusillade!' Mr Kaspar chimed in, and then they sang on in chorus: 'On to the pyre we cast our lot! On to the pyre!' I heard them toast Marshal Piłsudski, and then there was a sound of breaking glass.

Later on I caught sight of them on a wide lane running between the apple trees. They were strolling towards the river.

'Of course I'll help you,' my father was saying. 'Mind you, I've never done it before.'

'Yes, yes,' the carpenter replied, 'I always wait until after dusk; because it's not a simple job. You've got to be careful!'

The red disc of the moon was rising in the sky as the two gentlemen disappeared into a large shed, closely planted round with forsythia and hazel. I sat down nearby at the water's edge. Further down the river, among the reeds and rushes, I could see the wreck of a barge, which had been driven into the bank like a mighty wedge. The air stood still, and I thought of Mr Polaske. Might he pay a visit to our flat while my father and I were at Mr Kaspar's? The last narrow-gauge railway train had left hours ago, and my mother was sure to be in our neighbour's flat by now, calling the police and the hospitals to confirm her worst forebodings. What if she met Mr Polaske in the dark stairwell, silent and pensive in his long overcoat? Or worse still, what if she saw him in the flat itself?

There was no sound coming from the shed, nor was the faintest ray of light peeping through the closed shutter, although I noticed a grey thread of smoke seeping from a small chimney. Then the air was suddenly pierced by an unearthly scream.

I was paralysed. I stood on the riverbank, staring at the black outline of the shed. After a few moments I crept up to it and gingerly pushed the door ajar. Through the chink I could see Mr Kaspar in a white apron splattered with blood. With both hands he had raised a big chopper, and my father was shouting loudly say, 'No, no—not like that!' The axe struck something soft which was lying on the table, and blood spouted in all directions. Mr Kaspar, wiping the red streaks from his face, said, 'Yes, maybe it really hasn't all flowed out as it should.'

A fire was blazing in a large oven. Mr Kaspar put down the chopper and, knife in hand, began cutting up red and pink steaks of the meat that was hanging from hooks around the room. Nearby on the floorboards lay the piglet's head, its open eyes gazing at me. The two men rinsed the cuts of meat in bowls, shoving some into earthenware pots and smearing others with a sort of powder, then hanging them up on an iron rail in the depths of the oven.

'We should be done by morning,' said Mr Kaspar, putting down his long, broad knife. 'It's lucky that you came today. My wife can't bear the sight of this.'

My father wiped his hands, and from a crystal decanter which stood on the shelf, he poured ruby-red liquid, thicker and darker than blood, into two glasses.

'Your wife isn't very talkative,' said my father, wiping his mouth. 'But she's got an unusual accent. Pomeranian, but different, somehow.'

'You noticed?' said the carpenter, setting to work again. 'You did notice, didn't you?'

Mr Kaspar began to tell of how he dreamed of *them* at night, of how he saw *them* passing through the entrance to the camps, dressed in black cloaks, and there, up above, the Lord God opening the gates and welcoming them in with a smile. They, who tilled the land and dug out canals, built floodgates, erected windmills, sang psalms and hymns, and would never, on any account, take up arms.

'They . . .?' asked my father hesitantly, as he set the oven door ajar.

Mr Kaspar gently sighed. He told him about the Mennonites, of whom hardly a trace was left, and of the house he had entered at the end of the war, thinking it would be empty like the rest. But after two whole days had passed he saw a pair of shining eyes up in the deepest corner of the attic. They were her eyes, the eyes of a Mennonite, the last on the earth.

'Ah, yes,' said my father.

I stood in the doorway gazing at the ruby-red liquid in the crystal decanter and the cuts of meat hanging on hooks, while Mr Kaspar went on with his story. He had stared into those eyes and known at once that they understood him, although for months he had been unable to explain to her exactly where he had come from, and why he had taken the train so far westwards. He couldn't describe his city to her, for she—at this point Mr Kaspar put the bowl aside and reached for a bag of cereal—she knew only one city, the one she used to sail to for the market; it was completely different from his own. And now it had been burned to the ground.

'But even the ruins looked uncanny,' said my father, holding up the intestine for the carpenter to stuff. 'When I paddled my canoe out on to the Motława River and first caught sight of the ruins from a distance, the whole place looked like a city on the moon.'

Mr Kaspar shook his head and tied up the stuffed intestine with some fine string. At that precise moment my father looked up and saw me standing in the doorway.

'Aren't you in bed yet?' he cried in amazement. 'What on earth's the time?' But Mr Kaspar gestured to him to be silent, asked him to keep an eye on the fire—since there's nothing more ruinous for cured ham than an uneven stream of smoke—and set off across the garden, leading me along the path towards the house.

'What's happening about the table?' I asked timidly.

Mr Kaspar replied that it would all be fine, that there was a right time for everything.

In the distance, from the direction of the river, several voices were hoarsely crooning: 'And then you'll pity me a little, and then you'll give me a kiss, my pretty!'

'That's the Ukrainians from the collective farm across the river,' explained the carpenter. 'They drink, they sing, they have a sad time.

'Do you know why they're sad?' he then asked unexpectedly.

We stood in front of the house, watching the long shadows of the trees as they spread across the garden paths. I didn't know why.

'It's because of the moon,' said Mr Kaspar. 'When it's full, they drink and sing. Even in winter. A long time ago, perhaps ten years, they walked across the ice to this side and set the shed on fire. The moon seemed bigger then, as it always does when there's snow on the ground.'

I wanted to talk to Mr Kaspar about our table. My father certainly wouldn't have told him about the Polaske brothers from Zaspa. But the carpenter hurried away before I had the chance, vanishing like a shadow among the trees.

The wrinkle-faced woman took me up to a room in the attic and showed me my made-up bed. But I wasn't sleepy. As soon as I heard her footsteps on the stairs, I went up to the window and opened it wide. The roof of the shed, the trees and the bright ribbon of the river were all clearly visible in the moonlight. Only the wreck of the barge was lost from sight somewhere round a bend among the reeds and rushes. On the far shore the Ukrainians had lit a bonfire. I could see their figures weaving in and out of its light, and I was sorry I couldn't hear their song.

Suddenly I was seized with longing to know everything.

Where does the river flow to? Where was Mr Kaspar's city? Why weren't the Mennonites willing to take up arms? Did they really all go to heaven? I'd forgotten all about Mr Polaske, my mother and the round table, for which we'd come over the pontoon bridge across the Vistula.

I noticed a wardrobe with carved legs and opened the door. Inside I found a hat. It was black, with a huge brim and felt edges. I put it on and stood in front of the mirror. I could see my reflected face, obscured by the brim's shadow, my eyes and lips barely visible. And then the hat seemed to grow larger. It got bigger and bigger. I seemed to be growing too, until I was as tall as my father and as broad-shouldered as Mr Kaspar. I crossed the moonlit garden to the river and stepped aboard the barge. I guided my ship through locks and floodgates, until at last I sailed out on to the Motława River and dropped anchor at Long Harbour amid the throng of masts, chimneys and ensigns. I asked the Ukrainians to unload. Sacks of grain, baskets full of apples and plums, barrels with live fish swimming in them, pieces of cloth scented with summer and with herbs, several pound tubs of butter—all this made its way from the hold on to the jetty. The Ukrainians crooned plaintively as they worked, a song in which a Mr Potocki, 'that son of a dog, betrayed Lithuania, Poland and all Ukraine.' Although I didn't understand all the words, I listened as if they were a familiar refrain expressing inconsolable yearning and anger.

The black hat gradually regained its depth and sharpness in the mirror, when suddenly I caught sight of a candle flame. Above the broad brim the woman's wrinkled face appeared. She was standing behind me, holding a candlestick, and the hem of her dressing gown fell to her ankles. I didn't know when she'd entered the room or for how long she'd been watching me at the mirror. Could she have seen me on the barge? Tears were pouring down her cheeks. With a delicate movement she took the hat from my head and turned it in her hands.

The wrinkle-faced woman stared into the blackness of the

hat. She was lost in thought. Then she left the room, clutching the black brim with both hands.

I blew out the candle. The starched bedlinen enfolded me with soothing coolness, and yet I was burning hot, as if I were standing by the oven in the shed, where Mr Kaspar and my father, busy with their illegal butchery, had forgotten all about the passage of time and the world outside.

I didn't exchange a single word with the wrinkle-faced woman the next morning, as the two men discussed the particulars of the order over a breakfast of smoked bacon and black pudding: diameter of the table top, the leg height and the colour of the veneer.

I didn't tell my father about the black hat as we travelled by narrow-gauge railway along the River Tuja past overgrown canals and closed-down locks. Nor did I tell him later as we streaked across the pontoon bridge over the Vistula in a sky-blue bus, nor even when the brick church-towers loomed ahead in the suburbs of Long Gardens.

As my father unwrapped some juniper-scented ham from a greasy piece of paper, and my mother nursed a migraine with a damp towel round her head, they each let fly with words such as 'duty', 'table', 'thoughtlessness' and 'opportunity'. I looked at their angry faces and in my thoughts I was with the wrinkle-faced woman: I would never forget her.

A week later there was a knock at our door and some strange men carried Mr Kaspar's table into the living-room. It was round, with a walnut veneer, and utterly enraptured my mother. The squabbling and bickering stopped completely, and that day dinner went on for ages, just as if Grandma Maria had come to visit us.

And once the chestnut trees along our street were in bloom, and I was bent over Mr Kaspar's table, slogging away at the first letters of my ABC, getting to know the fortunes of Ala, who has a cat, Mr Polaske knocked at our door. He was bashful and awkward and told us how he'd found our address and what troubles he'd had with his visa and with the officials at the Ministry of Foreign Affairs. He sat at Mr Kaspar's table and took out some coffee, cocoa, chocolate and a tin of English tea as he talked about his journey and how very happy he was to be here.

'Will you have dinner with us?' asked my mother, but Mr Polaske was in a hurry to get to his hotel. He said thank you, apologized and left quickly, bid farewell by my father in the doorway.

'He didn't notice the table,' said my father.

But I wasn't so sure. The presents which he left did not disappear this time. I turned the pages of the primer. Ala went to school. Father went to work. Mother cooked the dinner. The workers smelted steel. The miners extracted coal. The pilot flew over the motherland. The Vistula flowed to the Baltic. The woman took away the black hat. The Mennonites went straight to heaven. Mr Polaske sold a table, and Mr Kaspar made a new one.

'What are you reading? He's making it up, isn't he?' asked my mother.

'Yes, he is,' said my father, lighting a cigarette and placing the palm of his hand on the table top as the light skimmed across it, 'it's all made up. Every single world of it!'

I gazed at the trail of smoke wafting up towards the ceiling. From then on time went by differently, and only I knew why.

(*Translated by Antonia Lloyd-Jones*)

Ida Fink

In Front of the Mirror

On a gloomy December afternoon Adela decided to alter her dress, so she put on her father's shoes and ran over to her dressmaker-friend Nisia's place. Nisia had been living near Adela for a year. Everyone had become close neighbours in the past year. She ran into the little room on the ground floor, completely out of breath. Nisia was sitting near the window, which looked out on to an empty stone courtyard. A clean piece of cloth lay across her knees and a frying-pan sat on the cloth. Nisia the dressmaker was eating her dinner of warmed-up potatoes. A large, heavy shovel was propped against the window-sill. Nisia's hands were rough and cracked, and there was no sewing machine in the room at all. Nisia had sold it; she hadn't done any sewing for a long time, but just wielded her shovel constructing a huge bridge across the small river, just like Adela, in fact, who also had at home a shovel that she used while loading coal at the railroad station.

Adela closed the door behind her, stamped her feet on the floor to knock the snow off her shoes, and sat down on a stool that had once belonged to Nisia's father, who was a tailor. Nisia did not interrupt her dinner; with slow, measured movements she gathered the potatoes from the frying-pan and chewed them painstakingly. There were four beds in the room, three of them unused. First, in the summer, one of them was vacated; then, in early autumn, the second; and later, the third. The fourth was for Nisia, who, without interrupting her dinner, listened to the rapid speech of Adela, sitting there on her father's stool.

When she had finished eating her potatoes, she stood up. She was tiny and still pretty, even though three beds had been vacated one after the other, and the fourth would be vacant, too, before you knew it. She rinsed the pan in cold water and hung it on a hook above the unused stove in which the fire had long since grown cold. (She warmed her potatoes over a small, confined fire.)

'You say it needs to be shortened?' she said, and Adela eagerly nodded her head, yes.

'It has to be shortened and taken in at the hips, because I've lost weight.'

They went over to the big mirror, which, in the depths of the dark room, seemed like a yellowish lake with rippling waves.

'Right there, you see . . .' Adela whispered, 'that's where it bunches up.'

Nisia gathered the material with an expert movement of her fingers that was only slightly too rough and too abrupt for a dressmaker. Their eyes met beneath the opaque yellow surface.

Of Nisia, just a bit mockingly.

'Do you know, Adela, there is no one left but me in this house?' she said to the large, feverishly glittering eyes of the other girl.

'Do what needs doing, Nisia, don't say anything to me, I don't hear what you're saying.' And Adela put her hands over her ears.

But Nisia insisted. 'Did you hear? No one but me. . . .'

'Do what needs doing.' The other girl cut her off.

So she knelt down beside the girl who was pretending to be deaf, reached out her hand for the bristling pin-cushion that she still kept here from her former tailoring days, and, picking out a rusty pin, glanced up at the face looming out of the yellow abyss. The face was glowing. Adela's face was full of light.

'Adela, don't tell me you can . . . Aren't you ashamed . . .? Adela . . .'

'You're a fool! What a fool!' Adela burst out laughing and brought her shining face close to the surface of the mirror, as if she wanted to get a better look at herself. 'This is my first love. My first and only.' She smiled at her own face.

At the sight of Adela's full, moist lips parted in a smile, Nisia felt a sudden pang and squeezed her eyes shut.

'I know everything, you fool,' Adela continued. 'In my house, too, beds have been emptied . . . I know everything, everything. And I don't want to know a thing.'

She bent over the girl kneeling at her feet and, with the self-assurance of someone who is absolutely certain she is in the right, added benevolently, 'Do what needs doing, Nisia, and don't get so upset over it.'

'Tell me,' the kneeling girl whispered humbly, 'tell me, is it possible . . . you are . . . happy?'

Seeing the light in those eyes and the radiance of that face that confirmed such an incomprehensible, cruel possibility, Nisia the dressmaker was overwhelmed by the horror of it and broke down in loud and despairing sobs.

When she calmed down, she shortened Adela's dress with quick, adept movements of her hands, now rough from the shovel, and then, to check the effect of her work, she raised her eyes to the mirror.

Night had descended over the yellow lake, the water had turned black, the dark abyss had swallowed Adela and her happiness.

(*Translated by Madeline Levine*)

Hanna Krall

A Tale for Hollywood

I

A certain woman, unknown to me, phoned up to say that a woman, unknown to either of us, would like a book written about her. A book to be written by me.

'Does her life deserve to be written about?' I asked, but my caller had no idea about that woman's life.

'Will she pay me?' I asked. The caller had even less idea about her financial circumstances, but she dictated the address. The person in whose name she phoned lived in Israel. I wrote to her. It was a short, matter-of-fact letter, with commercial intent. *'Apparently, Madam, you'd like a book about yourself'*, I wrote. *'If your life is suitable for a book, I'll write it. But, of course, it'll cost money.'*

I'd never written a letter like this before, but on the other hand I'd never before had an emigrant daughter. My daughter and grandson had recently settled in Canada, and a ticket to Canada isn't cheap. To be precise, two tickets, one for my husband as well. For two tickets to visit my daughter, I thought, I can hire myself out to ghost anyone.

'Ghosting'—that's the name for the service I was supposed to provide.

In the West this is a frequent occupation for impoverished writers. Ghost writer. Writing anonymously, for someone else, for money.

In reply, my prospective heroine and employer suggested I come to Israel.

It so happened that I'd been invited to a conference in Jerusalem on the subject of the history and culture of Polish Jews, so everything was falling into place. I wrote to tell the prospective heroine that I'd visit her after the conference. She could tell me about her life then, and I'd offer my terms. If we didn't strike a deal, it wouldn't matter. We'd get to know each other, have a cup of tea together and say goodbye nicely. Who knows, we might even get to like each other.

For a week I lived in Jerusalem. From time to time I talked with my prospective heroine on the phone. I soon learned that she'd only recently come to live in Israel, where her two daughters lived, and that she'd spent the war in Auschwitz.

'There've been a lot of books about Auschwitz,' I said, disappointed.

'I know,' said my prospective heroine, 'but it was different for me.'

'Nobody could improve on Borowski and Primo Levi . . .'

'I was also in a few other places,' said my p.h. (prospective heroine).

One day she phoned up to tell me that someone at a party had asked her how often they changed the sheets in that Auschwitz place. 'It was a young person,' she added, 'but all the same . . .' (I had the impression she was close to tears.)

'Don't be upset,' I consoled her. 'Yesterday a certain journalist from Tel-Aviv asked how to spell the name of Mordechaj Anielewicz. She was a young journalist, but all the same . . .'

'Exactly,' she sighed, and we both fell silent.

The conference over, I went to a kibbutz. I spent a whole hot day looking at people, factories, gardens, cow-sheds, houses and museum exhibits. In the evening, exhausted, I was taken to the town where the prospective heroine of the book (that was and was not to be mine) lived.

We drove in darkness, past gardens and suburban villas. In front of house number 98 I got out and rang the bell.

An elderly woman opened the door.

She stood inside, in bright light, as if caught in the beam of a spotlight which isolated her against a black backcloth. She had thick, grey, upswept hair, large brown eyes, an uncertain smile, and an attentive gaze.

'That's exactly the way you should look,' I said, feeling reassured, 'but I must go to bed now.'

She served me tea in a beige parlour, she showed me the pink bathroom, as big as my biggest room in Warsaw, and took me to the white bedroom. In the morning I read her written testimony as submitted to the Memorial Institute, Yad Vashem, in Jerusalem.

'Fine,' I said. 'About this I could write. How much are you offering?'

'Whatever you ask.'

I named a sum which was exactly the cost of two return tickets to Canada plus long-distance phone calls—also to Canada.

'Fine,' said my p.h., and I immediately wished I'd named a slightly higher sum.

'You'd pay a Western author ten times more,' I added magnanimously. It was a fact.

'I know,' agreed p.h., 'but I don't have the money for Western authors. This is my daughter's house. I only have a pension to live on. To pay you, I'll take on the job of looking after an old, blind, half-deaf woman; she can only hear low notes. I speak to her from my stomach, like a ventriloquist . . .'

'I'm better off than you,' I reassured myself. 'Anyway, why d'you need this book?'

She needed such a book for a film.

The book should become a bestseller, and the film should be made in Hollywood.

Her life, she told me, was extraordinary, her problems were extraordinary, she'd like people to know about them, and besides she'd like to earn money for some things. Like a residential apartment in an old people's home; to support her elder daughter who isn't doing very well; for plastic surgery; to take care of her husband when he became bedridden...

'My dear woman,' I confessed, 'none of my books has ever become a bestseller. Except for one, possibly, but it was about one of the leaders of the Warsaw Ghetto uprising. After all, let's face it, there is a difference between the two of you. Anyway, even with that one I didn't earn much... Are you sure it's me you want as a writer?'

She wasn't sure but she had no other option. She'd made an earlier offer to a famous Polish writer living in Israel, but he refused. He said he told only his own stories, no one else's, and he advised her to write it herself.

'It's very simple,' he explained. 'Let's take the scene where you're going to Vienna smuggling tobacco in a black lacquer suitcase. You enter a compartment, put the suitcase on the rack, and take a seat. After a while a tall handsome SS man comes in, carrying a yellow pigskin suitcase. He puts it next to the other one and sits down opposite.'

'And what next?' my p.h. asked the writer.

'That you have to invent all by yourself,' the writer explained. 'You've got a riddle that has to be solved. That's what literature's about.'

'But at least tell me what he had in that suitcase,' insisted my p.h.

'How am I supposed to know?' huffed the writer. 'It's you who are supposed to know, not me.'

'But if I can't even write about my own black suitcase, how am I supposed to describe his invented yellow one?'

'That's what literature's about,' the writer repeated, spreading his arms. 'I've already told you a lot.'

So ended her attempt to win over a famous writer for a Hollywood blockbuster. I was her last resort. Because I was the author of *Shielding the Flame*, which indicated that I understood Jews, and also because I wrote *The Six Shades of White*, a reportage, which indicated that I understood love. And these are the two subjects I had to grasp in order to write a book about her. The book that will buy her a residential apartment at the old people's home, plastic surgery, and soon.

To be honest, I felt a bit insulted that I was not her first choice, but I quickly multiplied the fee by the black-market dollar rate, divided it by the price of a ticket to Canada, and worked out that if my husband and I made fewer long-distance phone calls, and if we generally lived more economically, we should get two visits to our children out of this.

'Fine,' I declared, 'I'll write the book for you. But you must know one thing. That famous writer and I, we have different views on literature. It seems to me that literature is about something else . . . Won't you mind that?'

'No,' replied p.h., 'so long as the end result will be a Hollywood film.'

I asked for some paper and milky coffee, made myself comfortable in the beige armchair and asked who her parents were.

II

A book about Isolda R—this is my heroine's real, prewar name; now she has a different name and as the book's author she wants to hide behind the pen-name 'Maria Pawlicka', which was, incidentally, one of her numerous false names, during the Occupation—so a book about Isolda R, written for me, not for Hollywood, should begin as follows:

'Isolda R, a shortish brunette, with quite long legs and with thighs which she liked to describe as "full and round" (she believed the sturdiness and length of her legs added to her height), met her future husband in the first year of the Second World War. Soon after their wedding a ghetto wall started to rise around the Jewish district. By their first wedding anniversary the wall was closed. Isolda R, the daughter of a chemical engineer—the owner of a fair-sized tenement house on the corner of Ogrodowa and Zelazna—had to learn how to look after typhoid patients. She was good at it. During the day she worked in a hospital, at night, with private patients. The private ones died as frequently, but in clean sheets, with their family around, with the doctor, and she preferred the luxurious dying of the rich to the death of poor wretches in hospital. At dawn, on her way back home, she saw those who couldn't afford even a funeral, let alone a private nurse. Relatives carried the bodies out of the houses, placed them on the pavement, covered them with newspapers, and secured the newspapers round them with stones against the wind. Later the funeral carts went round the town picking up the bodies, but Isolda R would come back before the municipal undertakers had set to work.'

That's how it should begin, but it became clear straight away that it couldn't begin like that, for two reasons. Firstly, no American reader would understand what was going on: what typhoid? what wall? what about these corpses? Who knows, perhaps one should even indicate the date next to the words 'World War II': (1939–45). Secondly, organizing the material that way, I could do a reportage, even a decent one within the limits of eighty pages, whereas I was expected to produce a massive novel.

'A really fat blockbuster, Hania,' the heroine explained. 'At least as weighty as *Ingeborg* by Kellerman. Haven't you read it? A most beautiful story about love. You can really feel everything in it—that kind of despair, of love, of pain . . . Do you understand now?'

I understood.

I also understood that I had no idea for a fat blockbuster, in which one can feel despair and love.

Back in Poland I phoned Krzysztof Kieślowski. He had become a world-famous film director and should know how to write for Hollywood.

I told him the story of Isolda R.

'Not bad,' he pronounced. 'American Jews are fed up with victim-Jews, humiliated-Jews, passively dragged to death. Your heroine fights and wins—and this subject's *en vogue*, just right for an American producer.'

'In that case, Krzysiu, do me a favour and write the

beginning for me. Nothing long, a few sentences, a typical Hollywood, so I can see how it's done.'

Krzysztof Kieślowski is not only world-famous but also very obliging. He went home, took his own script out of his typewriter, rolled in a clean sheet of paper and wrote:

> *His hands were exactly like those in an Italian art book, of sketches by Leonardo da Vinci. How had Leonardo known that he of all people would have such hands? And that she, who would, ever since her childhood, every now and again, when father wasn't home, climb up on the chair and take the book down from the highest shelf to look at these hands— that she would meet and touch them. Slim, distinct palms with long fingers that would be ideally matched by the thin gold wedding ring, the thinnest she had ever seen, on the finger of her dead aunt as she was dressed for the coffin, only such a ring, nothing else. It would also match him because it would be hardly visible—his skin was the colour of gold. Not tanned, not swarthy, just the colour of gold, all year round, in winter too . . . The hands looked like a decoration when he put them on the back of the armchair, and now—without realizing it—the hands glorified her arm, her hand . . .*

Yes, this was it. Quick to learn, I filled up the text with the first chapter's scenery: a birch coppice, flaming moss and hot light flickering among the branches. '*He moved his hand along her neck . . .*' I added, and after that came the description of gold skin. It was only at the mention of the dead aunt, dressed up for the coffin, that I revolted and crossed her out.

Isolda R's husband, whom I met later on, in Vienna, had exactly the hands described by Krzysztof Kieślowski.

III

When—according to Isolda R's testimony—the ghetto was being closed off, when corpses appeared on the streets, dead from hunger and typhoid, covered by newspapers that she passed at dawn, I thought for the first time that I would probably forget about Hollywood. It's quite possible that the Americans could make a film like that—build a mock-up ghetto, populate it with emaciated people, arrange dummies covered by newspapers along the street—the Americans can do anything, but I no longer felt capable of writing a fat blockbuster. However, something else began seriously to preoccupy me. Namely: what sort of newspapers covered the corpses in the ghetto? There's mention of them in all the diaries—the newspapers weighted down with stones against the wind—but no one ever specified what sort of newspapers they were. It may not be very important, perhaps, but all the same, what newspapers? Prewar ones? People in the ghetto changed addresses many times, but they couldn't have dragged old papers with them. Occupation publications? The *New Warsaw Courier* in Polish was sold in the Jewish district only to start with. Later on distribution was prohibited, and it was smuggled in from the Aryan side at a higher price. Would someone who couldn't afford a funeral buy a newspaper on the black market? Occupation newsletters don't come into it: they were too small. How can you cover a body with *The Information Bulletin* or *Ojf der Wacht*, A4 size, like a sheet of typing paper? Arranged straight, it would cover the arm below the elbow, without the fingers of course; sideways, at most it would cover a hand.

In addition, I became aware that in spite of all the books I'd read, in spite of my own book about Marek Edelman, I could never imagine the reality of ghetto life, as lived by Isolda R.

I asked Ruta Sakowska, Poland's foremost expert on the ghetto, about relevant literature. She said, 'Read the *Jewish Gazette*.'

The *Gazette* was published for two years, in Polish, with the authorities' consent, so it was a 'reptile paper', which wouldn't be touched by decent people at the time, but may be a valuable source of information today. I didn't expect any files to have survived, but Ruta had had them in her hands, bound, while researching at the Jewish Historical Institute.

I went to the JHI. Neither in the library catalogue nor in the archive was there any mention of the files. The original files of the ghetto newspaper, unique and priceless—and no mention anywhere?

'Sorry, we certainly don't have anything like that,' said the archive staff.

'You have,' I insisted. 'Ruta Sakowska saw two files.'

'But we haven't.' The staff were at a loss.

'Yes, you have,' I said. 'And you know what? I'd be very grateful if both volumes were waiting for me tomorrow morning in the reading room.'

I haven't a clue what I would have done if the files hadn't been waiting, but on the following morning at eight o'clock, the bound *Jewish Gazette*, which was absent from every catalogue, lay on the table. Beforehand it had lain in the cupboard belonging to one of the institute's bosses—probably stored secretly for years, because neither Jarosław Marek Rymkiewicz collecting materials for his book *Umschlagplatz*, nor I, working on *Shielding . . .*, knew it existed.

It turned out the *Gazette* ran to eight large-format pages daily. It cost thirty groszy, so the price wasn't impossible. It was the only paper with current communiqués and—although they condemned it—people did read the thing. Wasn't this the one that later served another purpose, as a shroud? Eight pages—two large sheets . . .

The *Gazette* printed 'disinfected' news. You could find no mention in its pages of hunger, transports, Treblinka. On the contrary. The *Gazette* was to pacify and reassure about the normality of ghetto existence.

Here is the news that covered corpses in the streets of the ghetto.

On food rationing:

In March the Office of Distribution will dispense 51 ration cards (yellow) for 50 dekagrammes of sauerkraut and 10 dekagrammes of pickled beetroot at the total cost of 1.50 groszy per coupon . . .

Ration of 4 kilos of bread per person per month—for employees of Aryan companies; special ration of 2.6 kilos— for persons performing useful tasks . . .

As previously stated, in the month of April we shall be receiving bread for the coupons numbered 3 to 8 only. We have already collected two April numbers in the period before the festival.

On the definition of the concept 'Jew' according to the Legislative Declarations of the Governor-General, No. 48, section 1:

A Jew is a person at least three of whose grandparents are, in respect of race, of pure Jewish descent.

A person two of whose grandparents are, in respect of race, of pure Jewish descent, is considered to be Jewish

a) if on 1 September 1939 he or she was a member of a Jewish Religious Community

b) if at the time of introducing this regulation he or she was in a state of marriage with a Jew

c) if he or she is the product of an extramarital congress with a Jew and is born after 31 May 1941.

By the term 'Jewish half-breed' should be understood . . .

On kosher saccharin:

In accordance with the statement of the Rabbinate it is permitted at the approaching Easter Festival to use only crystalized saccharin dissolved in water and strained prior to the festival.

On the anniversary of the destruction of the Temple in Jerusalem:

1870 years ago we lost our country. We lost the land . . . The tempest of history blows and tosses the boat of our existence on . . . Who knows, perhaps towards a safe harbour . . .? 'Sits in silent solitude'—saith the prophet Jeremiah on the position of a nation in misfortune—for it has put on its destiny with dignity . . .

On accidents:

At 13 Zamenhof Street an unidentified 17-year-old girl jumped through the window, meeting her death on the spot.
   David Feldmacher, a resident of 105 Gesia Street, jumping from the fourth floor into the asphalt yard . . .

On first aid:

Hanging. The hanged should immediately be cut down and artificial respiration administered . . .

On funeral directors:

Natan Wittenberg. Well known for his long-established work, the director of The Last Service before the war has opened a new Funeral Office, The Last Way, and conducts it with great efficiency at Grzybowska 23.
   The Jewish Funeral Service Eternity announces that it has introduced the first bicycle hearses in Warsaw, designed by the owner of the Service. The four-wheel bicycle hearses operated by two cyclist-mourners are aesthetic and practical in many ways. They can accommodate four coffins at a time. In this way the funeral cortège does not cause traffic obstructions and the Service saves time.

On the lost and found:

At Zamenhof Street a four-month-old male child has been found. A note was found with the child: 'To human charity, still believed in by—the unhappy mother'. The child has been handed over to the orphans' home.

On the Rabbi of Sasow:

He said once: 'If someone comes to you and asks for help, act as if there were no God and as if there were only one creature in the whole world able to help him, namely you yourself.'

On souvenirs:

For officers of the Service for Civil Order, the nicest souvenir—an artistically produced commemorative signet ring with the insignia of rank. Engraver Jakubowicz, Leszno 65.

On fashion:

The signal from London announces a return for men to the top hat for occasions of great prestige. Accordingly, the owners of unworn top hats should promptly deliver them to Keller's. There, besides top hats, they darn holes in sweaters, tablecloths and the entire wardrobe.

Neither Aristotle nor Socrates ever dreamed that from the most grease-stained gentleman's hat a new one could be made, but it's true. Contact—Keller

On starred arm-bands:

You will avoid the penalty for the use of an unauthorized arm-band by replacing it with an authorized one, made of rubber, with an impressed and indelible yellow star, with practical clasping mechanisms.

On clairvoyants:

Clairvoyant—psychographologist explains all matters, also missing persons. Foretells the future with astounding accuracy.

On Alaska:

Unexploited treasures and only 500 Jews. We enclose a review of the structure of the country which, who knows, may become a new motherland for many of our readers. The rivers and lakes of the tundras hide a wealth of salmon . . .

Miscellaneous:

> *Fleas exterminated radically with gas under guarantee.*
> *Inoculation against typhoid for displaced persons and*
> *victims of duty.*
>
> *Doctor-Israelite-bachelor seeks wife with permit to leave*
> *for USA or other country overseas.*
>
> *'New Azazel'—theatre, 72 Nowolipie Street—'God of*
> *Vengeance', daily.*
>
> *Friday, 17 July 1942, candle burning in Warsaw—20.36.*

IV

When Umschlagplatz and the transports began, Isolda R
realized her reason for living. It was to save her husband.
Herself too and the rest of the family, but somehow that
seemed less important. The only one who HAD to survive
was him. It's hard to explain why. Because of his slender
hands? Because of his thick, straight hair that clung to his
head like a gold helmet? Not only his skin was gold; his hair
was too. And perhaps there was no explanation. He had to
survive, that's all.

Isolda R was the first to get out of the ghetto, to prepare
the hiding-places. (She spent the last day before getting out
of the ghetto at Umschlagplatz; she sat through the last
night of deportations, already on the Aryan side, on the seat
of a public lavatory, trembling with fear that someone might
need to use the toilet and discover her.)

She went to Zofia Romerowa, someone she knew from a
prewar holiday camp.

Zofia Romerowa wasn't surprised by the sight of her, nor
scared. She stroked Isolda's dirty, tangled hair and said,
'Don't cry. We mustn't cry.' She said *'We'*. To Isolda. As if a
person who tries to hide in a barrel in Umschlagplatz and
then trembles on the seat in a public lavatory were the
equal of someone who's the wife of a Polish major, taken

prisoner of war, and who keeps a weapon and Underground leaflets in the drawers of her table. Isolda R had no doubt: cowering on the Aryan side, where a different kind of people lived, a better category of people, since they were so much better off, and no one drove them to the square or into cattle wagons—and Zofia Romerowa, with the short word 'we', included her among them.

The very same day Isolda R visited her prewar hairdresser, a confidante, and transformed herself into a blonde. With dark eyes, it's true, but she hoped that the length of her ash-blond hair and her shapely legs would divert the attention of the most consummate Jew-catcher. She came back from the hairdresser's pleased with herself, and entered Mrs Romerowa's kitchen—just when the caretaker was visiting—and, with the flamboyance of a big blonde, she put her bag on the table.

Later, Mrs Romerowa said strictly, 'Marynia, remove that bag, you've put it down like a Jew.' Later still, Mrs Romerowa explained that such a line was supposed to allay the care-taker's suspicions, should he ever have any, so it had all been for her benefit; but from then on whenever Isolda R put her bag down she'd think, self-consciously, Am I putting it down like a Jew?

After the caretaker left she started to practise the Aryan way of *Putting it down*: on the floor, on the settee, on the stool, on the chair ... Each time she took a close look at herself and the bag: is it *put down* the way a Jew would do it? In the future she was to practise some other 'Aryan' habits too: the Aryan walk, the Aryan voice and even the Aryan bending in front of the blackboard (that came later, after the war, at the nurses' college, when one of her class-mates remarked as a joke, 'You bend in front of the blackboard like a Jew')—but the first lesson happened there and then, in Mrs Romerowa's kitchen. Because the visit to Mrs Romerowa's was to affect Isolda R's entire life. After that particular visit Isolda R decided to belong to the better, the Polish world. And during that visit, with this banal state-ment about a bag, she was at once rejected by that world. It was to stay like that. The yearning for Polishness—and the rejection.

Transformed into a big blonde, Isolda R led her husband out of the ghetto; they moved out through the sewers, alongside Polish workers employed legally in the ghetto, engaged in house demolition. She also led her mother out. Later on his parents and sister got out through the same sewers. She found a flat in Nowy Swiat for his parents, who looked Semitic and spoke bad Polish. They were not allowed to raise themselves above floor level, in case someone should see them through the window. She herself settled with her husband and her mother, in a small summerhouse in Wesoła. The room next door was occupied by a woman who had a daughter. The girl was mentally handicapped but she had a beautiful voice and she sang songs (preferably Brahms's 'Lullaby': 'Tomorrow agaaain, if the Lord allooows, you'll wake up happy and heaaalthy . . .') travelling on the train from Warsaw to Mińsk Mazowiecki, while her mother collected alms in a small cotton bag.

One day Isolda R, carrying a bundle of bed-linen, took a rickshaw to the railway station. In the Aleje Jerozolimskie they were stopped by a policeman. He took a quick, practised look at Isolda R and ordered the rickshaw driver to go to Chmielna Street. There was a hotel there. In a hotel room the policeman said, 'You're a Jew but I don't want to hurt you. Take off your clothes.' It wasn't a rape. Isolda R undressed and laid her things tidily on a chair. From the bed she watched the policeman take off his uniform and put away his gunbelt. When he was on top of her, she thought she could move her hand and take the gun out of the holster. She thought every decent woman, for instance Mrs Romerowa, would do exactly that, but she lay still. The policeman finished, got dressed, and said, 'You're lucky you bumped into a decent man.' He saluted and left. She took the bed-linen to the station and boarded the train. In the middle of the journey she heard her neighbour's song approaching: 'Tomorrow agaaain, if the Lord allooows'. She put five whole złotys in the cotton bag. In her joy that it hadn't all taken long and that she'd bumped into a decent man, who didn't want to hurt her. She got home, kissed her husband hello, served him dinner, and when he went out washed herself and changed her underwear.

My heroine told the story about the policeman without embarrassment and without hysteria. She talked like that about everything—precisely, to the point, as if she herself kept forgetting that a surefire blockbuster was supposed to come out of it. Sometimes she reminded me of Marek Edelman, when she tried to comprehend herself living in those times. Or rather, when she gave up on comprehending, assuming, and rightly so, that today understanding is no longer possible, all she can do is be as factual as possible. The quiet detachment from 'Over There' created the impression of a transparent, invisible curtain hanging between her past and her present—like the curtain put up by Krystyna Zachwatowicz in the play *The Dybbuk* at the Old Theatre.

So we sat in the beige parlour, sipping tea, crunching chocolate-coated nuts, and from behind the transparent curtain came the memory of Isolda R saying goodbye to her best friend Basia Gajer. She who believed it when the Germans said Jewish holders of foreign passports would be allowed to leave Poland. It took place in the Polski Hotel, in Długa Street. Basia was wearing a sweater made from multicoloured wool remnants, which she had knitted herself for the journey, and she was showing Isolda the stitch and the pink lining with which she meticulously finished off the inside, full of knotted ends. (Later, when Isolda R found herself in Auschwitz, she spotted Basia Gajer's sweater on the very first day. It was worn by another woman prisoner performing quarantine duty. Beyond any doubt, it was Basia's sweater; finished meticulously with a pink lining.

In the morning the Germans surrounded the Polski Hotel. They divided them all into two groups, Polish and Jewish. Isolda R showed her Aryan documents as Maria Pawlicka and stood with the other Poles who had come to see people off; the Jews were taken away to Bergen Belsen; the Poles to the Pawiak prison. Behind the transparent curtain of the elegant beige parlour, full of paintings, books and records, a Pawiak cell materialized with twenty-four women prisoners. Every morning after breakfast they took turns scrubbing the floor, and when it was Isolda's turn it turned out that she didn't know how to scrub. Amazed, twenty-three women watched how clumsily she plunged the floor rag into the bucket, how clumsily she wrung it out, and asked, 'Haven't you ever scrubbed a floor?' Truthfully she said she hadn't, the maid did it for her. There were other rich women as well among the prisoners who, however, could scrub the floor efficiently, and nobody stared at them. It filled her with anxiety, because again she was different from the rest. Though she didn't possess a handbag to handle like a Jew, it turned out that even a floor rag can be handled in a different way and that her scrubbing surely wasn't done the Polish way.

The Pawiak corridor was long; there were long rows of cell doors on both sides. As they were walked to the lavatory, it was possible to shoot a quick glance through the spyhole into the cell they knew was a Jewish cell. Isolda R used to glance every time, and one day she saw her mother-in-law, whom she'd recently placed in the Nowy Swiat flat. The mother sat facing the door, as if she'd been looking straight at her through the spyhole, shaking her head from side to side. She was left with that permanent twitch after a minor stroke, and it gave her face an expression of cheerful disbelief. The face, watched through the spyhole, now said, 'I'm in the Pawiak. Can you believe it?'

Isolda R returned to her cell. They had two new young women prisoners there, brought into the Pawiak the day before.

'Who else did they bring in with you?' she asked. 'Was there by any chance a man, sort of blond, tall and handsome?'

'Yes, there was,' answered the girls.

'And how did he sit?' asked Isolda R. 'Were his knees wide, did his hands hang limp?'

That's exactly the way the handsome blond man and the elderly, grey-haired one next to him sat. Only the young, bleached blonde woman wasn't there with them.

All became clear: they had caught her husband and his parents; only the sister managed to escape.

Isolda R wished she could die, immediately, right in the cell. She looked round. Would they—she meant the other women prisoners—wish to die too in my position? Do women who can wring the floor rag properly also die of love?

In all honesty Isolda couldn't see any connection between the floor rag and dying of love, but she was sure it must exist. The other women in the cell came from a 'better world'. In the 'better world' one puts the bag down in the proper way, the floor is decently scrubbed . . . In the better world one reaches for the policeman's gun lying next to . . . In the better world one lives after one's husband's death because one lives for a good cause. Was it her fault that she had no other cause except the survival of her husband?

Next day they were taken out for exercise.

Halfway through exercises, five women were led from the prison building to the forecourt. They came from the Jewish cell. They were led out to be shot. One of them was her mother-in-law. The Jewish women were led through the precinct, down the steps, then turned into the yard.

Isolda R was terror-stricken. If they turned left, Mother-in-law might catch sight of her. Make a sign of recognition. Might betray her . . . Isolda R wore round her neck a chain with the Madonna, given her by Mrs Romerowa on the first day with the words, 'Now you're under Her protection and nothing bad can happen to you.' Isolda R touched the medallion and started to pray. 'Holy Mother,' she prayed, 'don't let her look my way. Holy Mother, just don't let her look at me . . .'

While the Jewish cell was still going through the yard, while her mother-in-law walked to her death, she pleaded with the Holy Mother that they might die a little more quickly. At last she saw her mother-in-law's back disappearing behind the building with the rest of them. She felt relief. After a moment she heard five shots. She thought, 'In a moment they'll bring my husband to be shot.'

Two days later she received a note smuggled in from her husband. It turned out that it was another beautiful blond man with his hands hanging limp who had been driven to the Pawiak.

On our side of the transparent curtain, my heroine lifted herself up from the armchair and switched on the lamp.

'That morning I wished I was dead, and when I saw my mother-in-law go past I felt relief... Can you make any sense of it, Hania?'

I didn't even try to make any sense of it, because I was preoccupied with another thought. I felt invaded by a familiar sensation, a sensation known to me for years, ever since I'd started to write reportage. It presented itself when I had a fierce protagonist in front of me. When I knew I had a STORY. Isolda R was telling me how she had prayed in the yard of the Pawiak for a quicker death for her mother-in-law, and here I was thinking it was a wonderful scene. 'Can you, Isolde, make any sense of this?' I might have asked, but I was too ashamed, so I asked her to sketch the Pawiak yard for me. 'As if my drive to describe were more important than their death...' I thought with remorse while Isolda R was explaining the topography of the event. 'As if they had to march to their death so that I could write about them... And yet,' I tried to find an excuse, 'this thing should be put on record. Mother-in-law marching to her death, and Isolda's prayer... If it must be recorded, it should be recorded in detail so that if someone, some day, reads about it... Hannah Arendt read all the books in the world, and she still couldn't make sense of why the Jews went to their deaths. Is it remotely possible to describe it so that the world would understand?

I recall a story told to me recently by a composer, an Auschwitz prisoner. When the camp evacuation began, several hundred men were lined up in fours and led to the

trains. The first in the line broke into the 'Warszawianka'*
song; after a while the whole column was singing. At this
point the Germans decided to play a trick and at the place
where the roads divided they directed the prisoners not to
the cattle trains but in the direction of the gas chamber. The
Poles were singing, 'Hey! Every Pole fix your bayonet . . .';
but at the line 'Long live freedom, long live Poland', the
group in front stopped singing. They fell silent as they turned
towards the gas chamber. Then the group behind them fell
silent. Then the ones after them. The whole column kept
walking—not marching any more but simply shuffling their
feet—all in complete silence, numbed. 'My mind was blank,'
the composer told me. 'Later on I often tried to remember
what I thought, and I came to the conclusion there was
nothing. Not about my wife nor my parents. My legs moved
automatically, my body moved quite unconsciously. A few
yards before the gas chamber the Germans, laughing, turned
the column back. The prisoners stayed silent. They were
taken to the barracks, where they were to wait for transport.
In the barracks they threw themselves on the plank beds,
covered their faces with their arms and wept. The entire
barracks was filled with the muffled sobbing of several
hundred men, saved from the gas chamber. 'Ever since,' the
composer finished his story, 'I have understood how the Jews
felt when they were led to die.'

Can we blame Hannah Arendt for never having sobbed,
with her face covered, on a bed of planks?

Can we, never having walked down the yard of the Pawiak,
make sense of Isolda R's prayer?

Can we, having recorded that prayer on paper, help
anyone to make sense of it?

That's what I was thinking when Isolda R finished sket-
ching the yard and lifted herself up from the armchair with
the invariable question.

'Hania, what shall we have for dinner?'

* A nineteenth-century Polish patriotic song.

V

The actual story of Isolda R—the real plot of the guaranteed blockbuster—starts with her husband's arrest. He was caught working for a Mr Lampart, who smuggled people across to Hungary. Isolda R's husband delivered the fugitives to Kraków and then other intermediaries drove them into the mountains. One day things went wrong in Kraków and Isolda R's husband ended up in the Montelupich prison. After she found out about it, Isolda R immediately knew who to turn to—to Terenia, Mrs Zofia Romerowa's sister. Terenia could read the cards. On hearing the news, she reached for a pack without a word, laid out the cards and cried: 'Fantastic! The king of hearts is on the move.' (She took Isolda's husband to be the king of hearts, since he was loving, married, and fair-haired.

Later, this 'hasty departure' kept coming up repeatedly, because first he was sent from the Montelupich to Auschwitz, then from Auschwitz to Mathausen, eventually from Mathausen to Ebensee. Other cards, the nines of spades and clubs, also kept turning up. Not the best cards, Terenia admitted, yet not foretelling tragedy. The worst of all were the three spades next to each other: the king, jack and nine. 'Aha! Here we have a dangerous figure,' Terenia sighed. 'You should warn him somehow ...' ('The Gypsy,' the husband guessed straight away when, six weeks after the war, in the woods of Ebensee, Isolda R passed on the omens to him. 'Nobody else. The most evil Kapo in the whole camp.')

Terenia read her the cards day after day.

'Well, I see trouble, but there's also some happy news from a journey.' And sure enough, there was news, a letter. From Auschwitz, to be sure, but with the number which allowed him, as a Pole, to be sent parcels.

She sent him one kilo of sugar, one kilo of lard, a loaf of bread, bacon, onion and salt. It was expensive, a hundred and twenty złotys. They allowed one parcel a month, and even at the cost of her own life or if she had to sell herself, she must manage a hundred and twenty złotys month after month.

She and her husband had often dined together at The Bouquet. It was a once-elegant restaurant, since the outbreak of war the favourite place of smugglers and black-marketeers. For less elegant guests there would be a choice of two dishes: cabbage dumplings or beetroot dumplings. She used to take the cabbage, her husband the beetroot, and the waiter, who liked them, would serve her husband a double portion for the price of one.

She entered the restaurant as usual at dinner-time. The waiter put the cabbage dumplings in front of her and asked, 'Shall I serve your husband now, or wait?'

'My husband's in Auschwitz,' said Isolda R. 'And you know,' she added, 'I'm going to get him out of there. I need a lot of money now. Do you understand?'

The waiter nodded.

He was an old waiter, already a bit slow, with distinctly flat feet which made him walk pigeon-toed, the way waiters do all over the world after many years of work. He sincerely liked the couple and would sometimes pour rich meat sauce over her husband's double dumplings, for free.

'Will you help me?' she asked.

A few days later, while serving her dumplings, the waiter said, 'There he is. Waiting over there.'

She finished eating, got up and went towards the door leading to The Bouquet's *chambre séparée*. Behind the door, a man sat on a worn-out settee. He was bald and fat and he sat with his legs spread wide apart, giving support to his drooping belly, and the button of his waistcoat was undone. Apart from that he had an engaging smile; after all, he was quite nice, a jovial kind of old man, waiting for a woman. She sat down next to him. The man touched her leg with his hand and lifted her skirt. On her thigh, the stocking had a run. She feigned surprise, though she'd known about the ladder for a week. The gentleman stroked the ladder and said, 'Don't worry, we'll buy you a new pair of silk stockings.'

Isolda R put her hand on his and asked, 'Do you like me?'
He said affectionately, 'Oh yes, very much.'

'Then please don't buy me anything . . . I'll do everything
you want. And the way you want. And as many times as you
want. But I need a lot of money, because my husband is in
Auschwitz and I must get him out of there. Do you accept
such a deal?'

They looked at each other—she with her thigh exposed
and the nice old gentleman with a pink bald head, in a grey
fil à fil. In this man's eyes the interest in her beautiful eyes
and voluptuous thighs was gone. He echoed sadly, 'In
Auschwitz . . . Aah . . .'

Then she smiled at him, got up and, walking past the
waiter, whispered. 'Unfortunately, Roman, this is not what I
had in mind.'

Feverishly, she looked for money and protection. She
trusted people who later robbed her. She clung eagerly to
everyone who raised her hopes. She travelled, traded, got
caught, was sent to a forced labour camp in Germany,
escaped, searched again—lonely and excluded from the rest
of the world which wasn't hers because it was better. She
knew Poles suffered too, but that suffering was superior and
enviable. Her suffering was worse because she was inferior.
The whole world deemed her an outcast, and it must be
impossible for the whole world to be wrong in its assessment
of good and evil. The world had to be right. She was a reject
and therefore seen, through her disguise. She again changed
her name, the colour of her hair and the way she put down
her handbag, and only in that disguise did the world accept
her. So, if it preferred her disguised self to the real self, it
follows that the person whose disguise she assumed was
better than her real self.

From Auschwitz, Isolda R's husband was transferred to
Mathausen. Mathausen is in Austria, so Isolda R decided
to go to Vienna. She began to inquire among her friends.
Someone knew an address; someone else said, 'I know a
man in the *Todt* Organization,' and that in itself was the
right track because the organization carried out building

work for the German army and issued work permits—valuable and safe.

Isolda R picked up a permit for Dalmatia, and in return was only asked to deliver a package of tobacco to Vienna. She delivered the tobacco and she realized that she shouldn't head for Dalmatia, however safe. She should go back to Warsaw and smuggle more tobacco into Vienna. From the sale of tobacco she should buy Italian silk. This silk, sold in Warsaw, would earn her enough to get her husband out of Mathausen and possibly even enough for a flat for her mother, father-in-law, sister-in-law, for herself. She made a few journeys like that—four or five. Each time she carried twenty-five kilos of tobacco, in leaves, packed tightly in a suitcase. She went back with the silk in the same lacquer suitcase, hidden under her nightshirt. (it was the same suitcase she had told the other writer about, and beside which the handsome SS man was to put his yellow one.) One day she arranged to see a man from the *Todt* Organization in Vienna, in the Pruckel Café, but instead of her known contact two strangers arrived. They grabbed hold of her, one on each side, and took her to the Gestapo.

Isolda R was accused of working for the Polish Home Army and of visting Vienna in connection with General Anders in Italy.

It was an absurd accusation, because working for the Underground was the last thing that would ever have occurred to Isolda R. The Polish Underground was none of her business. Her business was her husband, and conspiracy would only hinder her in her efforts to free her husband. If the Home Army had been interested in helping her husband, maybe she'd even have done them a favour, but since they didn't give a damn for him, she was indifferent to the fate of their couriers, their General Anders and the whole Home Army.

First they beat her, as was customary, on her face and kept asking questions about Anders and the Home Army. Then they beat her so that after each blow the back of her head hit the wall. Then they hung her from a hook—she was slung from the hook, handcuffed and twisted backwards, by her arms . . .

From the Vienna Gestapo she was driven on to Auschwitz. She passed through the quarantine; after three months—she couldn't stay any longer because there in Mathausen her husband was waiting—she approached Dr Mengele on the loading platform. She said she was a nurse, and asked to be included in the departing transport. (It was the period of the camp's dissolution, which the composer who sang 'The Warszawianka' told about; people were sent away in over-crowded cattle trucks, but each train had a nurse in it: there must be order.) Mengele—handsome, polite—conducted a short examination on the platform.

'How do you distinguish a venous haemorrhage from an arterial one?' he asked. She knew that because, of course, she had learned nursing at the typhoid ward in the ghetto.

'How many times a minute does a man breathe?' Dr Mengele kept asking. She didn't know that and got scared.

'How many times a minute does the heart beat?' he asked like some understanding professor, who doesn't like to fail you in an exam.

'It depends,' she said, 'if the man is afraid, and to what degree.'

Dr Mengele burst out laughing, and she noticed then that he had a gap between his front teeth. Diasthema—she remembered the information from her nursing courses. Such a gap is called a diasthema . . .

She was recommended for the transport and left Ausch-witz for Guben. In Guben she stole a coat from a German worker and ran away (there in Mathausen her husband was waiting, wasn't he?). She ended up in another camp, Schwetig am Oder. In Schwetig she was picked out to go to Auschwitz, but she never got there: on that very day Auschwitz was liberated. They were driven to the West. She escaped on the way (in Mathausen . . . and so on). Via Berlin she reached Vienna and worked in a German military hospital as a nurse. In April the Russians came to the hospital.

'Nu, siestra, katoryj SS? (Which of them is SS?),' she was asked by an officer.

She knew katoryj SS because she changed their dressings every day, but she said, 'Nie znaju. (I don't know.)'

'Now you can take your revenge,' the officer explained, when she clarified that she was Polish and presented her arm with an Auschwitz number. 'Who's from the SS?'

'I don't know,' she repeated with a stubbornness that surprised her. 'I can tell you who's got no eyes, who's got no hands, but who's from the SS—I haven't a clue.'

The soldiers left. She took off her cap, rolled down her sleeves and ran out of the hospital. The Second World War was over.

She found her husband in the barracks of Ebensee, in the mountains, above Mathausen.

'Six weeks since the war ended, and no sign of you,' he said reproachfully, though she was the first wife to reach the camp. Then he bent down to her ear. 'No one here knows that we're ... that we're ... Jews.'

She nodded. 'Same with me. And it'll stay like that. Now we'll always be Poles ...'

They left the barracks.

She told him how the others had died. 'There's no one left,' she said and started the count: her parents, his parents, his four sisters, his nephew, brother-in-law ... While naming them she bent the fingers first of one hand and then of the other, then she ran out of fingers; at which point she straightened out two fingers, the index and the middle one: 'We are left, you and I. I knew you'd survive. I was saving you.' (She said then, for the first time, 'I was saving you.' From then on she would repeat it more often: that if he'd survived twenty-two months of a camp, of a camp like Mathausen, if out of five hundred men who were building the camp in Ebensee sixteen survived, and if he'd found himself among the sixteen, it was thanks to her, it was the power of her love that kept him alive. 'I carried him inside me as a pregnant woman carries a child in her belly,' she told Mrs Romerowa, and Mrs Romerowa said, 'Don't tell him that. Don't tell him again that he survived thanks to you.')

They returned to Poland. They retained, naturally, their Aryan papers. Her husband opened a private weaving workshop; she went to a school for nurses. They baptized both daughters and went to church with them in an exemplary way. One day her husband was summoned to the police. On the officer's desk there were several yellowing sheets of paper. They weren't documents connected with weaving. One sheet turned out to be the original, prewar certificate of his parents' marriage, the other was her father's tax statement. The husband touched the sheets carefully, as if afraid they might crumble in his hands, but the officer seemed reassuring:

'It's good, old paper, it'll withstand a lot. So,' he added with a sigh, 'when are we going to assume our real names? It's high time, Mr Pawlicki.'

Soon afterwards they filled in the appropriate forms and handed them in at the Passport Office. The officer asked about their nationality.

'Polish,' she said.

'And your parents?'

'Polish.'

'I didn't know that a pair of crows could give birth to a falcon,' laughed the officer.

At the Ministry they were informed that if they put down 'Jewish nationality', they would receive their documents within seven days. They put down 'Jewish nationality', and after a week they were handed sheets of paper, the size of a school certificate, with the note 'Travel Document'. Underneath there was the following information. 'The owner of this document is not a Polish citizen.'

They settled in Vienna. The younger of the daughters, who had never missed a Mass when in Poland, and on fast days wouldn't even drink a drop of water, went on holiday to a kibbutz. After her return she informed everyone that, together with her fiancé, she was moving to Israel. The elder one went on a holiday to visit the younger and stayed too.

So they lived in Vienna without their daughters, exiled from Poland and the familiar world, and only one thing turned out to be immutable—her love. She was, as in the past, caring and tender, considerate and meek, and keen for any sacrifices. In fact she was even more devoted and more eager to make sacrifices, because she was left with only one object of affection: her husband.

One morning Isolda R went into the kitchen. She reached for the coffee and noticed a sheet of paper, folded in four, lying on the sewing machine, just under the maker's name-plate, 'Singer'. She put the coffee on, reached for her glasses and started to read. It was a letter from her husband. In the letter he informed her that he was leaving her forever.

'I'm leaving never to return,' he wrote. 'I'll be paying you fifty dollars per week. I'll also be paying your rent and telephone, provided the bills aren't too high. Janek.'

She moved to Israel. She settled in the house which her elder daughter and her husband bought and furnished specially for her. Her husband rarely rings. She stopped pretending to be a Pole. She no longer cared if others ever accepted her as a Pole. She realized what a great relief it was to stop thinking what others . . . She realized she should be very happy—no longer pretending, not to be thinking 'If . . .' And she is happy, except her husband's phone calls have become less and less frequent, and only in connection with their daughters.

Her husband suffers from kidney problems; he tends to be depressed, has already had a heart attack, and must have a prostate operation. One day he may need kidney dialysis, the coronary disease may get worse, depressions will recur . . . Then he'll come back to her, and she, luckily, is a nurse. She knows about the kidneys and the heart, and she's just started learning about dialysis. Her husband will have the finest professional care.

VI

I wrote the book. Exactly the way it should be. I sent off the typescript. After a long silence, when the phone finally rang, I heard an uncertain voice:

'It's strange, Hania. I keep reading. I've already gone through it four times . . . Well, Hania, I don't know. Well, we'll talk about it.'

We talked in Vienna. First in the Pruckel Café, then in her husband's flat.

The Pruckel Café was where the Gestapo picked her up. She showed me the table where she had waited for the man from the *Todt* organization: by the mirror, opposite the door, next to the potted palm. The mirror still hung there, the table still stood, the palm still grew.

She said, 'I was sitting opposite the entrance, and that was a mistake. I should've sat with my back to the door.'

'They'd have spotted you in the mirror. You'd have gained a few minutes at the most.'

'That's true.'

We were sitting close to that table, by the window, eating apple strudel and whipped cream. The cake was hot, the cream cold—the best cake I'd ever had in my life. We were eating the sensational strudel, and my heroine was explaining which way the Gestapo led her out.

'We turned left, oh, this way.' She pointed through the window. 'We went towards the canal and turned left again. I'll show you later.' (Later she showed me a monument and a plaque stating that here was the Gestapo site, here was the site of suffering and death.)

'Hania, that novel, it's terribly slim,' she said suddenly. 'It was supposed to be a big fat blockbuster, and what's come out is a booklet.'

'That's the way it ought to be,' I explained. 'The book about Marek Edelman was even shorter. By sixty pages, by a third. And that was a book about the ghetto fighters.'

'It was all so horrible,' she went on, as if she had not heard what I said. 'All my despair, my heart, my tears—and in your version? A few sentences. Is that really all?'

'The greater the despair, the fewer the sentences needed, Isolda.'

(I didn't say Isolda, because in reality the heroine's name is different. No, in reality her name is Isolda, but she uses her 'Aryan' name, uglier and simpler. How can you, being an Isolda, give it up in favour of something more common?)

'I told you so much. I thought you'd be able to use it.' She spoke with growing confidence, with a more striking note of reproach.

I was getting angry. My heroine was starting to behave like a client who'd brought some fabric to the dressmaker, expected a creation with pleats, tucks, puffs and frills and is delivered a classical dress that's simple and modest.

'The more exquisite the material, the simpler the line should be.' I repeated my previous idea in other words. 'You're a wonderful person, Isolda,' I added, 'but you have bad taste. Perhaps not bad,' I corrected myself, 'but anachronistic. Or conventional, perhaps.'

The next day I went to her husband's flat, where she was staying for a few days, while she was in Vienna. It was a nice, bright flat, far from the city centre.

Her husband was still at work.

I looked around. The walls of all the rooms were covered with blown-up photographs. Some were black and white, some colour but retouched from the original black and white. The photographs showed women—some dark, some light, all cheerful, smiling, young.

'My husband's sisters,' explained Isolda R. 'This is Tusia, That's Hela. In reality the sisters' names were Estera, Chaja, Nachama and Sara, but at home they were called by their Polish names: Tusia, Hela, Halina, Zosia. I knew them all from Isolda R's story and from the book which was and wasn't entirely mine.

Zosia, the youngest of the sisters, married in Lwów, died first.

Tusia and Hela. (Both Hela's summer frock and the toque

on her head were tinted pink; her hair was golden, her *décolleté* tanned, and her waist slender, but that wasn't visible in the photograph.) They both committed suicide after Hela's husband died. They poisoned first the child, then themselves. The last time Isolda saw them was when she was fetching their mother from Chelmno. Hela kept repeating, 'Save them. Save my Mummy, my father, my sister.' She didn't ask for her brother because she knew her sister-in-law would save him anyway. Isolda R couldn't forgive her. She was so fair, so pretty, so unlike a Jew, and didn't even try to save herself, whereas she, with dyed hair, with eyes that a policeman could recognize with no trouble, even from a moving rickshaw—she had an obligation to live and save everyone.

Szymek, Tusia's little son. He was six years old. They gave him poison. They said . . . What can you say in such cases? 'Be a good boy, and swallow, please'? The owners of their hide-out found the three of them after several days. They had a huge problem with the funeral.

Halina. She was dark and plainer than her sisters; her legs weren't shapely, but in the photograph she shows them off with grace (I think Isolda slightly exaggerated about those legs; they weren't so bad after all). She dyed her hair an awful yellow. She met someone. She used to say about him, 'We understand each other without words.' Isolda R was very anxious about it. Who on earth could get interested in Halina? With her legs? With her hair dyed yellow? 'Look after yourself,' she used to say. When she came back from Vienna the second time, she was told that some gentleman came for Halina and their father and took them along with him, and they disappeared without a trace.

Father. The first time he managed to escape: when the landlady of the flat in Nowy Swiat threw them into the street. She threw them out in broad daylight—two old people who for the whole of last year hadn't risen from the floor, who had to crawl to the toilet on all fours, avoiding the window, and Halina, with her black, sad eyes, with her hair dyed yellow. The mother was caught and driven to the Pawiak, the father and Halina escaped. The second time they didn't manage to escape: when Halina's gentleman acquaintance arrived; they understood each other without words.

Father has a smooth, shaven face in the portrait. In real life he wore a beard, but after the war, when they changed everything into Polishness—even the names of the parents and old photographs—they gave Father's photograph to a woman photographer they trusted. She made a negative, blotted out the beard and Father emerged with a strange, alien face they hadn't known before. With a beardless face—which would be his forever.

Isolda R and I sat together, as we had done in her parlour in Israel, only now without the transparent curtain. Perhaps because of the faces, which gazed from all the walls and were with us.

So we were sitting, and Isolda R was reading her comments from notes.

Add the dumpling scene. She meant the dumplings served on her plate by a peasant woman near Łódź, when she was fleeing from forced labour in Germany. Her hostess welcomed her, and while she served the dumplings she kept explaining where all the evil comes from: from the Jews.

Add the restaurant scene (never mind the details).

On the whole: add, add, add.

'It was there, Isolda,' I kept saying. 'I wrote about it in the first version, but I had to cross it out because it was getting tedious.'

'*Tedious?*' cried Isolda R. 'Hania! What do you mean, tedious? The dumpling scene shows the whole problem, doesn't it!'

Next: take out some words, for instance, 'humble', 'submissive', 'eager to please', 'devoted'.

They was about her. With these words I characterized a heroine who was brave and stunning in the face of the whole world, but who turned, in her husband's presence, meek and quiet. Submissive.

'Never, Hania. Meek? *Me?*'

'Oh yes,' I was told later by Isolda's friend. 'She was

incredibly brave, braver than all our girls in the Home Army. Behind us we had the organization, contacts, friends, and she acted on her own and her heroism was greater, there's no comparison. But when she heard Him turn the key in the lock, she went quiet, small, flat, she'd get shy and scared.'

I was very proud that I'd guessed right about Isolda R. She didn't tell me about the humility, but I sensed it while writing. Obviously, writing must be a cognitive process.

We heard the key in the lock.

In came the husband. He was tall, very handsome. Introduced himself politely. He had beautiful slender hands.

'Are you hungry?' Isolda R asked and hastily rose from her armchair.

After coming back to Warsaw, I gave the typescript to Wiesia Weissowa, an experienced editor at a leading Polish Literary Publishing house. Not to print—I don't have the copyright—but out of curiosity, to get a competent opinion. In the meantime I was introducing the changes Isolda R requested.

'Are you writing?' she asked, this time phoning from Israel.

'Yes, I am.'

'Are you adding?'

'Yes, I am. But I'm reducing straight away, because what's added turns out superfluous.'

Silence fell on the line. A silence like that is expensive. Isolda R must work hard for it, using her ventriloquist's voice, from the stomach, to entertain her old lady who can't hear high notes.

The silence lingered.

'What about your husband?' I asked.

'Nothing.'

'Does he phone?'

'No.'

'What about your daughter?' (The daughter had been abroad for some time.)

'Nothing.'

'Does she phone?'

'No.'

Silence.

'So what's new?'

'Nothing's new, Hania.'

I felt sorry for her again.

'Isolda, I'll still try and add something.'

'Will you?' In Isolda R's voice I heard a note which in my book she used when speaking to her husband. 'I'm begging you, give it a try.'

Wiesia Weissowa rang. She said they'd like to publish *The Triumphant War of Isolda R*, that it's one of the most interesting books about the Jews.

'I've only one comment,' she added. 'Structural. Shouldn't that husband leave her much earlier? For the novel's sake, it really would be better.'

(*Translated by Basia Plebanek*)

Stefan Chwin

The Touch

So who was this man, Stalin? The man whose terse signa-
ture had changed my erroneous position on the map to
one which had been deemed more correct, the co-author of
my father and mother's biographies, invisible, yet always
there?

The hand which had, from above, redrawn frontiers and
relocated cities on maps, was it the same hand which could
set the earth trembling, let loose earthquakes, orchestrate
sunrises and sunsets, blow in the clouds over the sea? How
was one to understand the hidden harmony (or dissonance)
between the triangle-framed eye which glittered with gold
over the entrance to the cathedral in Old Oliva and the
decisions which shaped my destiny from afar—at least in
terms of topography and climate—seemingly real, and yet
still unclear, open to the possibilities hidden in the ink signa-
ture laid on the documents signed at a big table in a small
place near Berlin, where the three Most Powerful Men in the
World, each with a fountain pen in hand (albeit of different
makes), met over a sheet of paper as clean as a freshly
washed bandage? Had the golden pen-nibs awaited for cen-
turies those three autographs which were to bring order into
the world, as if it had all been pre-ordained and what
remained now was merely to fulfill destiny? Or, did they
wilfully produce these elaborate ink letters—meaningful
tracks of the fate-shaping Hand?

The Hand that I could understand was the Hand of Stefan
Batory, which I saw in one of the pictures in the cathedral,

in which the Polish king was represented as carrying the cathedral on a tray, and handing this Gothic edifice to the Virgin Mary, who glistened amongst the clouds over 'Karlsberg'. The cathedral the king was offering her became a portable trophy and I had always admired its walls (particularly the one between the square and the granary building which bore traces of German bullets) because they were high and permanent (could there be anything more permanent in the world than a cathedral?). Now, I understood the secret of transferability of cities—that they, too, could be carried on a tray and offered to fate so that they could be relocated to a better, more suitable place. This act of offering up the cathedral on a tray, symbolizing, as it did, the gift and the offering, could be seen reproduced elsewhere in the cathedral. That is why, standing beside my father on the stone floor of the presbytery decorated with the bishops' tombstones (granite testimony to immutability and permanence), I could, without the slightest effort (or fear), imagine the moment when this floor would suddenly begin to shake under our feet, the cast-iron candle-holders hanging in the main nave would start swinging to the left and to the right until the cathedral itself would be lifted up into the air, together with Father and me and all the other people from Old Oliva as well as those from the part of town which lay on the other side of the railway line, all of whom came here for the eleven o'clock Mass. Then this someone would hold it up in the air like a moneybox, with all of us inside holding on to the pews so as not to lose our balance, and, having decided to make a gift of that white building, he would at the same time transport us into the distant regions of the sky ... and now he carries the cathedral on a tray above the moraine hills towards Sopot ... or perhaps even to Malbork.

But the Hand which shaped my destiny—did it have much to do with the Hand of the king, or was it rather the Hand appearing out of the clouds to accept the gift from the imposing man in the golden royal fur-lined coat—the man who appeared taller than the nearby hill of Pacholek and touching silver-grey clouds with his head? In the cathedral picture this Hand, illuminated by golden rays, emerged from the hole in the clouds in order to receive the building of the church with its two pointed spires protruding above the entrance, as if it had been a cardboard model, and yet, lo and behold, painted on this tray, you could clearly see huge, real trees growing.

If the Hand's existence was so distant that it appeared a dream, could I have, if only intuitively, grasped a distant shape of the power that had determined my existence in time in space? What was the link between St Michael (equally impressively dressed up and well armed) and the man in the plain military tunic with no decorations, whose black moustache could just be made out in the far distance, above the spires of the Town Hall and St Mary's Church, looming faintly on the eastern side of the horizon, beyond the buildings of Wrzeszcz?

Stalin? I had first learned of his existence from a song.

This I sang, dressed up in a lovely Cracovian-style hat decorated with feathers, my nice costume conferring solemnity on a nursery-school ceremony in the basement of a house in Gdynia's Świętojanska Street to which Mother used to bring me every day. The song took the form of a dialogue: some of us asked a question, which the others answered. As for me, I invested the questions with additional emphasis by the gesture of my hand and the rustle of my feathers.

'Children, by whose design was the sun decreed to shine?' I sang in a treble voice, a little embarassed, gazing at the pink and violet lamps high up under the ceiling above the walls of the room, which were decorated with cut-out letters. I could sense fixed on me the eyes of some tens of parents gathered before me in slightly unnatural poses (as everybody had to sit, their knees almost touching their chins, on long gym benches, not more than several inches high).

My question would be followed by a moment of silence. The windows were ajar and from behind the curtains the

noise of passing trolley buses would rise and fall. My friends'
faces would turn towards the teacher waiting for a sign,
which she would give by nodding, whereupon the boys and
girls dressed up as ladybirds and fireflies would sing the
answer: 'Staaaaaliiiiin.' On the wall painted with crude green
paint a lovely white papier-mâché pigeon spread its wings
above freshly watered wall-ferns (our tender feelings towards
these plants having developed during our daily rota of wat-
ering them) which trailed from the window-sills, just as they
did from the praesidium table at Party conferences.

How did I come to be singled out as the one to ask the
questions? This was because of my talents which I accidentally revealed during the class when, with a purple crayon
on the back of an invoice (which our playschool used to
receive from the accountancy firm 'Dalmore', I drew a lighthouse and a warship, and signed my drawing with my full
name.

Full name and surname. This was a mistake but also a
stroke of luck. Until then I had been one of many children,
but now, when the teacher looked at our work, my full name
signed in the corner of my drawing (the children could not
yet sign their names) suddenly catapulted me in front of the
others and the finger of fate pointed at me. I was assigned a
Cracovian hat and the role of a public interrogator.

The song itself, which we intoned with our clear voices,
ran through many verses. It dealt, in turn, with rain, good
harvest and newly built houses, but it only appeared an easy
song, since the teacher had deemed it necessary to add a few
words of explanation. While we were memorizing the words,
it was explained to us that the song was really about the
fight for peace (which was not at all obvious at first). So it
was that, standing between the wall-ferns hanging from the
window-sills and the wall bearing the noticeboard with the in-
house newsheet, I learned that the basic function of the
Hand was to fight for peace and that I could take an active
part in this fight by asking these questions. ('In this way,'
the teacher added, 'you will also give pleasure to Bolesław
Bierut.') So I kept interrogating my friends with active

involvement and it wasn't till afterwards that I wondered what connection there could have been between my inquiries about peace and the talents which I displayed when I signed the picture of a warship and a lighthouse rising against Oksywie. A portrait of Bolesław Bierut surrounded by smiling children, which had been cut out from a popular magazine, hung on a noticeboard in our room, and, while eating milk soup from thick earthenware plates, one could have a good look at it.

But as for Stalin himself, I became more closely acquainted with him only later in the fresh air.

The month of May. A clear sky. Sparrows twittering in the birch trees. Fresh, green leaves. The shining trumpets of the navy cadets' brass band, whose thunderous sound could be heard from the direction of the the street full of people. Father usually carried me on his shoulders (not always, as he tired quickly), so I had a good opportunity to see things well. I was sitting comfortably, protecting myself from the sun by fanning myself with a paper flag which was fixed on to the same kind of stick as they use for candyfloss.

Whenever in winter I cast my mind back to these May days, I could always recall the sweet taste of candyfloss, its distant memory merging with the image of birch trees covered with new leaves, the brick-red of the flag fluttering in the wind, and the picture of the moustached man in the uniform without decorations whose portraits decorated the building next to the railway station. So it was that usually, while marching perched on Father's shoulders, I held in one hand a fluttering paper flag, while with the other I gripped a sugar cloud which I nibbled at slowly, opening my mouth wide and biting at the fluffy sweetness which never seemed sweet enough (the 'raczki' sweets, ah, well, that was something else!), even though it was made of nothing but sugar. (This I could see for myself, while observing the rotating machine under a glass cover, into which a fellow in a white hat kept pouring little crystals every so often).

So I kept eating and looked around. The eating and the looking became one with the blue of the sky, with the thunder of music, with long hold-ups when the crowd had to stop and the road before us was empty. It became one with the quickening steps, so that sometimes one was almost running, when the men with arm-bands on their sleeves would encourage us with energetic gestures to link up with the next group; they were fond of order and tidiness.

Candyfloss ... The very act of eating it to the accompaniment of the sea cadets' brass band had a metaphorical value and helped you to grasp some secrets of the world which were unfolding before your eyes. As you ate it, you had to be careful not to touch it with the tip of your nose or your eyelashes, as there was such a lot of it and it was so sticky. Yet, every time when you tried to get your teeth into the white cloud wound round a stick, you felt as if you were nibbling at a sweetened wind. It was as if the candyfloss was and wasn't there at the same time. Can something be there and not be there at the same time? My mind was troubled with difficult questions again.

Marching among the fluttering flags and slogan boards, all featuring the same face with a moustache, I was imperceptively entering into an unsettling dispute.

So, can there be a non-sweet sugar which is not sugar at all, but its barely distinguishable approximation? Well, perhaps, I answered myself, as I could taste it for myself. And what about unsalty salt? Can it exist or not? If, however, there can be sugar which is not sweet and salt which is not salty, can there also be iron-free iron, steel which does not contain steel or cement without cement? Can there or can't there? Didn't Father complain every so often about those 'steel' nails which came from the shop in Red Army Street and which, when you drove them in, would bend as if they were made of butter? Didn't the cement slabs that covered the platform of the railway station in Oliva crumble as if they were made of sand? Slowly, I began to grapple with the complicated questions. The candyfloss, rather like the cement which went into the making of the platforms and factories, was not to be taken seriously. So I kept eating my candyfloss and gazed at the picures adorning the walls of houses on both sides of the road.

On the pictures which hung high up above our heads, Stalin did not move and was of huge proportions—big. On the newsreels in our local cinema he did move about, but that was something entirely different. What, however, could the mysterious words I happened to overhear in Mr Jasniew- icz's garage one summer afternoon have to do with these gigantic portraits which glorified the May parade? We were standing in the open doors of his garage, watching the mech- anic's oil-smeared hands, while he was fixing something in the underbody of an ancient Warszawa car, and we heard him singing, with a strange smile: 'Sweet are the lips of Uncle Joe, Sweet as raspberries, or more . . .'

In the Dolphin cinema, I watched the Builder of Commu- nism kissing children time and time again. Wearing a white uniform jacket and a cap with a large round crown, he would kiss all the children in turn, and then push them away. I myself must have had lips sweeter than raspberries after having sucked my 'raczki' sweets, not to mention candyfloss. But raspberries and sweetness? I could not see the connec- tion, even though I could sense the strange charm exuded by the words of this song. When Stalin smiled, his face froze in that gentle smile and little wrinkles appeared round his eyes, the same wrinkles I could see in my father's face and, later, in my own. But the sweet lips of the Builder of Com- munism?

On the screen the children, dressed in their neat uniforms with neck-scarves, crowded round the man also wearing uniform, stretching out their hands, in which they held posies of flowers, and ran lightly towards him. Father would say that all this had been rehearsed and he didn't trust the sincerity of it, but what reason had I to doubt it?

The smiling man with a moustache and eyes narrowed to slits looked straight at me and I stared back at him—he standing in Red Square, I seated in the darkness of the Dolphin cinema, a very small distance away, quite close, in fact, as my seat happened to be in the third row.

The boy on the screen clung to the uniformed chest for a moment too long, only to be immediately pulled away from the Builder by the security people. He was pulled away discreetly but decisively (the contact was meant to be very brief and that is why it was so pregnant with meaning). I accepted the necessity of parting, but despite this couldn't help a sense of something tender and weepy creeping into my soul. I knew that the contact could last only for a moment; how many more boys like this one were awaiting this touch? The whole stadiumful of them! In the Dolphin cinema I saw, many times, thousands of boys whose bodies would, together, form themselves into various bright patterns and slogans, waiting for one gesture from the hand in uniform raised above the world, the hand which was to play its game of patience with them.

I could not tear my eyes away from the scene which would normally precede this parting. My heart quickened its beat. Here, we could see the man touch the boy—the hand in the white uniform pressed the slender body of the boy to his bemedalled chest, and the boy cuddled up to it. The vague meaning of this image slowly penetrated my senses and sweetness seeped deep into my heart. There were no women around (at least not in the vicinity of the white uniform), at best only girls with ponytails in military-style aprons, running towards the man with posies of flowers, but they, of course, didn't count.

On the stone tribune, which doubled as the tomb of the embalmed body of the Builder's friend, the power which was capable of bringing into being the T-34 tanks and the roaring hydroelectric stations, of redrawing state frontiers with a thick pencil and of transferring thousands of people from one place to another, softened movingly. The boy clung to that strength which was capable of lifting him up as a wind picks up a dry leaf, and he surrendered softly to it. Wasn't this a real meeting of father and son, such as we could only dream about? Isn't this what Abraham and Isaac looked like after their ordeal?

Every time Mother told me the story of the Biblical father, who, for the sake of a Higher Purpose, was prepared to kill his own son, only later changing his mind, I felt greatly, greatly moved. Here was the knife glinting in the hand of the parent, lifted up above the boy's curly head, his hands tied behind his back, the glistening blade ready to fall down any moment on to his bared neck but I knew that nothing could happen, and that the angel would hold back the raised arm gripping the sword. This moment brought such sweet relief after a terrible tension, that I always felt overwhelmed with gratitude to Abraham, as I looked at him as represented in the picture, which hung on the left of the cathedral's main altar; the gratitude that it all ended well, at least so far . . .

And now, too, in this meeting of the boy with the Hand in uniform, I also felt this gentle suspension of Purpose. I felt this even though I knew that this Hand had very nearly hit Father and made him flee Vilnius (so I ought to feel resentful, if not outright hostile). Despite this, I still drank in its power and gentleness, which made the picture shining in the darkness of the Dolphin cinema three metres away, so very close and appealing.

And yet, while capable of identifying with the boy's feelings and even ready to accept an obligation (as yet unclear), I remained unmoved.

This was because the cuddling to the chest in uniform was usually followed by patting on the cheek.

This I did not like.

Why do they have to do this? I thought, looking at the moustached portrait which gently waved above the platform opposite the railway station in the breezes of May wind blowing from the direction of the Oliwa Gate, with the Gdańsk dockyard cranes just coming into view behind the bridge over the railway line. Why couldn't they refrain from this pinching of the ears?

Because suddenly, the Power adopted the patronizing pose of an uncle, the provincial, sweet solemnity spread over the faces of the dignitaries, delegates and the security men. Was the secret of the lips sweeter than raspberries to be found there? Was this the small gesture which invalidated everything? The truth about it, at first obscured by the props of the staged meeting, would suddenly reveal itself to me in the same way as did the stuffing which came out from underneath the embroidered cover of the sofa in Grandmother's room. Everything seemed unreal as if made of cardboard or plywood. Even the medals and the ceremonial uniforms.

But the portraits, well, that was something different—so, in the end, I preferred them to the cinema. More serious still were the white plaster models. The huge portrait hung above the podium, but right next to us, by the Rail Workers' Hostel, which we were just passing by, in a big photograph in a glass show-case, I could see four huge heads which looked like a fanned-out hand of cards, with one profile protruding from behind another. The two nearest heads sported bushy beards, one a pointed one, but only the head of the Builder of Communism could boast a moustache. The heads were made of plaster and stretched over half the width of the wall in the hall, in which about a hundred men sat in three rows, while in front of them stood a man in glasses, reading something: his name was Bolesław Bierut. A minute later, looking towards Hucisko, I noticed the same foursome on a piece of cloth stretched over the façade of the Railwaymen's Health Centre by the station.

Huge faces ... Oh, to see a face like this over the heads of the crowd was quite an experience. Around me, red flags fixed on long poles fluttered, the plywood rectangles covered with letters waved. I had to take care not to get hit by one of these plywood boards, as—when the wind came from the dockyard—they all started leaning in the direction of the station and one could easily get hurt.

'Here, on the wing of a song, comes our Polish youth,' somebody shouted very loudly through a gigantic megaphone just as we were passing, and a radiant choir of girls' voices broke out into the air: 'Here comes youth, youth, youth!'

I looked around carefully. I saw before us 'our youth' marching towards the Railwaymen's Health Centre, but they were not singing. So what was happening? You could hear the singing quite clearly from the loudspeaker, but who was doing the singing? I lifted my head to see the singing youth, but could see nothing! 'Where are these singing young people, Daddy?' I was about to shout to Father who was underneath me (as I was still sitting on his shoulders), but I gave up unable to hear myself shout, so loud was this strident voice intensified by the thudding of the band and the girls' singing. 'The young people are cheering the heroes of socialist labour!' thundered the voice. You could hear clapping, but, again, I couldn't see anyone clapping. Everybody's hands were busy trying to resist the wind, which was blowing from the dockyard and tugging at the red canvas with big white letters on it. Who would bother to sing in this wind, let alone to clap? Who was clapping, then? And yet I could hear the applause quite clearly. I would have joined in if not for the candyfloss, which I had to keep an eye on as the wind was tugging at that, too.

We turned right, went under a line of rope and found ourselves right by the loudspeaker. Ah, it was very nice to stand there, in the first row, just behind the rope cordoning off the pavement from the road, close to a militiaman in his newly pressed uniform. Behind us we had Gdańsk railway station and the lorry from which hot dogs were being sold. There were crowds of people, some women in scarves tied up under their chins, even though the sun was getting hot. The militiaman in his tin-peaked cap kept his hands behind his back and stared with the others at the parade. The heat mixed with the cold wind blowing from the dockyard, the band played, the drum thundered, the voice echoed.

It was only at this moment that the holiday really began for me, as until then everything seemed not quite real. In the morning, about ten o'clock, Father would plunge into the crowd, and, so that nobody could suspect him of playing truant, casually and quite loudly say 'good morning' to some gentlemen I didn't know, so they would take note of his presence, but later, when the marching started in earnest, we walked in the crowd by ourselves, which is to say as if together with them and yet on our own, a few steps further away, just ahead of the singing young people. We walked quite quickly, even though this was fairly difficult, as I was sitting on my father's shoulders, which allowed him to keep his hands free (those who carried children were exempt from carrying flags or something heavier still). From this height, I saw a lot, but mainly people's heads and the banners (which I saw from behind, from where all you could see was the paint and the glue with which the cut-out letters were stuck to the thin fabric). The flags waved, the cloth fluttered and frequently got in the way of my vision, a few times the banner hit my face. The march was not conducive to thinking.

But what now? Now we stood just behind the rope and we could see everything that was going on. Taking the rope under my arms, and leaning against it, I nibbled at my candy-floss and began looking around again.

On the other side of the road, above the podium, the huge faces decorated with fir tree branches waved in the sea breeze. The podium too was decorated with branches of fir and birch tree, nice and spring-like. The faces on the flag were a nondescript brown. Next to the podium there was a small scaffolding, from which a man in a white shirt and a tie roared to the silver microphone in the rectangular frame: 'I can see the happy faces of the working youth! Let's cheer the working youth!!!' The sea cadets' trumpets and kettle-drums thundered. 'The working youth' indeed had smiles on their faces, which were beaming, for what else could they do when it was warm and the music was playing. So 'the youth' smiled, but as for me, I looked around and again felt troubled by a difficult question.

The 'working youth' may have been genuinely happy, but you couldn't say the same about the huge faces. I have never seen a hearty smile on any of those huge faces painted on canvas and hung up high above the street. Has anybody ever? 'The May day of joy!' shouted the man with the loud-speaker. 'Hurraah!' some voices answered. But the huge faces did not change and wore the same expression throughout—of general goodwill, if a little absentminded.

Strange. Down there such good cheer—and up on high? Boom, boom, boom, a sea cadet's drum ushered in a crash of trumpets and cymbals, which rolled over the crowd. Pink and blue balloons waved this way and that on strings and wires. From the side of the lorry behind us, a moist smell of hot dogs with mustard wafted in, the stoppers on the bottles of fizzy lemonade popped with a loud fizzle. 'The day of joy!' shouted the man. Even the men on the podium, in their suits and uniforms, would smile to those marching below—and there, up high? There, nothing changed, only now and again the painted cheeks shuddered, when the wind from the Bay of Gdańsk stirred the flags and shook the white canvas with the grey-brown image. The moustache remained still, the half-smile frozen. To the right: bushy beards. At once, I thought of what I liked doing best: and that was messing about with people's faces in the pictures.

Who didn't like that? It was great fun, this lesson meted out by us to the powers that be of today and yesterday, even if our headmaster, K, and our teacher were on their side. The teacher would hit us with a wooden ruler, she would hit at an angle so as not to make any noise, otherwise she might have got into trouble. But did it make any difference? You only needed to open my satchel, capacious, made of waxed black cardboard, studded with what resembled drawing pins and with leather buckles; it rattled when I ran because of the wooden pencil-case in it. The same went for Zbyszek Relski, whose satchel smelled strangely of ammonia, or for Piotrek B, who had his stuffed with breadcrumbs and little pellets of gunpowder which he had picked out of the cartridges scattered around the practice ground.

'Why are you looking so uneasy, Napoleon?' a voice from within the satchels would call. 'And you, King Bolesław, why are you looking so stuffy?' 'And you, Wera Kostrzewa, what's wrong with you?' And, wasting no time, armed with a nib dipped in a round glass inkpot with a wooden cover, we would set to work to make them feel better. Even Rosa

Luxemburg was made to give us a full smile, showing all her teeth.

So the pen went to work with a black blob at the tip—and, hey presto! Page after page! The city railway went past, its carriages (adapted from a design for the Berlin metro) rattled noisily, whereas the Polish-made lorries, stacked with empty bottles, thundered past the school in the direction of the fizzy drinks factory in Beniowski Street. And straight away Tadeusz Kosciuszko, wearing a rough overcoat from the time of the Polaniecki Manifesto, burst out laughing; Edward Dembowski brightened up, Adam Mickiewicz raised his eyebrows, which resembled a gooseberry bush, as if he was quite fed up and all he wanted was revenge (without thinking twice about it, we gave him a steel Wehrmacht helmet into the bargain).

So, nibbling at the candyfloss and looking up at the huge faces stretched out on the wall of the Railmen's Health Centre, I thought, perhaps one might just. But what would they do to my father if I did colour in the moustache on the big canvas which stretched out in front of the station, just a little, here and there.

(*Translated by Teresa Halikowska*)

Tadeusz Różewicz

The Tip

Fyodor Mikhailovich sat by the huge window looking out over the boulevard, watching the animated streams of people flowing past and the great carts. From time to time, a heavy flat wagon loaded with barrels of beer trundled by, and its massive dray-horses, in their carved wooden harnesses bearing the insignia of the brewery, clattered over the paving-stones. Fyodor Mikhailovich knotted and unknotted his fingers, and clenched together the palms of his hands, which were moist and warm and chafed him as if they were alien hands touching him. He was wearing a jacket, and hadn't noticed that its collar was turned up. Anya had been quilting a topcoat since yesterday in her skilful, rapid way, but hadn't managed to finish it. She was in a good mood, and had forgiven him for losing that money the night before; she just wagged her finger at him like a mother scolding a naughty boy. In his pocket he had some small change, enough for a cup of coffee and a tip for the waiter . . . The Swiss, the French and the Germans feel they have the right to a tip running in their blood. The Russians have a different, 'broader' nature—they wait for a bribe, the biggest they can get, and they accept it without any scruples. Whereas the Western soul has been formed, as it were, by the '*donner un pourboire*' mentality. You would think that all of them, from the waiter and the porter to the bishop and the president, were waiting for their '*pourboire*'. Fyodor Mikhailovich wrung his hands and waited for the waiter. The café, probably for reasons of economy, was neither lit nor heated, though the day was quite cool; there weren't many people, and in a remote coner of the big room some fellow was sitting entirely concealed by a spread newspaper. A cup and a cream jug stood in front of him.

At the other side of the window sat an old woman wearing a huge pink hat with a white ribbon running right round it. Brightly coloured birds nested on its brim, together with flowers and red cherries intertwined with leaves. The lady was drinking some kind of liqueur in small sips from a crystal glass, and feeding sponge fingers to a little dog with a flat muzzle. The waiter, a great fat fellow, smiled at the dog, and even gave it some signs of recognition; but neither the dog nor the lady deigned to notice the obsequious, over-assiduous waiter. The waiter stared intently at the ceiling, where a solitary fly sat, and paid no attention to the foreigner addressing him in broken German. The waiter had taken against the turned-up collar of his customer's jacket, and had decided to teach him a lesson. Fyodor Mikhailovich cleared his throat impatiently, indistinctly stammering something in this barbaric, ridiculous tongue. Between the customer and the waiter a mutual feeling of dislike and exasperation was growing. Sometimes this comes about for no particular reason, or rather, for a reason hidden deep in that part of the human brain which has retained the largest number of cells from its reptilian, amphibian or Stone Age past. The fact that people dress in tail-coats, waistcoats or trousers, or look at their watches, read newspapers or drink coffee, has a strictly limited significance ... they could equally well be gnawing bones in a cave sitting round a camp-fire. This waiter was a typical Western product, treating the poor with disdain, but complaisant, attentive and even submissive when people had money ... This is the difference between East and West. Of course, our Russian aristocracy takes only its worst features from the West; and the link or conduit between these feelings is furnished by those Poles who crawl at the feet of the West while treating Asia, or Russia, with contempt. It goes without saying that they have no idea what contempt the West feels for *them* ... That waiter! He knows me pretty well. He's had a fair number of tips out of me at various times, even if he did accept them with almost no thanks or acknowledgement, as Anya, who was sensitive to such trifles, noticed... 'Son of a bitch,' said Fyodor Mikhailovich, in Russian or in Polish, as he looked at the waiter, who was picking at his ear and smiling at the wretched dog. The dog looked uglier and uglier to Fyodor Mihkailovich. Anyway, it wasn't a dog at all, it was some sort of little monkey, sort of Chinesey... as if someone had taken a proper-looking dog and shoved its mug in till just its eyes stood out from its head, swollen and full of hatred. He looked at the old lady whom he (mentally) called 'the old moo', though if the dog was anything to go by, not to mention the hat and the waiter's exaggerated, sugary attentiveness, she must be some kind of fine lady, maybe even a baroness or the widow of a general. 'Bitch,' he thought to himself, meaning the waiter, who had melted away like morning dew. Could such a fat pig of a man melt away like dew?... What the hell had dew got to do with all this? Fyodor Mikhailovich licked his lips and bellowed, 'Waiter!' The word filled the interior of the empty café. Nobody replied, only the dog growled once, then again. This monster of a dog had nothing doggy about it, nothing amiable, nothing wise or submissive, like normal pooches have. It was just pure malice and arrogance. Even where dogs are concerned there is a difference between East and West. Fyodor Mikhailovich put down his paper, pulled out of his pocket a clean, carefully folded and ironed handkerchief and, holding it in the palm of his hand, began to wipe his forehead with it. Anya took care not only of his linen and his shirts but also of trifles like ironing his handkerchiefs. He looked up at the ceiling, put his hands in his pockets, and felt once again the touch of cold metal coins on his fingers. He guessed by the feel of them how much each was worth... those big fat ones were worth least. Anyway, it was enough to buy not just a coffee but some sort of cake as well. An Apfelstrudel, perhaps, or some other sort of *Kuchen*. It's not just their bellies but their hearts and heads as well they have full of those dreadful cakes. *Kaffee und Kuchen*... Terrible! Not Faust or Kant but Apfelstrudel!

And to think that Turgenev, who was a Russian landowner, real gentry to boot, had renounced his nationhood just so that these Westerners would give him a breathing space and let him eat *Kuchen* or oysters... Yes, renounced, for how else could you describe his confession that he 'felt he was a German'? Bah! And a Westerner he remained, even when his stories were about Russian peasants, Russian forests, the Russian sky, Russian women. He had abandoned his soul to the Paris salons and the German spas. Mammon was his god now. So completely had he lost his sense of pride, and perhaps his memory as well, that he kept on and on about me giving him back those fifty 'rhinelanders' I borrowed, even though I sent him back the money I owed him by post... well, if not the whole sum, then part of it! Where the hell did I put the receipt? And when all's said and done, I'm a gentleman as well as him: so if I ask for an extension of the repayment date, I'm only asking my social equal... Ivan Sergeyevich, if you are trying to tell me that I didn't give you back my loan, I'll give it back all over again, but you really will have to be civil to me, even if you *have* renounced your nation! I know that a Parisian or a Swiss waiter is closer to you now than any Russian writer. What has become of that great oaf? Fyodor Mikhailovich thought to himself. They're scoundrels and cheats, the whole lot of them. Just look at it, the flower of Western civilization, that Turgenev is so impressed by. Yet a waiter in a Russian restaurant, or even any old tapster in a pub, has more soul in one dirty finger—devil take him if he *does* dunk his finger from time to time in the soup he's serving you with... because this Russian waiter of ours isn't just the automaton we call an excellent waiter, he's a sinner too, like you, he is your brother... and God knows what else besides... Switzerland! Whether German, French, or Italian... the German sticks out like a sore thumb. One simply cannot fail to observe it: the more expensive the restaurant, the more soulless the service, and the more complete the absence of human contact between waiter and customer. The elaborate, ornate menu, the tableware and the smiles, it's all done just for the money, for the *pourboire* . . . and their whores are just the same. To think that this world without dignity, with its stunted little soul, dares to treate us with contempt, and even despises us Russians . . . for them we are just Mongols, Asiatics. Of course, here everything is cleaner; but alongside the cleanliness, atrocities have taken root, the cleanliness is all on the outside. The cleanliness and the hygiene of an expensive prostitute. Fyodor Mikhailovich struck the table suddenly with his fist. The violent movement and the thud made the little dog jump off the old lady's knee. It stood one pace in front of Fyodor Mikhailovich and started barking viciously. But this wasn't the barking and snapping of a normal dog, it was the gibber of a sort of mouse, plus a kind of wheezing. A French dog, Fyodor Mikhailovich thought with amusement, a real French mollycoddle dog, called Bijou no doubt, everything of theirs is 'bijou', wife, mistress, dog. The dog barked as if someone was skinning it alive. The old moo didn't budge from the spot, just called out 'Poochikins' . . . Fyodor suddenly started up as if he'd been scalded, stamped his foot at the dog, and roared, 'Who the hell do you think you are? Why don't you barking well bark off!' He was seized by a desire to give the dog a taste of his boot and chuck it out of the window, along with the old moo, the palm tree and the whole of Western civilization. At the same moment a tall, comely girl, wearing a white lace cap on her black hair, and checking a smile which played over her lips, gave the stiff curtsey of a girl straight from finishing school, and said:—Did you ask for something?

Fyodor Mikhailovich looked at the girl in surprise, as if she came from another planet, and said softly—Yes, my lady, I've been waiting for a coffee for half an hour . . . that 'Ober' is simply . . .

—He's left, sir, gone off duty . . . Would you like something with your coffee? An Apfelstrudel?

—Bloody penguin.

—I'm afraid there's only strudel. Penguins is off.

—Yes, right . . . strudel—he answered mechanically—yes please, thanks—and he sat down at the table. Meanwhile the dog, which had been lured back by the old witch, had returned to her lap . . . that miserable little dog . . . there you have the values of Western civilization, the darling little doggy scrounger, which has a better life than some lad working twelve hours in an English factory, that overfed 'bijou' is better off than peasant lads in Russia . . . but your poor Mr Turgenev sees Russia and the Russian village through rose-tinted spectacles. And that is precisely why the bourgeoisie and capitalism do such harm to children, and socialism will prevail . . . I loathe socialism, and revolution, and I am afraid that with the spectre of communism the rule of the hooligan draws near . . . My God, why do these revolutionaries not believe in God?—because if they believed in God they could change the world. But without God everything is permitted. Murder, pillage, rape or eating dog . . . Fyodor Mikhailovich smiled. Sometimes even I have my doubts about whether, if there were no God, 'everything is permitted' would really be a truth that could wreak havoc in our vale of tears . . . maybe it's the case that, without God, everything depends on the individual conscience. If you don't sin, it isn't because there's no God to absolve you, it's because self-absolution is an impossibility. I don't know: sometimes someone will say something that really seems to be true . . . of course, I am a believer . . . but perhaps that's something else altogether. Here, even in church they give tips, on a silver salver . . . They give tips to the chaplain and to the Lord God himself.

Fyodor Mikhailovich didn't notice the cup of coffee and the cake in front of him; he didn't notice, either, that the old lady, cuddling her little dog, had left the café. As she left, she weighed up with a single glance this foreigner with his pale, alien face, his massive forehead, and his downcast eyes . . . some sort of ape, she thought with disgust; an Asiatic. Fyodor Mikhailovich sat with his eyes shut. Turgenev, he thought with disgust, he couldn't even fall in love and get married in Russia, when he wanted to fall in love he had to go to Baden-Baden or to Paris, and as if that wasn't enough he had to fall in love with a French singer of Spanish extraction. He had searched and he had searched and lo! he found love at the Opéra: and as if *that* wasn't enough, he had got to know the woman of his choice in the part of Rosina in *The Barber of Seville*. Pauline Viardot. 'Tourgenieff, Tourgenieff'—that's the way the French say it, and the way he seems to like it. The singer leading a Russian bear around her salons. A gypsy going the rounds of Paris with a huge Russian prisoner . . . and the bear, wearing its customary tailcoat, dances in time with the Spaniard or gypsy's singing and playing . . . and probably he hasn't so much as touched with his tongue his Parisian 'bijou' . . . the café suddenly became quiet, and Fyodor Mikhailovich distinctly heard the drone of a fly looking for a resting-place between the blind and the window . . . the elderly lady with her wizened little dog floated away, left the café . . . a dog like that isn't a dog at all . . . it eats sponge fingers and probably drinks coffee with cream, perhaps a liqueur as well . . . Kutiapka, Cunty Katy, Fyodor said out loud to himself . . . Kutiapka, he repeated, as if proclaiming some living truth . . . but this was a fabrication from the world of the dead, as utterly remote from this town and this canton and Ivan Sergeyevich as the sea on the moon was from Lake Leman, or the Orthodox God from the Roman Catholic God . . . Kutiapka was a dog and a half! And so was Whitey . . . and Grey. Kutiapka . . . one ear stuck up, projecting just like a wolf's ear, and the other hanging down . . . he seemed to feel suddenly the warmth of the blind, squealing puppy he was warming with his own body . . . Kutiapka had a shaggy coat the colour of a grey mouse . . . then they lost Kutiapka, when she was already full-grown; then Nestroyev killed her, skinned her to make a fur cap and ate her . . . without Kutiapka's barking the House of the Dead seemed empty . . . and there's Turgenev sitting (no doubt) at the feet of Mme Viardot, reciting French poetry . . . Fyodor Mikhailovich laughed out loud . . . French lyric poetry! The Parnassians . . . Heredia, Leconte de Lisle . . .

The elves are crowned with marjoram
The elves are dancing, whirling in the meadow
They bind him fast in their airy dream
Rising in song amidst the silent air
—O gallant knight, on this starry night
Whither wanderest thou, at this tardy hour?
Evil spirits encircle the massy oaks
Dance, dance with us—saith the elfin queen . . .

and there he sits in his tail-coat babbling this nonsense . . . I really know nothing in literature more ridiculous than French lyric verse . . . O gallant knight! yet they have a writer of genius as well, the man who wrote *The Mysteries of Paris* and *The Wandering Jew* . . . Elves, elves . . . Salvador . . . Fyodor Mikhailovich sat over his newspaper with his head on one side, with his eyes half shut, as if he was listening to the dying buzz of that fat old Swiss fly. He was preoccupied by the feeling that in some other place, in some other café, someone was waiting for him: not Anya, but that other woman, whose name was branded on his forehead as clearly and shamelessly as some scarlet letter. There were times, when Anya looked at him with those startled, plaintive eyes, like an injured child, when he had the impression that that name really was burned on his forehead like a brand . . . and it seemed to him that in a nearby house, a few paces away, Apolinaria was waiting for that person, just waiting, in a room in some third-class hotel, waiting for her young man: that fiery, fascinating, elegant young student . . . Student! My God! . . . I still have to go through all that . . . She is waiting for a student, and I am simply the 'pangs of conscience', old, worn-out, a convict, just some Russian scribbler . . . Apolinaria is lying in bed. The room is full of a 'bohemian' disarray . . . yes, they're all writers and artists . . . they adopt a colourful manner of dressing, they have long beards, they chatter on *ad nauseam* about 'what they're working on' . . . and of course do nothing. A has a sort of careless way of lying, but very contrived and deliberate at the same time, as if she was posing for one of those thousands of mediocre artists who spend their time here in Paris squandering their youth and their bourgeois parents' money. A. is reading something, not one of my books, of course, one of those Parnassian lads . . . but the book falls from her strong, beautiful hand on to the floor, she lies back with her eyes closed, carelessly rocking her childish, slippered foot, until the slipper falls from her toes on to the book . . . a long shapely leg in a black stocking almost touches Fyodor Mikhailovich's lips . . . Anya is stitching my overcoat and that's why I'm so cold, he thought, she is stitching my overcoat and I gambled away the last fifty francs I took from her to pay for the wedding rings, and the ear-rings and brooches I gave her for her birthday . . . and . . . I staked her overcoat as well . . . Anya, for the first time since the beginning of our acquaintance, gave me a really hostile look, and said, in a voice quite unlike her usual voice, 'Go, and never come back' . . . so I went, and here I am sitting in this café, and where am I supposed to go? . . . even the birds have their nests . . . and I have nowhere to lay my head . . . everyone needs somewhere to go . . . Paris is only a few hours by rail from this boring Swiss town . . . I'll get on a train and be with her tomorrow morning . . . He felt a strange weakness overcoming him, a fleeting smell of perfume mixed with sweat, the harsh coldness of silk fitting tightly to a leg swaying back and forth and sending him secret signs, on the tips of the toes an old, worn, Turkish-style slipper with a yellow, dirty, crumpled pompom hung, swung, is that how you spell it, 'pompom', not 'ponpon' . . . on the tips of the toes it looked like a big fish-hook, or like a big yellow insect caught on a hook . . . the leg bent at the knee and the light shining on the taut black silk, cold, glistening like the light on the blade of a knife . . . but, he thought, the 'bait' is in my head, in my thoughts, which have sort of swallowed both the slipper and the foot and the reflection of light from the stockings; smell, taste, sight, touch, and another sense as well . . . there are five senses, anyhow . . . what is the fifth sense? I hear: hearing is what it is . . . all the senses participated in the transformation of vision, the transformation of the whole organism . . .

the senses swapped over, transformed themselves, one stood in for another. Fyodor Mikhailovich distinctly heard the rasping light on the stocking, touched the smell of perfume mixed with sweat, felt on his tongue the throaty, dark, moist voice. Despite the fact that his eyelids were lowered, he saw her shining black eyes, as if without whites altogether, her lips, the lock of hair touching her eyebrows ... a big shapely foot rocked and signalled for him to draw nearer ... and he went forward slowly, feeling suddenly feeble and confused he knelt down on the worn carpet (in places there were holes) ... the hotel was second-rate, the furniture no more than sticks ... a French double bed took up half the room and was reflected in the shadowy, unwashed mirror. In this mirror he inspected the back of his head, the thinning hair that scarcely covered the scalp, like a layer of damp straw stuck to the head of a porcelain doll; in all of this there was something so wretched that he shut his eyes and crawled in the direction of the perfume on all fours ... the foot came to rest against his breast and thrust him away ... but he seized the cold harsh shape in his hands and desperately pressed his face to it ... he felt a powerful scent, as if the foot, which he began kissing reverentially, was a flower on the end of its stalk ... he soaked up this scent, he felt on his cheeks the harsh sensation of her hair, and a peal of laughter rang out, he opened his eyes, startled, and raised his head. The waitress was standing over him. 'What were you dreaming about?' she said. 'Something nice or something nasty?' She started to laugh. 'You almost spilt your coffee.' Fyodor Mikhailovich moved his hands as if he was taking a spider off his face. Anya, I have been sitting here for an eternity and I haven't got the nerve to go home, you are mending my overcoat, and I haven't redeemed your pawned coat, though the mornings are already cool ... the overcoat is at the pawnbroker's; and I lost; so here I sit, with nowhere to go. I sit, and count with my fingers the metal coins in my pocket. On the wall there is an etching of Lord Byron ... they say that Byron ate breakfast in this café, though of course that was a long time ago, probably before I was born, but the proprietor is keen on the idea of putting up a plaque in memory of the late poet. Lord Byron deigned to take breakfast here, English breakfast of course . . . tea with milk! What a primitive race they are, they pour milk into tea, or even worse . . . cream with tea . . . and they probably have sponge fingers with their vodka . . . and they don't know what a salt cucumber is, our kind of cucumbers, the slightly salted kind. I look at that young man of genius, and what genius . . . with the beautifully curled hair over a forehead which is as fine and broad as some heraldic device . . . and hidden among the splendid curls his aristocratic little ears, not like the ears of any old mongrel, the extraordinary eyes under the well-defined arches of the eyebrows, the shapely but projecting, manly nose, and the soft, feminine, almost childike oval of the face . . . the poet was a young man in the full flower of his years, a flower, really . . . nineteen years old! A mouth made for kissing . . . curving, slightly swollen lips . . . large eyes, protuberant, what colour were his eyes? I look into the eyes of this young genius . . . and (don't laugh, Anya!) I feel as if I could fall in love with him, this lad . . . and me? with my big ears, hair like straw, sunken eyes, commonplace nose sort of plonked between two eyes . . . and you know, Anya, he hated England and the English, I'm not surprised, I don't like them either . . . and he couldn't stand literature either . . . what an aristocrat! He didn't have to earn his living by writing . . . probably what he really wanted to say was 'What the devil have I to do with writing? but it's too late now to worry about that, all regrets are useless' . . . because when you think about it, it really is hard to understand why a lord or a count or even Turgenev, a rich landowner, writes stories and poems . . . I write because I need money to buy shoes, an overcoat, a shirt, food, fuel . . . Lord Byron . . . well yes, the title he inherited as a child, 'Sixth Lord Byron of Rochdale', and the motto on the family coat of arms, '*Crede Byron*', or 'Trust a Byron'; and a Turgenev can't even trust a Dostoevsky, and even that idiotic head waiter doesn't trust me . . . A real lord like him can afford a confession: 'The resurrection of the body just seems such a strange, even a ridiculous, idea ... unless it's meant as a sort of punishment.' An English lord can afford not to believe in the resurrection of the body ... of course, a Russian lord may equally not believe, but I have to believe, because if I doubted that, I'd buy a rope and string myself up today, right here. A poor man, even a prostitute, in Russia, believes in the forgiveness of sins, the resurrection of the body, life everlasting ... Let him be! what he was, he was, but he was splendid: and what a poet! He wrote those long narrative poems, pure genius, and on top of that he could ride a horse, swim, handle a pistol, be the lover of scores of women, and perhaps of young men too, write thousands of lines of poetry, climb mountains, listen to Lord Grey's most beautiful daughter make music, and even box with Jackson, the professional ... he spent two months in Turkey as the guest of the sultan and various pashas, swam the Hellespont at its widest point in an hour and ten minutes ... he hunted snipe, wrote with a golden pen which Dr Butter gave him, had a hundred and fifty lovers, conquered the Jungfrau, the Dent d'Argent and the Wetterhorn. Goethe wrote poems in his honour, and added a dedication in his own hand ... but this eagle had his weaknesses, too, yes, Anya, a man is a feeble creature ... Lord Byron was always in danger of getting a bit plump ... his distaste for bodily functions might be called an *idée fixe* ... Stendhal used to gossip about him a lot even though he claimed to be his friend, but whether a Frenchman is capable of friendship ... it's not friendship but good food and the glory of France that take pride of place in a Frenchman's life, along with Napoleon and 'my bijou' ... Stendhal, who was as ugly as the seven deadly sins, said in his journals that Byron spent at least one-third of every day like a dandy whose main concern was not to let his paunch be seen; he took care to conceal his lame foot and always moved in such a way that women would not notice his physical defects ... he had a hundred and fifty lovers, but he could treat love and matters of the heart with total disdain if they threatened to get in the way of his daily horse-riding ... How could you say to

me 'Go and never return', I fall on my knees before you . . .
I kiss your footprint . . . feet don't leave prints on carpets,
he thought to himself, self-critically, that was a realistic attitude to things, Gogol's way of seeing the world: while those
others babble on about elves! one Eugène Sue is worth the
whole bunch of those salon scribblers, yet they think of him
as second-rate . . . but of course the reading public prefer
Rinaldo Rinaldi to *The Sorrows of Young Werther* . . . I like
both of them, but I've never said so, not in the context of
our literary salons . . . Byron was bored all his life, he used
to say that a simple pinch of salt would give him as much of
a high as champagne would . . . but wine, alcohol generally,
made him gloomy and savage to the point of frenzy . . . so
you see, Anya, it's a good thing, for me as well as for you,
that you didn't marry Lord Byron . . . Fyodor Mikhailovich
smiled, pulled a handful of small coins out of his pocket, and
spread them on his napkin . . . then he counted them out
and put them in two separate piles, one for the bill and one
for the *pourboire*.

He hadn't noticed the waitress staring at this funny old
bloke's bizarre antics. That was how she saw him: not a
gentleman but a bloke. 'The bill please,' said Fyodor Mikhailovich, more or less to himself. He put the first pile of money
into the girl's hand, then he took the girl's other hand and
tried to press a few small coins into her large, strong palm . . .
'*Pourboire, pourboire*,' Fyodor Mikhailovich repeated, but
the girl broke into peals of laughter . . . he looked at her
young face, which was so full of life and so open, and smiled
at her; the girl took the tip, curtseyed, and then with a few
indistinct words she pushed the tip into Fyodor Mikhailovich's pocket, and with a swift, almost furtive movement,
caressed him on the shoulder. The girl went off, and disappeared behind some door, from which there came the clatter
of washed dishes. Fyodor Mikhailovich looked into the
mirror and made out his shadowy likeness. As he left, the bell
over the door burst merrily into song.

The door to his flat was open. There were no thieves in
this country. Anya only locked the door, and its shutter, at

night. Fyodor Mikhailovich walked around on tiptoe, as he often did, so as not to disturb Anya . . . but he was also in the habit of sneaking into his own flat by day as well as by night when (for example) he'd lost at roulette, or had in his pocket a letter from 'that woman' (now the property of some gilded youth, a student named Salvador). Anya was sitting in the armchair holding Fedya's overcoat in her arms; she had already started mending it the day before. She was asleep, with the coat cradled in her arms like a person. Her face in sleep suggested to Fyodor the face of some unknown, defenceless young girl. And yet, wonderful to behold, she was smiling in her sleep. Fyodor Mikhailovich stood motionless: the big belly under the overcoat moved rhythmically in irregular exhalations. Their child had been breathing in Anya's belly for several months. For a while he had the impression that Anya was looking at him with a strange smile, from under knitted brows; but she opened her eyes slowly and looked at him with a somewhat vacant and distant gaze. Fyodor Mikhailovich pulled out of his pocket a parcel wrapped in paper.

—I've brought you a cake . . . Apfelstrudel . . .

Anya smiled and repeated—Apfelstrudel . . . with a comical sort of stress on the beginning of the word, so that it sounded like 'Ap-felstrudel'.

Fyodor Mikhailovich was holding the parcel in both hands.

—Maybe you'd like it with your tea . . . you know, Anya, this strudel . . . I just can't stomach it, to me it's just tedious, just like this lovely country we have to cross in order to get to Russia . . . tedious! I have my mouth as full as if someone had put a gag on me, I can't stomach it . . . what a tedious cake.

Anya burst out laughing.—What *are* you on about this time? A 'tedious cake' indeed . . .

—Yes, yes, these Swiss cakes are as tedious as German cakes, it's the same family of cakes . . . see, it just goes tedious in my mouth, so I quickly have a drink of coffee, and it goes down somehow or other.

—And I think it's lovely, it's got a lovely smell when it's still warm, and it just melts all over your palate.

Fyodor Mikhailovich put his parcel on the table and sat down next to his wife.

—You know, Anya, it seemed to me that I saw Ivan Sergeyevich . . . in fact he's in Paris of course. But sometimes you can be in two places at once . . .

—I don't know, I'm always in one place, and I'm not going to give up my place as long as I live—said Anya solemnly, and she closed her eyes.

(*Translated by George Hyde*)

Natasza Goerke

The Third Shore

Stop pulling faces, pleads Kalsang. We don't know the hour of our death and were yours to come, let's say, this very moment, you'd get stuck like that and that's how I'd remember you. And then I'd blame myself for the rest of my life: that I didn't rise to the occasion, that I didn't stop you in time.

Kalsang rises to the occasion, he stops me in time, makes tea. 'Here you are, drink. It's a special tea from Tibet via Paris. A friend of mine bought it thinking with you.' 'Of you,' I correct him. 'And besides, I don't understand why the Tibetans buy their tea in Paris.' Kalsang smiles, looks through the window. 'See?' he says. 'In this country December looks the same as July.'

I've had enough. 'Listen!' I yell at him. 'How am I supposed to stop pulling faces when you talk to me in *koans*?' Now Kalsang pulls a face; he is surprised. 'But Treasure, I've only stated that in Denmark it rains all the time.' I defend Denmark: 'In England it rains even more. And if you want a change of climate, let's go to Poland—there are no communists there now, nobody will deport you to China and you can have everything: tea shop, the classic four seasons, there are even Buddhists.' Kalsang looks at me, horrified. 'I met Polish Buddhists in India. They marched around a temple, chanting something. I thought they were an army platoon, but they were only chanting a mantra.' 'Don't be stupid,' I say. 'They must have been German Buddhists. The Polish ones are a bit like those in Denmark—they too have beards but they don't carry those little Fjällräven rucksacks, and they stoop more.' 'Maybe,' admits Kalsang, but without conviction. 'Whichever,' he sighs, 'they didn't look happy.' I smile. 'Kalsang, Treasure,' I explain, 'the West is not Tibet. Here you're not born a Buddhist. Here you convert to Buddhism when you're really, really unhappy. One day you simply discover in yourself a space which makes you scared: you feel evil, more and more evil, while around you, just to make it worse, everyone's ever so good and saintly. So instead of making them sad, or being a pain in the arse and a source of anxiety, you start pretending to be one of them. Till something snaps and all hell breaks loose: you want to get hold of a nun and smash in her jolly face, you feel like shaking a cardinal out of his habit, throwing him into boiling water and, while reading aloud from the Holy Bible, closely observing him for behavioural changes. Of course you don't do that, but you have to do something instead. You take to drink, you open a shop or, just then, convert to Buddhism.' 'And do you really want to go back to that Poland of yours?' asks Kalsang; he is very pale. 'I don't know,' I say, 'but we can't stay in Denmark, can we? And from Australia or Canada everywhere else is too far.' Kalsang reads the future from his beads. He counts them, rolls his eyes.

'We shall go to Tibet,' says Kalsang and begins to hum. 'It's the love song of the sixth Dalai Lama,' he explains. 'We used to sing it as children when tending yaks on the meadows.' 'Lovely,' I sigh, 'but I've really had it up to here with foreign languages, and besides, I'm not sure if I could stand a country which has more Buddhists than Poland.' 'You would stand it well. Tibetans are simple people,' Kalsang assures me. 'And if you really want to complicate things, we can settle near a Christian community. You could practise your English, go to Mass, the nuns would give us rice and biros.' 'In Poland you can have rice and biros just as well, and you don't have to go to Mass for it,' I shout and fall silent, while Kalsang pours milk into the tea and stirs very loudly.

'I'm going to meditate,' announces Kalsang and leaves the

room. 'I'll send you some good vibrations, to calm you down. Later, we can go out for a walk,' he adds. He shuts the door and begins to send good vibrations.

I pour out the tea and pour in the cognac. I feel sick at first; then blissful. I start drawing: all the Buddhists in the Chinese book get moustaches. 'I'm turning them into Padma-sambhava,' I call out to Kalsang who, I'm sure, has by now meditated out so much calm he shouldn't take it too badly. It's his book. He got it from me last Christmas. I got hand cream and a rosary, and talc to stop my creamed fingers slipping off the beads. Once I start praying that is, for at the moment I'm going through this weird phase in which instead of prayers my lips pour out obscenities. Obscenities are the words I always learn first with any new language. One day, by way of an experiment, I let rip in Tibetan. Kalsang's eyes nearly fell out of his head. Then he mumbled out a mantra and staring at me full of admiration asked: 'Do all Polish women speak like that?' 'Not all,' I admitted. 'Polish women are like Indian women: hypocritical, they hide in their clothes, which are not saris, true, but serve the same func-tion—they simulate innocence.' 'That's a shame,' laughed Kalsang, 'for that's how Tibetan women swear, not in the presence of their husbands but with strangers.' 'As it happens, it's the opposite with Polish women,' I sigh. 'Their canons of femininity oblige them to be graceful, thus afflicting their expressive powers. In public life, the Polish woman opts for euphemism, but at home, when she lets her husband have it from the heart it knocks the stuffing out of him.' 'Hm,' hmmed Kalsang, made me some tea and went off to medi-tate. I stayed lying on the bed and, as always, started making greeting cards.

The world is full of holy days. Of New Year's Eves alone there are two hundred every year. I already have a nice pile of those cards. I just don't know who to send them to, so that I don't hurt anyone's feelings. For they are horrible cards—a reflection of my present state of mind. Collages are the best: Christ on the lotus, Buddha on the cross ... I can only send them to the Rajneesh commune; they think along similar lines.

'Listen, this book of yours,' I call out to the kitchen. 'May I cut it up? We'll send them moustachioed Buddhas!' After a moment's silence, Kalsang puts his head through the kitchen door. He says, 'Before you throw a grain of dirt at Buddha you need to rise at least to the level of the first *bhumi*. *Bhumi* is a step on the path of *bodhisatva*. If you reach it you can laugh at the sacred till you burst and you won't go to Hell. But, in order to laugh at the sacred, you have to meditate for a very, very long time, and not drink cognac.' I hide the cognac under the table and make sure: 'Was Christ a *bodhisatva*?' 'If he acted for the good of other beings he was,' says Kalsang. I show him a holy picture that my grandma's just sent me. The picture is not a collage: Christ is lying in the cradle, *sans* moustache. 'How tiny,' marvels Kalsang. He places the picture on the top of his head. It's a blessing, and if you believe in it it works straight away. I think it really works. Kalsang rolls his eyes, smiles and states with conviction, 'Christ is a *bodhisatva*. Do you know his mantra?' I take a piece of paper and write down a fragment of Our Father. Kalsang tries to read it, it twists his tongue. 'Transcribe it into Tibetan,' he asks. 'I will include it in my prayers. Maybe Tibet will be free sooner and we'll leave Denmark.' 'Treasure,' I cry, 'stop messing things up! Christ cannot answer contradictory prayers. I've just asked him to help us settle in Poland.' Kalsang shrugs: 'Poland, Tibet— what's the difference?' he says. 'The important thing is to leave here. If we agree, at least in this respect, they'll come to an understanding too and all will be well.' 'Who they?' I cry. 'My God forbids other gods and in your pantheon there are so many of them that I'm sure to end up in some horrible Hell. I'm earning that Hell living with you. I'm pulling myself out by the roots from my native soil!' Kalsang grows sad. 'But it's only one great symbol. We are different only on the symbolic level,' he explains. 'For in fact God is Buddha and he won't mind if instead of Our Father you say mantras.' I press on the Padmasambhava's forehead a stamp that

Kalsang gave me last Christmas: it's a little swastika; in Sanskrit *su asti*, the ancient symbol of happiness. 'Now, try and send it to Poland,' I say. 'You'll soon find out about the differences on a symbolic level.' Kalsang nods and goes out to the kitchen. 'I'll pray and all will be well,' he assures me. And I feel that in a moment I'll go mad.

At the last moment I don't. I pick up my cognac and imagine that my cheek is being gently stroked by Piechocki. He's a bloke I met once, years and years ago in Poland. His name is not Piechocki, of course, but I had to encode him somehow, to let him enter my memory in such a way that in case of my death, which may come at any moment, he won't be compromised. Now it's enough that I think 'Piechocki' and straight away I feel glowing warmth; that's how I've programmed myself. I talk to Piechocki all the time. I made him free of all his shortcomings and the man's grown so attached that he won't leave me for a minute. When Kalsang strokes me Piechocki turns up and instantly I feel more passionate. One could say—doubly passionate, for I love them both at once. I only have to be careful to keep my mouth shut, so that I won't cry out all of a sudden—Come, Piechocki, come!

It must be some sort of reaction to the cultural differences, the only touch of local colour in this exotic life of mine. Piechocki is my entire childhood. It was with him that I smoked my first joint. He deflowered me on the Persian carpet when mother went to a congress of hiking doctors in Kościerzyna. Then he was a father who sent his teenage daughter to a convent school, and then, when he refined his taste, he became my professor. In his immaculate Polish he taught me about beauty. He would explain to me that beauty is in everybody and that everybody is a whole world, and that only an idiot could accuse the world of being ugly. The bloke I've called Piechocki in fact spoke in a slightly different way, more convoluted and partly in Latin, but that didn't put me off. Simply, I cut out of my Piechocki everything that was unworthy of my projection. I communicated exclusively with the beautiful side of his complex personality, and just to avoid making it too ideal I brought his wife into action. Slowly, the tragic side of the story unfolded: I tore Piechocki between heart and duty. And when in the end he followed his heart, I decided to reward him and took him with me to Asia. Piechocki looked at me with Kalsang's eyes and whispered: He, I—it's only a difference on the symbolic level. So I took Kalsang back to Europe.

Now Piechocki is simply my shadow. He strokes my back with that subtle wisdom of his, reminding me discreetly not to escape into cognac, and when Kalsang goes off to meditate Piechocki starts praying. 'Oh Lord,' he prays, 'restore the little one to reason, bring a happy ending to this painful crisis in her identity.' And when I listen to it, I get all confused and I begin to pull faces: now I have the face of Madonna, now that of Mahakala. My fingers slip off the beads, I knock over the candles, fall into the fire. 'No, Kalsang,' I cry, 'I can't live either in Poland or in Tibet! Let's find a less religious place, a secular dimension where you live once, die once and whence you don't have to go anywhere else.'

Kalsang runs in and picks me up from the carpet. 'What's the matter, Treasure?' he asks. 'Have you been attacked by a demon?' 'No, it's simply confusion on the level of values,' explains Piechocki through my lips, and he winks at me to keep my chin up. I do. 'Kalsang, darling,' I say, 'it's nothing. My ego flooded out. For a moment I believed it was not a dream, that I really existed. But now it's all right,' I add. I stroke Kalsang on the cheek and do a sit-up. I no longer exist; it was merely a funny crisis of illusory values.

Kalsang nods and murmurs, 'Yes, egos are funny things. You have to be careful what you identify yourself with. If you feel like a mountain then you'll start climbing yourself, and just before you die you reach the top and you notice the sky above your head. You want to soar into it but it's too late and you die of anger. Such a state of mind at the moment of death does not augur a happy future. You may be reborn as a donkey or even a speck of dust on some terribly unpleasant mental plane.' I start crying. Kalsang's eyes grow misty too; he identifies himself with a mirror.

It's like this: he reflects everything as it comes nice and clean, and likes every reflection. A Buddhist, as it says in the books, does not evaluate but loves everything. Kalsang makes tea. 'You've been mother a million times,' he says. 'So now drink.' I drink tea, grow silent. Behind my back Piechocki lights a cigarette. 'What do you think about it?' I ask, waiting for him to embrace me, to say: Rubbish, you have only one mother and she should be loved. Piechocki pulls a face like a Russian icon, stubs out his cigarette. 'I don't know,' he says, and disappears behind the cross.

Piechocki, just like Kalsang, is a mirror. I asked him once, 'Piechocki, do something with your facial expression, for if you die suddenly I will remember you like that and shall try not to dwell on memories of you.' And Piechocki says, 'You grow distant, I can't look any different.' I was lost for words. I asked, 'Piechocki, darling, what's brewing in that noble skull of yours? You're the only root of my past, the non-existent aspect of Kalsang, and without you I would've undoubtedly slipped into madness.' 'Return to Poland,' whispers Piechocki. He fixes his black eyes on me and disappears with the cross.

That is, what disappears is the text on my screen, the text I've been writing about him all this time. Simply, the computer censored it and gobbled it up. A moment later Kalsang enters the room and asks. 'How are you feeling? I've just had a vision that something bad is going on.'

It is. Kalsang puts his hand on my shoulder. I close my eyes with all my might, but instead of Piechocki I see the Pope. 'Children, do not participate in sects foreign to our culture.' The Pope wags his finger, pretends he is smiling, while the starving Buddha on the wall starts crying. 'No, leave it,' I tell Kalsang. 'I feel rather feeble today, as if I were drained of all dreams.' 'It's wonderful,' says the happy Kalsang, and embraces me more strongly still. 'One has to look reality straight in the eye. You have to create projections like bridges: right on to the other shore. If you want, tomorrow we'll leave for Tibet.'

I close first my eyelids, then my fists. 'Basta, Kalsang,' I announce. 'Basta! My bridge has gone down the fucking river! I'm leaving!' Piechocki grows pale. 'Where do you want to go?' he asks, his hands shaking. I make a face suitable for a departure and answer him: I'm going straight ahead. 'I'm going to look for a projection that will lead me out of you and out of Kalsang. I shall find my own shore, and one I won't have to emigrate to. Buddha will die on the cross for the three of us, the only season will be laughter, and I, calm and peaceful, shall bathe in a million holy rivers while bodhisatvas together with the angels, all merry, cast their nets to fish for the obscenities in all the languages of the world.'

'I don't understand women,' says Piechocki with Kalsang's voice and completely confuses the plot. 'Couldn't we have simply two faiths, two husbands, one moral system?' 'Maybe you can, Treasure,' I laugh. 'Maybe you can, but I can't. I, like you, am the chosen people, except we're chosen by someone else, and that's our problem.'

Kalsang knits his brow. 'I think I understand,' he sighs. 'A demon has possessed you and you want to die.' 'I want to live,' I say. I throw the rucksack on my back and begin to take my leave. I live leaving: Kalsang, Piechocki... I speak no tongues...

(*Translated by Wiesiek Powaga*)

About the Authors

Janusz Anderman (b. 1949) started out as a reporter for a students' magazine. His interest in and sympathy for ordinary people led to a steadily increasing political involvement, in particular with the emerging underground publishing movement. In 1978 he became co-editor of *Puls*, one of the first uncensored periodicals to appear in Poland. Later, he was the Polish Writers' Union Committee liaison officer with Solidarność (Solidarity). After the imposition of martial law in 1981, he was interned for six months in the infamous Białołęka camp. He gained wide popularity with a collection of short stories, *Brak tchu*, 1983 (*Poland under Black Light*, 1985), followed by *Kraj Świata*, 1988 (*The Edge of the World*, 1988).

Tadeusz Borowski (1922–51) made his literary debut in Nazi-occupied Warsaw with a cycle of poems *Gdziekolwiek ziemia*, published clandestinely in 1942. Arrested in 1943, he was sent to Auschwitz, where he worked as a hospital orderly, and later to Dachau. After the liberation of the camps he worked for the Red Cross in Munich, but in 1946 he returned to Poland and joined the Polish Socialist Party. In 1948 his most famous collections of stories, *Kamienny świat* [The Stony World], and *Pożegnanie z Marią* [Farewell to Maria] were published. It is on these two collections—translated into English as *This Way for the Gas, Ladies and Gentlemen* in 1976—that his reputation as a writer rests. Borowski committed suicide in 1951.

Stefan Chwin (b. 1949) is a writer and literary critic. He also teaches literature at the University of Gdańsk. He is especially interested in the connections between imagination and politics as well as in the psychological approach to literature. Fascinated by what he calls 'the psychoanalysis of place', he collects old photographs, maps and drawings of Gdańsk, tracing the interplay of cultural cross-currents as expressed in both individual and collective biographies.

Ida Fink survived the Nazi occupation of Poland. In 1957 she emigrated to Israel, where she still lives. Her first collection of stories was published initially in Hebrew, then in Polish (*Skrawek czasu*, London, 1987) and English (*A Scrap of Time and Other Stories*, 1988). She has also published *Podróz* (*The Journey*, 1994). All her work to date concerns the fate of Jews from small towns and villages during the Nazi occupation. In 1985 she was awarded the Dutch Anne Frank Prize.

Natasza Goerke was born in 1960 in Poznań. She studied Polish there, then moved to Kraków, where she studied Indian languages. In 1984 she left Poland for first Copenhagen, then Hamburg, where she took a degree in Tibetan. After three years' travel in Asia, mainly in the Himalayas, she published a series of short stories, later collected as *Fractale* [Fractals], 1994, which became a best-seller. She lives in Hamburg, and publishes regularly in the Polish and German literary press.

Witold Gombrowicz (1904–69) was born into the Polish landed gentry. When the Second World War broke out, he left Poland and went first to Argentina, where he lived until 1963, and then to France, where he remained until his death. His publications include *Ferdydurke*, 1937, the play *Princess Ivona*, 1938, and a Gothic parody, *The Possessed*, 1939. *Trans-Atlantyk*, 1953, *Pornografia*, 1960, and *Kosmos*, 1965, are darkly metaphysical novels; *The Marriage*, 1953, and *Operetta*, 1966, are 'absurd' plays. His *Diaries*, 1957–66, are the intellectual testament of this eminent but controversial writer.

Marek Hłasko (1934–69) first attracted attention as a writer of social realism, but he soon became a leading figure of the 'lost generation' of the 1950s disillusioned with the postwar world order. His position as the most prominent 'angry young man' of Polish literature was secured by two collections of short stories, *Pierwszy krok w Chmurach*, 1956 (*First Step in the Clouds*, 1956) and *Ósmy dzień tygodnia*, 1956 (*Eighth Day of the Week*, 1958), in which he exploded the cosy myth of a communist paradise. His courage in tackling hitherto taboo subjects—such as violence and sex—brought him instant recognition, not only in Poland but also abroad, notably in the USA. In 1958 he sought political asylum in West Berlin, and from then until his untimely death in 1969 he travelled restlessly between Western Europe, Israel and the USA.

Paweł Huelle was born in 1957 in Gdańsk, the city he celebrates in all his writing. His literary debut, which brought him immediate acclaim as Poland's most talented prose writer, was *Weiser Dawidek*, 1987 (*Who Was David Weiser?*, 1991), which won the prestigious Kościelski Prize. Since then he has written a good deal for periodicals and has published a collection of short stories, *Tygodnik Powszechny*, 1991 (*Moving House*, 1994).

Jarosław Iwaszkiewicz (1894–1980) was born into a family of Polish gentry in the Ukrainian borderlands and studied law and music in Kiev. He made his debut as a lyrical poet in the style of the Russian Symbolists in 1919 and continued to write poetry throughout a long and distinguished literary career spanning six decades. This enormously prolific writer is known to the wider public primarily as a novelist and a short story writer. Two of these: 'Panny z Wilka' [Maidens of Wilko] and 'Brzezina' [The Birch Grove], both dating from 1933 and expressing his deeply melancholic view of human life, have enjoyed enduring popularity. They have both been successfully filmed by Andrzej Wajda. The story included here dates from the 1950s and shows the writer in uncharacteristically humorous mood, lampooning the official dogma of socialist realist art.

Leszek Kołakowski (b. 1927) is Poland's most eminent philosopher and the author of the monumental three-volume *Main Currents of Marxism*, first published in Paris, 1976–78, English edition, 1978. Like a latter-day Voltaire, he has published, besides his scholarly writings, three collections of witty, iconoclastic, subversive philosophical tales, *Klucz niebieski albo Opowieści budujące z historii świętej*, 1964, *Rozmowy z Diabłem*, 1965, and *13 Bajek z królestwa Łailonii*, 1966. A selection from all three was published in English as *The Devil and the Scripture: Edifying Tales from Holy Scripture to Serve as Teaching and Warning*, 1973.

Hanna Krall first distinguished herself as a reporter for the influential weekly *Polityka*. She has published three volumes of reportage, of which *Zdżyć przed Panem Bogiem*, 1977, based on interviews with Dr Marek Edelman, a survivor of the Łódź ghetto, won high praise and by 1996 had appeared in twenty-two editions. She is also the author of a work of autobiographical fiction, *Sublokatorka*, 1983. These two books were published together in English as *Subtenant—To Outwit God*, 1992. Her other books include *Hipnoza*, 1989, which won a German Critics' Prize, and *Taniec na cudzym weselu*, 1993. All her writings explore the theme of the Holocaust in the context of Polish–Jewish relations.

Stanisław Lem was born in Lwów in 1921. He first studied medicine, but soon abandoned it for literature. He is pre-eminent in the genre of science fiction, probing the problems of contemporary civilization, notably those concerning the limits of scientific and technological progress. Lem's first publication was *Astronauci*, 1951, a collection of short stories anticipating space travel, and since then he has become internationally established as a prolific and highly popular author: his books have been translated into thirty-three languages. English translations of his work include *A Perfect Vacuum*, 1983, *A Chain of Chance*, 1984, *Cyberiad: Fables for the Cybernetic Age* and *Star Diaries*, both 1985, *Fiasco*, 1987, and, perhaps his best-known book, *Solaris*, 1987, which was filmed by Andrei Tarkovsky in 1972.

Sławomir Mrożek (b. 1930) made his literary debut in 1950 with a satirical piece in the hugely popular weekly *Przekrój*. He practised journalism until 1951, when the production in Warsaw of his first play, *Policja* [The Police] launched his career as a dramatist. His most important play is probably *Tango*, 1964 (translated into English under the same title in 1968). Also during the 1950s, Mrożek revealed his comic genius of the satirical short story. Those published here are from his first collection, *Słoń*, 1958 (*The Elephant*, 1962). Despite his enormous popular success, he left Poland in 1963 for first France, then Italy and finally Mexico, where he still lives. His work was banned for a while following his protest at the Soviet invasion of Czechoslovakia in 1968, but he soon resumed his place as Poland's foremost dramatist and satirist.

Tadeusz Różewicz was born in 1921 in Radomsko, central Poland, into a poor family. During the Second World War, he attended a clandestine military school, published in the underground press, and worked for the Polish Resistance. After the war he studied art history in Kraków. In 1966 he won a State Prize for Literature, and in 1971 young Polish poets voted him the country's most important living poet. He is also known for his significant contributions to avant-garde theatre.

Bruno Schulz (1892–1942) was born into a Polish-speaking Jewish family of shopkeepers in Drohobycz, Ukraine. He studied architecture at Lwów and painting at the Vienna Academy of Fine Art, then returned to Drohobycz, where he taught drawing at the grammar school from 1924 until his death. He was shot by a Nazi officer in the Drohobycz ghetto, in revenge for the death of another officer. Two volumes of his short stories were published before the war: *Cinnamon Shops*, 1933, and *Sanatorium under the Sign of the Hourglass*, 1936. In them, Schulz portrays a gentle, shabby provincial paradise, almost immune from the 'crocodiles' of the new mercantile power ethic.

Aleksander Wat (1900–67) was of Jewish extraction. He studied logic and psychology at Warsaw University. In 1919 he created a stir with a book of Futurist verse; between 1921 and 1925 he edited *New Art* and *Almanac of New Art*, and in 1927 published a collection of short stories, *Lucifer Unemployed*. He became literary director of the leading publisher Gebethner & Wolf and then (1932–9) editor of *Literary Monthly*. He was arrested in 1940, and served sentences in Soviet prison camps in Kazakhstan, being freed only in 1946. After his return home he was appointed editor-in-chief at Poland's state-run publishing house, PIW. His publications include his autobiography *My Century*, 1963, which was highly influential in Poland.

Permissions

Stanisław Lem, 'The Use of a Dragon', from a collection of Lem's work of the same title, 1993. Published by permission of the author.
Sławomir Mrożek, 'The Elephant' and 'Spring in Poland', reprinted by permission of Diogenes Verlag. Illustrations reprinted by permission of Daniel Mroz's widow.
Tadeusz Różewicz, 'The Tip', published by permission of the author.
Bruno Schulz, 'Birds' and 'Tailors' Dummies', from *The Street of Crocodiles*, Picador, 1980, subsequently published as *Fictions* (a collection of Schulz's work) Picador, 1992.
Aleksander Wat, 'The History of the Last Revolution in England', from *Lucifer Unemployed*, Northwestern University Press, 1990. Reprinted by permission of the publishers.

Serpent's Tail

1986 to 1996
TEN YEARS WITH ATTITUDE!

> "If you've got hold of a book that doesn't fit the categories
> and doesn't miss them either,
> the chances are that you've got a serpent by the tail."
>
> ADAM MARS-JONES

> "The Serpent's Tail boldly goes
> where no reptile has gone before ... More power to it!"
>
> MARGARET ATWOOD

If you would like to receive a catalogue of our current publications please write to:

FREEPOST, Serpent's Tail,
4 Blackstock Mews, LONDON N4 2BR

(No stamp necessary if your letter is posted in the United Kingdom.)